HUSH

HUSH

AMALEKA MCCALL

www.urbanbooks.net

Urban Books, LLC
1199 Straight Path
West Babylon, NY 11704

ISBN- 13: 978-1-60162-255-6
ISBN- 10: 1-60162-255-4

First Printing October 2009
Printed in the United States of America

10 9 8 7 6 5 4 3 2 1

This is a work of fiction. Any references or similarities to actual events, real people, living, or dead, or to real locales are intended to give the novel a sense of reality. Any similarity in other names, characters, places, and incidents is entirely coincidental.

Distributed by Kensington Publishing Corp.
Submit Wholesale Orders to:
Kensington Publishing Corp.
C/O Penguin Group (USA) Inc.
Attention: Order Processing
405 Murray Hill Parkway
East Rutherford, NJ 07073-2316
Phone: 1-800-526-0275
Fax: 1-800-227-9604

I dedicate this book to the men in my life—
Daddy, Edmund, and Aiden.
Thank you for your unconditional love.

Everyone has a story to tell. Some stories are best told from the grave. The dead speak volumes, and the living learn page by page.

Amaleka McCall

HUSH

Prologue

September, 2006

"In breaking news today, federal investigators report that after a one year undercover sting operation dubbed 'Operation Candy Shop', a multi-million dollar designer drug ring has been brought down. The ring, reportedly run by three of the most dangerous women operating between New York City, Newark, Baltimore and Mexico, were responsible for the illegal sale and circulation of prescription drugs like Oxycontin, Percocet, and Vicodin. The trio of woman were also reportedly running a large-scale methamphetamine distribution conglomerate. In recent years, these drugs have become just as popular and profitable as traditional street drugs such as heroin and crack-cocaine."

"According to the investigators, the drug ring was brought down by a joint effort between local police, the FBI, DEA, and ICE agents. The FBI credits the director of the Washington Field Office for the success of the operation. Investigators would not elaborate on the specific roles the women played, or their expected dates in court."

"We will continue to follow this story as it unfolds. For

channel 9 news, I'm Chynna Brown. Back to you in the studio, Ed."

Deidre stared at the television screen, anger welling up inside of her like hot lava in a volcano. Nothing shocked her anymore, but her heart raced as she listened to the reporter's words. She stood on wobbly legs, and the large vein in her neck pulsed fiercely against her skin. Months of lies, deceit and frustration sent a rush of heat through her bloodstream. "Argggghhh!" she screamed, sending the coffee mug filled with her favorite hazelnut-flavored coffee sailing into the screen. "Fucking liars! Fucking bastards!" she screamed. The thought of how her life had ended up sent hot tears streaming down her high cheekbones.

Deidre ignored the sparks flying and the damage she had inflicted on the television. Her mind racing, she ran up the creaking wooden stairs to the second floor of the cottage she had been staying at for the last three days. Reaching the top landing of the staircase, she bolted into the master bedroom. Panting for breath, she began frantically stuffing rubber banded stacks of money into a large Louis Vuitton duffel bag.

She looked down at the expensive brown and beige bag, and she felt her heart sink. The bag had been a gift from Chastity and the girls. A long row of Gucci, Manolo Blahnik and Jimmy Choo shoes peeked out from under the bed. Platinum and diamond jewelry sparkled from the dresser top. All had been gifts—tokens of appreciation for a job well done. Deidre couldn't help but think about the good times she'd had with the crew. All of the shopping trips, parties, vacations, and just the girl talk in general. Deidre felt sick thinking about how everything had played out. She thought about how perfectly she had fit in with the F.A.B.

Being the product of a mixed relationship—a half African-American and Irish mother and a half African-American and

Dominican father—she never seemed to fit in with any one group growing up. For the African-American girls, she was too light and too cute because her hair was wavy and long. They hated her and let her know it every day.

For the white Irish girls, just knowing she was part Black meant automatic exclusion. Besides, she wasn't loose and nasty enough to hang with them. They'd all started giving blowjobs at thirteen.

For the Dominicans, well, they couldn't really talk because she looked more Hispanic than most of them, but she didn't speak Spanish well enough to fit in.

Exasperated, Deidre flopped down on the bed, snapping out of the past. *Where the hell am I going? What the hell am I? Whose side am I on?* Confusion over her duplicitous loyalties mounted, and suddenly a sharp pain invaded her abdomen and she felt nauseous. Hand over mouth, Deidre ran toward the bathroom, but didn't make it in time. Warm vomit spewed between her fingers and ran down her forearms. Her nerve endings stood on end as she hunched over the old-fashioned porcelain sink and let the contents of her stomach empty into the basin. *I have to pull myself together and get out of here*, Deidre told herself, turning on the faucet to wet her face.

As she finished washing her face and cleaning up her mess, she heard several loud knocks on the cedar wood cottage door. The sound jolted her. Eyes wide, she listened intently.

"Bang! Bang!" Then a pause, and another *"Bang!"* The knocks were an all too familiar sound. They all had been trained to knock that way as a code for backup. They were conducting a raid like she was a common criminal.

"Shit!" she whispered, her survival skills catching her around the throat. "How did they find me?" Deidre muttered, her heart racing painfully against her sternum. She'd been taught to get out of situations like this. Looking up at the bathroom window, she contemplated climbing out, but her expertise told her that they probably had snipers surrounding the building. Deidre was now the enemy. The sounds grew louder and closer. "Fuck!" she exclaimed through clenched teeth. Her hands shook uncontrollably. Deidre knew that the information she held would surely cost her her life. *It's all over now*, she thought to herself. *There was no where to go*. However, Deidre didn't plan on going out without a fight.

She inched slowly over toward the bathroom door and locked it. She remembered that she kept her spare weapon hidden inside the Kotex box under the bathroom sink. She reached for the handles of the cabinet under the sink. Before she could retrieve the .357 Sig Sauer, her favorite gun, she heard footsteps and familiar voices thundering up the stairs toward her location. Instinctively, she got low to the ground, just as she had been trained to do, seeking cover as bullets whistled above her head and lodged themselves into the wood panels of the bathroom walls. She balled up into a turtle position, using her back as her shell. Glass rained down on her body, littering her hair, and shattering on her arched back. It was time to give up. If she didn't surrender, the undercover recovery team would surely kill her. In the eyes of the same people she worked for, she was just like the criminals they'd hunted together. What set her apart was that she held too many secrets to live.

Deidre stood up and raised her hands above her head as the door splintered open. "Aponte, it's over. You need to come with us!" a familiar voice yelled over the chaos.

Deidre looked into the eyes of the man to whom she had once professed her love. The jig was up, but far from over. The next few seconds seemed to move in *Matrix*-like slow motion for her. The lone figure stood before her like the Grim Reaper.

"Stay back! Stay back! The suspect is armed!" the man yelled to the other agents behind him, never taking his eyes off of Deidre. He wouldn't allow his backup of rogue agents anywhere near his location, and Deidre knew just why that was.

"Don't do it!" she screamed, throwing her hands up in surrender as he leveled the gun at the center of her chest.

"Drop your weapon!" he yelled deceitfully, drowning out her feeble attempts to elicit help from the other agents on the scene.

Deidre was unarmed; she never had the chance to retrieve her gun. Immediately, she knew what he had in store for her. She squeezed her eyes together, causing the built-up tears to escape from the corners.

"*Boom! Boom! Boom!*" The gun roared, hitting its intended target. The metal bullets seared through Diedre's skin. She stumbled backwards from the powerful shots, hitting her head on the edge of the old-fashioned lion claw bathtub her mother and father had bathed her in as a child. Her body convulsed as blood spilled from her mouth and cascaded down her face and onto the cold floor. "*Thump, thump, thump, thu . . .* " Diedre could both feel and hear her heartbeat slowly begin to fade. The pressure in her chest eased. She gurgled for air as her life flashed before her eyes.

VOLUME 1:
THE CALL

January 2005

Ricky grabbed a handful of Deidre's hair and yanked her head back, positioning her face right in front of his. "Ugghhhh," she grunted, keeping her eyes closed tightly. Ricky forcefully pressed his mouth against hers. His hot breath sent stabs of heated sparks down her spine. It felt like her vagina was going to explode, her juices dampening the insides of her bare thighs. She'd greeted him with just her robe on. Their tongues met, performing a wicked dance with one another. Deidre became so excited that she bit into Ricky's bottom lip and drew blood.

"Oww!" he yelped, followed by a seductive smile. "I love that shit . . . you nasty little bitch!" he said. Sucking the blood off his lip, Ricky released Deidre's hair from his grip and shoved her. "Get on the floor!" he demanded.

Deidre complied, stretching her body out on the fluffy throw rug in front of the fireplace. The orange and yellow flames produced a glow that made him look angelic.

"On your stomach," Ricky said, stepping out of his pants.

Before she turned over, Deidre examined his strong legs, the result of his daily five-mile run, and his long tool in between. *Who says white men ain't packing?* she thought to herself as she prepared to submit.

Ricky looked good for his age. He had a thin, muscular frame with six-pack abs. His hair was still full with not a single sign of baldness white men his age often suffered from. For a man in his late fifties, Ricky resembled a sexy Don Johnson in his *Miami Vice* days.

Deidre flipped her body over and slid her right hand under her stomach and fingered her soaking wet clitoris. "I like when you play with it for me," Ricky whispered, dropping to his knees behind her. He started at her neck, licking the nape, and then moved slowly across her shoulders and down the center of her back with his tongue.

"Ooh!" Deidre cooed. When Ricky reached her ass, the cooing turned into crooning. He placed his strong hands on Deidre's ass cheeks and gently spread them apart. She responded by gently pushing her torso upward towards his face, yearning for his long wet tongue to enter her.

"Ha-ha!" Ricky laughed wickedly. "You like when I lick you from front to back?" he asked, and then pressed his face between her ass cheeks while he held them apart. Ricky licked it from top to bottom, stopping at the hole for a minute and gently blowing.

"Agghhhhh!" Deidre cried out in ecstasy. Ricky gently pushed on Deidre's firm backside, urging her onto her knees. Once she got into position, he resumed his tongue massage. He bent his head and delved tongue first into her dripping hot box.

Deidre grabbed a handful of carpet in response to Ricky's warm tongue on her saturated labia. "Fuck me, please!" she growled. All of his tongue play had her overheated and panting. Ricky obliged. Lifting Deidre off the floor, he carried her to the bed and placed her in the center. Climbing onto the bed, he moved towards her, hungry for her loving. He kissed Deidre's erect nipples, moving slowly back up to her mouth. Wedging his hips between her knees, he entered her.

"Ohhh, Ricky! Right there! Right there! Harder! Harder!" Deidre pleaded as she grabbed a handful of Ricky's salt and pepper colored hair.

"Whose pussy is this?" he grunted in response, pumping his ass in and out with awkward rhythmless vigor. "It's your puss-e-e-e-e!" Deidre screamed as she climaxed, tightly wrapping her legs around his slender waist.

Before Ricky could return the favor, the sound of crashing glass cut through the air. The sound came from inside the house. "What was that?" Ricky huffed through labored breaths, simultaneously jumping up and reaching for his weapon.

"I don't know!" Deidre whispered, eyes wide, also searching for her weapon. She rolled over and got off the bed, spotted her gun and began frantically searching in the darkness for a T-shirt or any item of clothing to cover herself with. Neither of them were prepared for what they heard next.

"Deidre Aponte is a home-wrecking whore! Do you hear me? She wrecks homes and can't get a man of her own! She is in this house right now fucking my husband!" the shrill but slurred voice belted out like a wounded opera singer. Pain and hurt were evident behind each syllable.

Shocked, Deidre pulled back the thick chenille curtains in her bedroom window. Standing in the driveway of Deidre's townhouse was Lorna Blum, professing all of Deidre's sins to the neighbors in Deidre's posh, Fairfax, Virginia neighborhood. Clearly inebriated, Lorna continued to scream her profanities to anyone who would listen.

"Oh shit!" Ricky exclaimed as he fumbled with his pants, nervously stumbling around in circles as he tried to pull them on in a rush. His skin was red with embarrassment like a cooked lobster.

Before he could gather up the remainder of his belongings, Deidre heard more glass breaking. She watched from her bedroom window as Lorna sailed a brick through the windshield of her Mercedes Benz CLK 430. Deidre was powerless, and embarrassment kept her feet rooted to the floor.

"I'm sorry!" Ricky apologized as he ran down the stairs to placate his wife before someone called the police, never once looking back at Deidre.

"*Bzzz . . . Bzzz . . . Bzzz!*" Deidre jumped out of her sleep to the sound of her government-issued Blackberry vibrating on the cherry wood nightstand. Her mind still fuzzy with sleep, she fumbled with her fluffy down comforter trying to locate the nuisance. Blinking her eyes against the sunlight streaming in through her French windows, she blindly grabbed for her Blackberry, accidentally knocking it to the floor. "Shit!" she grumbled, offending her nostrils with hot, morning breath. She looked over at the cable box, and the red digital numbers read 11:55. It was almost noon, but having been up all night, she allowed herself to sleep in.

She slid her long, slender legs over the side of the bed and planted her feet firmly on the paisley Oriental rug covering the parquet floors. She bent over to pick up the annoying electronic device. Scrolling down, she retrieved the last urgent message: *Call Ricky Blum, STAT.* "STAT? Now he wants to get all official!" Deidre mumbled aloud. She rolled her eyes and tossed the Blackberry back onto the nightstand.

Flopping backwards on the bed, she rehashed the events of the previous night. She still couldn't figure out how Ricky's wife knew he was with her. Maybe it was that obvious. Who else knew? Deidre had put herself in this position, she reasoned.

She would surely be seen as the biggest home wrecking slut. Lorna was right. Deidre covered her face feeling ashamed and alone.

"*Ring! Ring!*" The sound of the telephone snapped Deidre out of her conscious nightmare. She sat up and peered at the Caller I.D. It was Ricky from the office. "Why don't you go call your crazy-ass wife? I should've never been fucking my boss, who is old enough to be my father in the first place!" Deidre yelled in the direction of the telephone, placing a pillow over her head.

"*Ring! Ring! Ring! Ring!* Ricky refused to give up. Frustrated, Deidre finally shut the ringer switch to "off".

Crawling back under the covers, she lay balled up in a fetal position. She thought about all of the consequences of last night's events. As she lay there stewing in her own juices, she received another urgent message on her Blackberry: *Call the office STAT, Business related.* She stared at the message, and curiosity finally propelled her into action. Reluctantly, she picked up her cell phone and pressed 1, the speed dial button to the office.

"Aponte?" Ricky inquired before continuing.

"Yeah, it's me," Deidre responded, defeated.

"I need to see you in the office now!" he demanded.

"Now?" Deidre asked incredulously. "It's my day off . . . my fucking vacation, remember?" she complained. They'd both planned to take vacation at the same time to furtively spend together. Ricky had told his wife that he would be away on business, and Deidre told her mother the same story. She still couldn't figure out how their plans had been foiled. *In all these years, had we gotten that sloppy?* she asked herself.

"This can't wait," Ricky said flatly, hanging up the phone before she could utter another word.

"What the hell is up with him? Wasn't it *his wife* who fucked up my shit?" Deidre asked herself aloud. Nonetheless, she dragged her feet into the master bathroom, wincing as she sat on the cold ceramic toilet seat to relieve her aching bladder. Standing up, she flushed the toilet, stretched, and yawned. She looked at herself in the large vanity mirror and decided she looked like shit. "Wake up, Deidre . . . wake up!" she pep talked herself, splashing cold water onto her face.

Deidre realized that the extra twenty-five percent she got in her salary called LEAP—Law Enforcement Availability Pay—meant that she had to be ready to work wherever and whenever the Bureau called, even if she thought it was her lover's ploy to see her one last time.

After taking a quick duck bath, washing her "coots and oots" as her mother used to say, Deidre slipped on a pink terrycloth BCBG sweat suit. Wetting her brush, she smoothed her soft, jet-black hair into a slick ponytail. "I'm not getting dressed up. This is my fucking vacation," she grumbled, as she slid her leather shoulder holster on, securing her weapon in place.

The crisp winter air bit at Deidre's face, causing her caramel colored cheeks to turn a blushed rose. Gritting her teeth against the cold and letting small puffs of frosty breath escape her nose, she bent down and carefully examined the damage Mrs. Blum had inflicted on her car. With every key mark, dent, and piece of broken glass, Deidre felt awful.

Guilt crept into her conscience. She'd been sleeping with Ricky since she was assigned to the Washington, D.C. field office three years ago. Although they were from two different ends of the racial divide, for some reason, he'd always made her feel safe. Deidre often wondered if she was drawn to Ricky because he had been a close friend of her father's since she was ten years old. During Deidre's times of struggle, Ricky stood right by her side. He attended all of her dance recitals, graduations, and even stood in for her father at Deidre's high school Father/Daughter Dance.

After taking a full inventory of the damage done to her vehicle, Deidre decided that it would be too embarrassing to drive her Mercedes to work. She had no choice but to drive her old Hyundai Excel. The hunk of junk Hyundai stalled, making a horrible screeching noise as Deidre pumped the gas and turned the key trying to get the ignition started. She hadn't driven the hooptie since she graduated from the FBI Academy in Quantico, Virginia five years earlier. After a few minutes of pumping and praying, the car finally emitted a sickening gurgle and came to life. "Finally!" she sighed. She hoped she didn't see any of her neighbors milling around outside as she switched the cars around, taking the Hyundai out of the garage and putting her battered Benz inside. Luck, however, was not on her side. "I knew she'd be outside!" she whispered as she spotted the nosey old lady across the street staring in her direction.

"Hey, Mrs. Zuberman!" Deidre sang out, waving and flashing a fake smile.

The old lady gave a short "Humph!" before she turned her humped shoulders in disgust.

"Wonderful! Just wonderful! Who the fuck is going to keep the kids off my grass now? Thanks a lot, Lorna!" Deidre said bitterly.

Interstate 66 was jam-packed as usual. "Damn, the traffic gets worse and worse every year!" Deidre griped, slamming her fist against the steering wheel. She needed to find a way to distract herself before she lost it. She reached toward the old car radio and manually turned the tuner dial. All she got was static. "Shit, no music and traffic. Oh, hell no!" she said, lifting the cover to the small compartment between the seats and frantically rummaging through old junk. "Aww yeah!" she exclaimed when she spotted a Mary J. Blige cassette tape. Mary had a way of curing any ill that Deidre felt. Throughout college and during the FBI training academy, she played Mary over and over again. Mary was the chicken soup for her soul. Deidre slid the tape into the cassette slot and the music started immediately:

"I'm goin' down . . . I'm goin' down . . . And you ain't around . . .

Baby, my whole world's upside down . . . Sleep don't come easy . . ."

The lyrics played as her car gradually inched forward. Deidre sang along loudly.

"*Be-e-e-e-ep! Be-e-e-e-ep!*" The sound of a horn blaring startled her. Traffic had begun to pick up. She immediately stepped on the gas.

VOLUME 2:
THE BRIEFING

The streets of Washington, D.C. always amazed Deidre. All of the buildings were wide and short. She read somewhere once that no building in D.C. was built taller than the top of the Capitol.

Deidre pulled into her place of employment located at the junction of Pennsylvania Avenue and 10th Street, NW. The J. Edgar Hoover Building was located on the corner, with its brown and copper façade. She knew that some of the most talented agents in the United States—agents that tracked criminals, including Osama Bin Laden—worked right alongside her every day. She was proud to be an FBI agent.

Stepping off of the elevator on the fifth floor, Deidre took a deep breath before she placed her right hand on the computerized identification system connected to the glass doors. A small red laser light scanned the fingerprints on her right hand. *"Good afternoon Agent Aponte,"* the computerized female voice chimed as the small red light on the door lock turned green, allowing Deidre access to the corridor leading to the offices.

Fellow agents bustled up and down the busy hallways, greeting her with, "Hey, Aponte!" Some of them gave each other the eye and snickered when they saw her. "Damn, they know already!" Deidre mumbled to herself.

"Aponte, aren't you on vacation?" a few of the agents inquired.

Deidre rolled her eyes. She hoped they would have overlooked the fact that she and Ricky took the same vacation time.

Rounding the corner at the end of a long hallway, Ricky's office came into her direct line of sight. The blinds were pulled on the large glass window, and the door was shut. Deidre knew that meant something serious was up. Since becoming the Special Agent-in-Charge (SAC) of the Washington field office, Ricky Blum practiced an open door policy. His door being closed meant bad news.

As slivers of sunlight escaped through the slots, Deidre watched shadows moving behind the blinds. "What the hell is going on?" she whispered to herself just as she looked up at the gold and black nameplate on the door—*Special Agent-In-Charge Ricky Blum, Capital Division*. Balling her fist, she knocked lightly on the door, hoping that Ricky wouldn't hear it.

"Come in, Aponte!" Ricky yelled from the other side of the door.

"Damn!" Deidre cursed under her breath, surprised that he knew it was her. She nervously stepped inside. She was met by Ricky and her direct supervisor, the Resident Agent-in-Charge (RAC), Bernard Baker. Baker sat on the long burgundy leather sofa. Ricky stood like a king behind his tall mahogany desk. Both were silent.

"Close the door," Ricky demanded dryly. Deidre complied.

"Have a seat, Aponte," Baker said, patting an empty spot on the sofa next to him.

Deidre had worked with both of them long enough to know when things were not good. She refused to make eye contact with either of the men. Sweat began to pour down her back. She knew she had walked into a trap. *Is Ricky getting me transferred because of the affair? Did Baker find out about us?*

"Well, I guess I'll begin," Ricky started.

Deidre continued to avoid eye contact as her emotions ran wild. As a welcomed distraction, she focused on the many awards and commendation plaques displayed on the walls. Ricky's office resembled a Bureau museum. She looked at a picture of Ricky and former President Clinton. Next, her gaze came to rest on the family portrait hanging on the wall of Ricky, Lorna, and their two daughters, Amanda and Heather, one of which was Deidre's god-sister. *Ughh!* The feeling in the pit of her stomach made her want to throw up, and she found it hard to stop staring at the picture.

"We called you in today because we want to talk about your work performance," Ricky said, taking in a deep breath.

Work performance! What the fuck is he talking about? Deidre's mind screamed, but she remained silent, staring at the family photo.

"Aponte, let me just give it to you straight," Ricky continued, calling her by the name he used when they were at work. Deidre finally looked over at his pale white face, which was slightly wind chapped from the cold weather, but she still couldn't look into those piercing blue eyes. Her nostrils flared and she became short of breath as she listened to him.

"You are one of the best agents we have here at WFO, and Baker and I think you are ready for a new assignment." He paused to gauge Deidre's reaction.

Her entire facial expression changed as a look of ease replaced her previously worried, furrowed brows. Relieved at the news, she finally took a good look at Ricky and couldn't believe her eyes. His right cheek was marked with deep red scratches. Being a bi-racial kid who was teased and picked on often, Deidre had enough experience with cat fights to tell that the scratches on Ricky's face had come from human nails—probably his wife's. She continued to scan his face as he spoke, surveying the damage. She noticed a huge purplish-red hickey on his neck peeking out from the collar of his dress shirt. Her heart jerked painfully in her chest. For the first time since she and Ricky had become lovers, she felt hurt. Deidre hadn't put the hickey on Ricky's neck. She knew her place as the other woman, so she never bit him or sucked on his neck. That passion mark must have come from Lorna, she reasoned. After he left from fucking her, he'd gone home to comfort his wife. He had probably said sorry to Lorna a million times and comforted her with soft kisses, not the rough, wild sex he always wanted to have with Deidre. Deidre balled her fist tight, so tight that her knuckles turned white.

Ricky continued with his speech, but Deidre couldn't hear his words; her ears were ringing. She watched Ricky's thin lips move, but she refused to listen to his words. Everything he said sounded like the teacher in the Charlie Brown cartoon; "*Wha-wha-wha* . . ."

Suddenly, she felt something land on her lap with a thud. Startled, she slowed her rapid breathing and fought against the tears burning at the back of her eye sockets. Looking down, she realized Ricky had dropped a *Washington Post* newspaper on her lap.

"Do you understand what's going on, Aponte?" Baker asked, noticing her vacant expression.

She glanced at the front page of the newspaper. In bold letters she read:

DAUGHTER OF NEW YORK SENATOR REEVES MISSING AND FEARED DEAD

"That's your new assignment. The media is all over it, but this one is going to require an undercover. We need the inside, Aponte. Apparently, this girl was involved in an illegal drug ring," Baker said to Deidre, rubbing his long chin as he usually did when he was uncomfortable with a topic.

Deidre stared at Bernard Baker's charcoal colored face, perplexed. She could see fear and anxiety mirrored in his beady onyx eyes. Baker was a notorious people pleaser. All high profile cases made him nervous. He inhaled deeply through his nostrils, which produced a sickening wheezing noise, and caused a feeling of disgust to come over Deidre. Weak men made her sick.

"So this is going to be a group II operation?" Deidre asked, confirming that she would be going undercover, maybe for longer than six months.

"Yes, we anticipate . . ." Baker began with his voice cracking before he was cut off by Ricky.

"Aponte, all we need is for you to go in and find out what happened to the girl. It's really not that big of a deal," Ricky said candidly.

"How could the possible murder of a senator's daughter not be a big deal?" Deidre asked, looking for clarification. She wanted to jump up and kick Ricky in his balls. She hated herself for loving and trusting him so much. She balled up her toes tightly inside her shoes and bit down into her jaw trying to hold on to her composure.

"Well, from what I understand, she was a drug addicted runaway to begin with," Ricky blurted out. At that, Baker shifted uncomfortably on the couch, causing the leather to crackle.

"If the shit is not important, why should I waste my time? For God's sake, Ricky, it says here she is only 22. Her life matters, regardless of whose daughter she is," Deidre commented as she stood to leave. She had never seen Ricky act like this over a case. He was always dedicated and concerned with the outcomes of their investigations. Just like Deidre, in her opinion, Ricky was not himself. She couldn't wait to get out of the office.

"Wait, Aponte!" Baker blurted out, uncrossing his legs and nervously fiddling with his tie as he stood. The tension in the room was thick. "Here are the alleged major players in this," he continued, handing Deidre three brown criminal profile folders.

Deidre silently read the names on each folder: Chastity Smith, Tori Banks, and Leticia Ruiz. "In this? These girls had something to do with Reeves' missing daughter?" she asked, confused.

Ricky interjected as Baker started to stumble over his words. "We don't know. That's your job," Ricky said flatly.

Deidre rolled her eyes at his sarcasm.

"There is a CI that will get you inside," Baker informed, diverting Deidre's attention away from Ricky. "We suspect that Amber Reeves may have been working with these three. What we don't know is why someone would kidnap or possibly harm her," Baker explained.

Deidre watched sweat drip from his shiny bald head and stain the underarms of his shirt. She knew he was usually a nervous wreck on high profile assignments, but this had to be the worse she'd ever seen him. Baker seemed completely unraveled. They all did, for that matter. Nothing about the meeting was usual.

"What about the DEA? Those are the dope boys. If she was involved with drugs, wouldn't they have jurisdiction?" Deidre asked, looking at Bernard like he should've known this.

"Agent Ferguson is going to be your case agent, and Denald and Buckwalter are going to run your surveillance detail," Baker continued, ignoring Deidre's question.

"Your meeting with the CI is tomorrow. From what I understand, these bitches are notorious. They've got New York City in fear," Ricky said, covertly scanning Deidre's slim waist and shapely ass and thighs with his lustful eyes. He couldn't hide the fact that she awoke something deep inside of him. His marriage had technically been over years ago, but with his salary, the house, the kids and Lorna not working, Ricky figured it was cheaper to keep her. He admitted to himself that his initial reason for sleeping with Deidre was to collect on an old debt, but the attention she'd shown him, Lorna could never match. He'd once heard a colleague talk about how exciting sleeping with a younger woman could be, but he never anticipated the sexual feelings Deidre awoke in him. If his father ever knew he'd slept with a Black woman, he'd be cut off for life.

Ricky was born and raised in confederate West Virginia. He grew up in a poverty stricken area of the state that resembled a third world country. No running water, a one-room shack, five siblings and a father who drank and abused the family. The son of an alcoholic coal miner and a submissive housewife, Ricky had a typical poor white trash upbringing infused with learned hatred for anyone who was not like him, especially, Blacks, Jews and gays. His father beat into him that "coons, Jews and faggots" were the reason he didn't have a television or toys, and had to work so hard chopping wood, shooting deer, and fishing for food to survive.

Ricky overcame the poverty. The death of his father from liver disease and a football scholarship gave him the chance he needed to get out of West Virginia. But the secret hatred for other races and religions lived on inside of him. Throughout his years of hard work, Ricky became a master at disguising his feelings, and he decided that he would use the very people he hated in his quest to be on top. He befriended "stupid niggers", as he referred to them, in order to get what he wanted, including Deidre's father and Bernard Baker. It was not so much the money that motivated Ricky, it was the power.

"Aponte, you have to bring your A-game to play with these females. To answer your questions, we have jurisdiction over everything, and we want this case. Undercover Operations has already begun setting up your living space, vehicle, and surveillance equipment. You will be Deandra 'DeeDee' Barnes from now on," Baker chimed in, breaking the awkward silence.

"New York, huh," Deidre said, her voice trailing off. New York City held many memories for her, both good and bad. She gathered the file folders, the newspaper, and her thoughts before she walked out of Ricky's office.

When Bernard Baker was certain she was gone, he looked over at Ricky nervously. "Aponte is more capable than you think," he said, his voice wavering. Of all of the things he'd been involved in during his career at the Bureau, this seemed the most risky.

Bernard Baker had grown up poor in one of Chicago's worst housing projects, Cabrini Green. His father was never around, and his mother worked two jobs to feed her six children. Bernard never spoke up for himself as a child, and his older brothers often got the best of him at fights when his mother was not around. He spent most of his childhood reading books; he would read anything he could find. His love for the written word helped him escape the violence and poverty that was his reality.

Bernard won a full ride scholarship to Georgetown University in Washington, DC, and he never looked back. After experiencing racism firsthand and being turned down for journalist jobs by all of the major newspapers, he became an

FBI agent as a part of the Bureau's efforts to diversify. One of his sisters once asked him if it bothered him to be a "token". His reply to her was, "Not as long as I get paid like everybody else. Somebody gotta force them to let us in."

Bernard was not driven by power like most of the agents he worked with. Instead, he just wanted to be able to provide for himself without working like a slave. He would take assignments no other agents wanted, he would work long hours, and he never complained. His dedication won him a spot on an elite team of undercover agents—the best and worst day of his life, he would often say.

Deidre left Ricky's office with a lot on her mind. She'd been briefed on her new assignment, but did not feel the usual fervor to go get the job done. Something didn't seem right about Baker's behavior and Ricky's apparent indifference towards the case. *A senator's daughter was linked to drug dealers? Very strange.* Deidre almost never ignored her instincts, but this time she was too upset about how things were going with Ricky to question the details of the case. She'd worked on small-scale undercover cases for a year now. She'd been successful at bringing down a few kiddie porn perverts and some low-level government computer hackers. She couldn't help but wonder why she was assigned to such a high profile case. Why wouldn't the New York field office be handling this case? Deidre decided that a high profile case with lots of kudos afterwards might be the thing she needed, so she stopped questioning Bernard and Ricky's intentions.

Deidre stopped at her cubicle to gather a few things. She looked over at a picture of her father. He was still her hero. It seemed like her father's death had happened just yesterday. What bothered her most about her father's death was that she could not figure out why a man with everything to live for—an exemplary military record, a great job with the

FBI, and a loving wife and daughter—would take his own life and not leave so much as a note or a letter of goodbye.

When Deidre first decided to become an agent, her intentions were to uncover the truth behind her father's death. As a child, teenager, and now as a grown woman, she still did not believe the story that her father had put the barrel of his own gun into his mouth and pulled the trigger.

Deidre returned to her car to retrieve her cell phone and call her mother. Since she had to leave right away for New York, she opted not to visit her mother. She knew her mother would most likely be indulging in the "Easy Jesus" (E&J liquor) that she'd grown overly fond of in the years after her father's death.

"Hey, Mom," Deidre greeted when her mother picked up the line. She held her breath, praying that her mother was sober. It was a high hope, and Deidre knew it.

"Don't 'hey, Mom' me! What the fuck is going on with you and Ricky Blum?" her mother yelled, slurring her words and hiccuping at the same time.

Deidre recognized the signs immediately. Her mother was clearly inebriated. Closing her eyes tightly, she continued. "Mom, we'll talk about that another time. I'm just . . ."

"Do you know how old Ricky is? Do you realize that Lorna and Ricky were friends of your father and I since you were ten years old?" her mother castigated, making Deidre feel like she was a fifteen year old that had just got caught kissing a boy behind the bleachers.

"Mom, I'm about to go to New York on assignment. I'll speak to you when I get back," Deidre said flatly, disconnecting the line. "Urgggh!" she screamed out in frustration, slamming both fists against the steering wheel. Her life was a mess. A new case and trip to New York was just what she needed.

Nothing was secret in the FBI society. The people who worked at the Bureau lived near one another, wives became friends with other wives, and children grew up and married other Bureau employees' children. It was like a cult, and Deidre had tried not to fall prey to it. It was no surprise to her that her mother had already heard about the incident with Lorna. Anytime she spoke to her mother when her mother was drunk, it reminded Deidre of painful memories from her childhood.

"How could you do this to me!" Cassandra yelled, tears streaming down her face.

"I never meant to hurt you," Ramon apologized.

Deidre lay in her bed listening to her mother cry and her father apologize. At ten years old, she didn't know what they argued about so much lately, but she did know that it was happening frequently.

"Who is she?" Cassandra sobbed.

"She is nobody," Ramon mumbled.

"Nobody? Nobody? Well I would think a woman who you've been sleeping with for this long, that has you damn near living a double life, is definitely *somebody*. For goodness sake, Ramon!" Cassandra screamed as she ran out of the bedroom and slammed the door.

Deidre quickly shut her eyes and pretended to be asleep. She knew her mother would be coming to sleep in her room again.

Running after Cassandra, Ramon grabbed her by the arm before she made it to Deidre's room. "Listen, it's all over. We are moving. I got the transfer. No more New York, no more women. I am all yours," Ramon declared, hugging Cassandra tightly and stroking her hair.

Cassandra melted into his arms. She loved her husband, but she was sick of his infidelity.

"Here, these are the keys to a new life," Ramon said, pulling Cassandra away from his chest and placing the keys to their new home in her tear-soaked hands.

The next noise Deidre heard was the sound of her mother moaning, not from sadness but from pleasure. That was their routine: screaming, crying, apologizing, and then moaning. Deidre had gotten used to it.

They informed Deidre the next day that they were moving to a big house in Virginia. "What about my friends?" she asked her mother.

"You'll make new ones," Cassandra consoled.

"I don't want to move!" Deidre groaned.

"It will be a better life," her mother assured.

As young as she was, Deidre felt that it was a bad omen. She wanted to stay in New York.

Two years passed quickly, the years seeming like months. Deidre was twelve going on thirteen, and she'd quickly adjusted to life in Fairfax, Virginia. Her parents seemed happier also.

"Give me a big kiss!" Ramon demanded, playfully grabbing Cassandra around the waist.

"A big kiss? Is that all you want?" Cassandra chimed, seductively turning towards her husband.

"M-m-m-m-m! Now that's what I call a kiss!" Ramon replied.

"What about me?" Deidre sang, grabbing her mother and father around their waists for a group hug.

"I was getting to you. *Dame un beso, mi amor.* (Give me a kiss, my love)" Ramon said, picking up his daughter. He always spoke to Deidre in Spanish. He wanted her to be a well-rounded bilingual adult. He also wanted her to remain in touch with her Dominican roots.

"I love you, Daddy," Deidre squealed, grabbing her father around the neck and holding him as if she never wanted to let go.

Ramon kissed Cassandra and Deidre on their foreheads before he left for work. *My two girls*, he thought to himself lovingly.

"Daddy!" Deidre yelled, running after her father.

"Yes, baby?" Ramon replied, looking over his shoulder.

"You forgot to say you love me back!" Deidre griped.

"Oh, sorry, baby. Daddy loves you more than anything in this entire, whole, widest world. *Recuerda, que tu eres mi muchacha favorita!* (Remember, you are my favorite girl!)" Ramon said with feeling.

"I'm your only girl, Daddy. *Gracias!*" Deidre said, playfully placing her hands on her hips. She knew speaking in Spanish made her father proud.

Later that night, Deidre was awakened by loud knocks. She crept out of bed and stood at the top of the winding staircase, watching and listening as her mother rushed to the foyer of their newly built home.

"Who is it?" Cassandra yelled from behind the door. A gruff voiced replied, and Cassandra immediately recognized the person on the other side. It was Special Agent Lewis, Ramon's partner. She pulled back the door, allowing him inside. Agent Lewis' facial expression was grave, his face and eyes swollen. "Lewis? What is it? What is the matter?" Cassandra's voice had risen two octaves, as she feared the worst.

"Cassy, I'm sorry, I'm so sorry! I couldn't save him! It all happened so fast!" Agent Lewis lamented, reaching out to console Cassandra, his body shuddering under her falling weight.

"No! No-o-o-o!" Cassandra emitted a blood-curdling scream, knowing exactly what he was trying to tell her. Her worst nightmare had come true.

Deidre ran down the stairs in response to her mother's screams.

Deidre couldn't focus any more on her mother, or on her father's death right now. She was about to embark on one of the most dangerous assignments of her career. With her mind heavy, she drove around D.C. for two more hours, stopping at the Cosi on 12th and G Street to eat her favorite salad. She didn't want to go home. She was lonely now that she knew Ricky wasn't going to sneak there in the middle of the night, or even call her ten times before she made it home. She'd grown accustomed to his routine of sneaking in during the middle of the night, and the way he wanted to keep tabs on her all of the time. With no place else to go, however, she decided it was time to head home.

She drove her hooptie up the driveway. The sky was dark and she could barely see the front of her house because Lorna had busted her porch light.

As she put the car into park, she noticed a shadowy figure running away from her front door. "What the fuck?" she mumbled, fear causing a hot surge of adrenaline to pump through her veins. Despite all of the training she received at the Academy, she screamed, "Hey!" and with shaking hands reached under her coat for her weapon. She frantically swung the car door open and exited, sliding on the thin sheet of black ice that covered the tar. Regaining her balance, Deidre rushed towards her house, gun in hand. But it was too late. The lone dark figure disappeared into the naked woods.

With her chest heaving in and out, Deidre swallowed hard and slowly approached the gaping front door with caution. *Scan left, scan right.* The only sound she could hear was her own heavy breathing. Dipping her head in and out of the doorway as if she were bobbing for apples, she cleared herself to enter, all the while maintaining a two-handed grip on her weapon. Once she felt the immediate area was clear, she stuck her hand inside and clicked on the light in the foyer. Inching around inside the house, making sure to keep her back against the walls, she searched the house. Nothing. She exhaled and grabbed her cell phone, involuntarily dialing Ricky's number.

"Hello?" Ricky's gruff voice boomed through the receiver.

Deidre clipped the phone shut to disconnect the line. "Shit!" she cursed aloud, angry at herself for calling him. She could've called 911. Instead, she called the person she'd come to depend on in times of need.

She shoved her gun back into the holster and walked down the stairs. Just as she rounded the corner at the bottom of the staircase, she bumped into someone. "Agggghhh!" she screamed and jumped, going for her weapon as the person screamed too.

"Mrs. Zuberman! Whew, you scared me!" Deidre gasped, placing her hand over her pounding heart. Little did the old lady know that she was about to get Swiss cheesed up. Lucky for her, Deidre wasn't like street cops—quick to shoot and ask questions later.

"I heard you scream, and I saw that person running from your house. They cut across my grass," Mrs. Zuberman said with a hint of scorn in her voice.

"Did you see what he or she looked like?" Deidre inquired.

"No, but whomever it was, dropped this," Mrs. Zuberman informed, stretching her wrinkled white hand out toward Deidre.

Deidre grabbed the silver chain link bracelet from her neighbor's hand. Examining it, she was sure she had seen it before. "Thank you. I'll give this to the police. Just keep your doors locked," Deidre responded, slowly ushering her neighbor towards the front door.

With Mrs. Zuberman safely inside her own house, Deidre walked back to the car. Bending into the passenger-side door, she retrieved all of the files, along with the newspaper article. As she lifted the stack of papers, a photograph slipped out from one of the folders. A cold chill shot through her body like someone had pumped ice water into her veins. Even in the dark, the eyes of the person in the picture seemed eerily familiar. Freaked out, she hurriedly

pushed the picture back into the folder, gathered the remainder of her belongings, and rushed inside the house.
"You've got too much shit to do tonight to be acting like a
scardy cat," Deidre mumbled, scolding herself. She had to
be in New York the next morning, and she still had to pack
some things, review the file folders, secure her house, and
most importantly, study her new persona—DeeDee Barnes.

The first rule of going deep under cover is to know the
role, and be able to answer questions at the drop of a dime.
Especially commonly asked questions like, *Where are you
from? Where did you go to school?* Deidre had learned never to
underestimate the criminal mind. One wrong answer and
her whole cover could be blown. She wanted to make sure
she had all her bases covered.

Diedre threw all of the assignment information on her
bed. She began to undress, deciding that a hot shower was
what she needed more than anything. As she pulled her
shoulder holster from around her back, her mind went to
the image of the eyes in the photo. Her curiosity was killing
her. She wanted to know, but then again, she didn't. "Forget
it!" she whispered, grabbing the criminal profile folders.

Sitting down on her bed, she spread the folders out and
opened each one, reading the headers aloud: "Chastity
Smith a.k.a. Chazz, Tori Banks a.k.a. T-Baby and Leticia
Ruiz a.k.a. Loca, all members of F.A.B. F.A.B? What the
hell does that mean?" Deidre asked herself. She would have
to read further about this all female crew.

VOLUME 3:
THE F.A.B.

"*Fight! Fight! Fight!*" *The crowd of unruly girls from the Mother of Grace group home chanted, urging on the wiry girl named Big Melinda, who cracked her knuckles menacingly.*

"*Please, I just got here! I swear I didn't roll my eyes at you!*" *the stubby, soon-to-be victim cried as she backed away.*

"*I saw you!*" *someone in the crowd yelled, instigating.*

Big Melinda balled up her fists and moved in for the kill. The teary-eyed victim, a chubby girl with big doe eyes, covered her head with her arms, preparing to take the beat down. Crack! Crunch! *The sound of bone hitting bone traveled through the air. Big Melinda held the side of her head as she crumpled to the ground like a crashed paper airplane, nothing at all breaking her fall.*

"*Ohhhhh!*" *the riotous crowd of girls voiced their astonishment. The short chubby girl unfolded her arms to find out what had happened.*

"*Now, who else wants some of this?*" *a husky butter-colored girl barked, flanked by her partner. Talk among the crowd buzzed, but it died down quickly as they began to disperse. Nobody wanted a piece of the crazy girl.*

The would-be victim looked down at the brute that had terror-ized her. Lifting her foot, she valiantly gave Big Melinda a sharp kick in the ribs before she turned to run.

"You don't have to run. That bitch is a fucking punk—always picking on kids smaller than her up in here. I ain't having that!" the husky girl announced.

"What's your name?" her pretty sidekick asked.

"Tori," the new girl victim said softly, lowering her eyes.

"I'm Chastity, and the person who saved your ass is Leticia," the partner said.

"Thank you, Leticia," Tori said genuinely.

"No problem. You can't be a punk in this place. You gotta hold your own. When you got here?" Leticia asked.

"Last night," Tori murmured, bowing her head in shame.

"So, you wanna be a part of our crew?" Leticia asked, feeling sorry for the little, fat weakling.

"Sure!" Tori beamed, finally making eye contact.

"We are the Fly Ass Bitches," Chastity informed her.

"Okay," Tori agreed, unsure if she wanted to call herself a bitch.

"Yeah, since you are so little and look like a baby, your tag name is T-baby. I'm Loca, because as you can see I'm one crazy puta. And this is Chazz, because her ass is cool," Leticia said.

Tori smiled as she walked with her new crew, glad to feel part of something.

"Inmate 990348BK, Leticia Ruiz!" the squat, big butted Corrections Officer screamed, breaking into Leticia's reverie. Leticia stepped forward from the line, hands and feet in shack-les. "Date and place of birth!" the CO screamed her ques-tion like a command.

"June 30, 1985, Brooklyn!" Leticia yelled in response.

"Release time: 1420 hours," the CO continued, while simultaneously snapping Leticia's picture.

Leticia let a huge smile spread across her attractive, but hard-lined face, which was marred by a single C-shaped scar over her right cheek. The CO unshackled her and handed her a stack of papers to sign. "What's all this bullshit?" she asked, screwing up her face.

"This is your release agreement and plan," the CO commented without looking up.

Leticia remained silent. She decided to get released first, talk shit second.

Once she scribbled her John Hancock on the stack of paperwork, the CO handed over her two-year-old possessions in three clear plastic drawstring bags. "Open the bags and take the things out one by one as I read them off the list," the CO instructed.

"Look, I don't need this old shit. You keep it," Leticia said, pushing the bags into the CO's chest. Taken aback, the CO looked curiously at Leticia. "And I don't need no fucking MetroCard and that bullshit release money either. You use it to buy yourself a new pair of shoes or something!" Leticia spat sarcastically, chuckling as she bopped away harder than a dude. She rushed towards the front gates of Rikers Island, where she had been transferred to from Bedford Hills Women's Facility three months earlier. The music she heard blaring beyond the gates put an extra pep in her step.

"What up, thug? What up, gangsta? They say I walk around like I gotta S on my chest. That's a semi-auto and a vest on my chest"

"That's gotta be those bitches!" Leticia whispered, her heart pounding with excitement. The Fifty Cent lyrics told her that her girls where outside waiting for her. Through letters and collect calls, Leticia knew her girls had her back.

She also knew they'd started a whole new life, which included many fine things. Tori and Chastity never let Leticia down while she served her two-year bid, but a lot of things had changed since then. They'd all come a long way from being three foster care runaways. All three girls came into the system under different circumstances, but over time, they formed a special bond with each other that was stronger than blood. They all brought something different to the table.

Chastity was the beauty and the brains. She could sell salt to a slug. Tori was the level-headed one, a bit jittery but always thinking outside the box. She kept them out of trouble on numerous occasions. Leticia was the brawn. She was down for whatever, whenever. Once she committed her first murder, there was no stopping her.

"Loca, my nigga!" Tori screamed, calling Leticia by the street name she'd earned for her constant display of erratic behavior. Leticia's light green eyes lit up when she saw her friends and their ride home. *Damn! I know they said shit had picked up, but I had no idea!* she thought to herself as she continued her masculine stride towards the gleaming silver Range Rover.

Leticia and Tori embraced tightly. "Damn bitch, you feel as hard as a dude! You been working out like a muthafucka!" Tori joked, referring to Leticia's muscular arms and almost flat chest.

Leticia's five foot seven inch muscular frame towered over Tori, who, with heels, barely reached five feet. Although Leticia wanted so badly to be a dude, her face was too damn pretty. Melted butter skin, combined with a pair of striking green cat eyes made her strikingly beautiful. With her dyed blond hair always in cornrows, she strongly resembled the old school female rapper, Yo-Yo.

"You look like a dude with those corn braids all going back and shit," Chastity commented as she extended her thick shapely legs from the SUV, placing her monogrammed Gucci boots onto the concrete and joining her crew.

"Yo, wasup, ma?" Leticia said with her gruff, wanna-be-a-dude voice.

"You, Loca! Finally back in the world," Chastity said, embracing her friend since childhood. At about five feet five inches tall, the two sized up well.

"Ya'll bitches lookin' right. Designer threads and expensive-ass jewels," Leticia commented, giving Tori and Chastity the once over. Leticia felt somewhat inadequate in comparison with her friends. With the exception of a fresh new pair of white Nike Uptowns, her clothes were very much outdated. Although all of her girls were naturally attractive, money had them looking fabulous.

Chastity's naturally long thick auburn hair was perfectly coifed without a strand out of place. Her bronze complexion, slanted chestnut brown eyes and long eyelashes made her look like a movie star.

Tori had a more homely look and remained on the chubby side with a couple of muffins hanging over her jeans. But Proactive Solution seemed to have worked wonders on the acne that once ravaged her skin. Tori was a shade lighter than Chastity, her skin the color of honey. Sometimes she wore too much makeup to conceal her old acne scars. But, the freshly done, long Yaki weave, along with the short mink jacket and close fitting True Religion jeans made her look like money.

"Don't worry, in a few minutes you gonna have your weight up too," Chastity said, finally opening the vehicle door for Leticia.

Leticia climbed into the soft leather seats of the SUV, and immediately noticed that the TV in the headrest in front of her was playing the movie, *Belly*. She smiled. "My girls know my favorite movie. Now get me some pussy and I'll be straight! Turn that shit up!" she yelled over the music. *"However do you want it, however do you need it. However do you want it"* blared from the Bose speakers as Chastity peeled away from the curb.

"I know exactly what you need," Chastity yelled over the music as she drove.

"Yeah, you got plenty of time to munch carpet. We've got some unfinished business with a certain someone who might not be so happy to see your ass out on early release. I got this one all mapped out too," Tori stated, peaking between the driver and passengers seats to talk to Leticia, who slouched in the backseat.

Riding with her girls again was relaxing, and Leticia took in the scenery as if for the first time. The streets looked different to her. Although she'd been gone only two years, shit had changed.

The girls quickly caught up on old times.

"So, tell me what the deal is? How ya'll cakin' off so lovely?" Leticia screamed over the music.

Chastity lowered the music and spoke. "Yo, you'll see. We ain't stuffing squirrel packs in our pussies no more, that's for sure. We got the jump on the new hot shit in the streets."

"The clientele got money. We ain't messing with no base heads no more. We got what the rich white people want—the fucking housewife drug, that crystal, baby, and straight chasers," Tori continued, laughing out loud.

"Ya'll ain't talking about that meth, right?" Leticia asked. In jail she'd heard about the homemade drug—methamphetamine—and she knew it was blowing up. She had also seen the devastating effects of meth while she did her time. An addiction to meth was harder to kick than any other drug on the street—even crack.

"Listen, we gonna put you on. Be easy!" Chastity assured,

her words settling over them like a comforting blanket, as usual.

"Yo, 'member that time we all got caught putting shit up the back in Macys on 34th Street?" Chastity recalled loudly, changing the subject. Tori and Leticia busted out laughing. They often played "'member that time" when they were all together.

"I got a better one. 'Member that time T-baby conned that white man outta his whole wallet, and we had to run like seven hundred blocks to keep his fat ass from killing us?" Leticia added. More laughter filled the air.

"No, no! 'Member that time you tried to steal a whole rack of jackets out of the North Face store in Woodbury, and Chazz punched the shit outta the security guard when he grabbed you?" Tori recalled. The girls laughed hysterically.

As the Range Rover eased off of the Jackie Robinson Parkway onto Bushwick Avenue, Leticia stopped speaking as she recognized her old neighborhood. The streets seemed a little more run down and a little more littered with trash. She'd noticed a few more fiends speeding down the sidewalks, and she immediately settled in her mind that things had changed. Her heart pumped with a dizzying combination of fear, excitement, and more importantly, nostalgia. She was home. "Yo, what happened to the Burger King that was right here?" she asked, pointing out the window.

"That shit been gone. It's a car wash now," Chastity answered.

As they rode down Bushwick Avenue, Leticia looked to her right and read the all too familiar granite sign, "Evergreen Cemetery". She lifted her hand and touched her forehead, stomach, and each side of her chest, making the sign of the Catholic cross. "Father, Son, and Holy Spirit," she mumbled, releasing her fingers with a kiss, sadness dampening her jovial mood. It was a sign of respect for the dead. Her grandmother's death was one Leticia would never forget.

"Abuela! Abuela!" Leticia called out, rushing into the third floor railroad-style tenement flat. Eleven year old Leticia was excited to show her grandmother her Police Athletic League World Series Baseball trophy. She was the only girl on her team, and they'd won the World Series. *"Abuela*! Come look!" Leticia continued, but received no response from her grandmother. The silence unnerved her. The house was always bustling with some kind of noise, usually clanging pots and pans from her grandmother's kitchen. *Arroz con gandules* and *arroz con pollo* were all of the traditional Puerto Rican dishes her grandmother loved cooking. Her grandmother had been her legal guardian and caregiver since her mother's abandonment and her father's untimely death.

Leticia thought it strange that the small statue of the Virgin Mary and Jesus surrounded by candles that usually sat by the door was missing as well. A feeling of dread washed over her as she made her way down the long, narrow hallway. Just before she reached the end of the hallway, which led into the kitchen, she noticed a man; her uncle, Papo.

Fear gripped Leticia tight around her throat, and she dropped her prized trophy. She had been afraid of Papo since she'd learned about the details of her father's death. When Leticia was three years old, Papo pushed her father, David—or Drago as he was called—off of the roof of their building. Papo had been in one of his infamous PCP-crazed states. He disappeared shortly after Drago's death, but occasionally popped in and out to wreak havoc on her grandmother's life.

Leticia blinked a few times to be sure that her eyes weren't deceiving her. Papo stood before her, laughing hysterically, butt naked and soaked in dark red blood. Her mind told her to run, but her concern for her grandmother kept her moving closer to the danger. An unknown force seemed to be pushing her forward. She tried to run past her crazy uncle, but instead slipped and fell on shattered pieces of porcelain. All of her grandmother's religious statues, which supposedly protected the house against evil, were broken into hundreds of tiny pieces. Leticia quickly scrambled in the debris and pulled herself up off of the floor.

"*Abuela*! Ahhhhhh!" Leticia let out an ear-shattering scream. The scene was horrific. Blood was everywhere, more blood than she had ever seen in her entire life. Her grandmother's eyes were still open, but fear and pain contorted the old woman's face. Leticia stared in shock at her grandmother tied to a chair with her throat slashed from ear to ear. Her head was barely hanging on by thin strips of membrane and muscle. The face of Jesus was gripped in her grandmother's rigor mortised hand. All Leticia could focus on was the pool of blood; blood was everywhere. It dripped a dark burgundy and smelled like raw meat gone bad. She began to hyperventilate as vomit crept up her esophagus. She could hear her uncle laughing out loud behind her.

Before she could move, Papo grabbed a handful of her hair and swung her around, hoisting her into the air in one motion. He sailed Leticia across the room. His strength was like that of a super hero. Slamming into a wall in the kitchen, pots and pans came crashing down on top of her body, producing loud clanging noises. Leticia couldn't get her bearings fast enough. Papo was right over her. He held a large blood covered knife, and without saying a word, carved a "C" into her cheek.

"Agggghh! Help!" she screamed in terror as his blood-covered genitals swung in her face.

Papo let out a hideous cackling laugh, and placed the knife's sharp tip to Leticia's neck. The rapid pulse of her jugular vein caused the knife to pierce her skin ever so slightly. Holding the knife in its menacing position, he eased himself down on top of her. Tears streamed her face, but she remained silent. Papo breathed hard as he struggled to keep his weapon in place while fighting to pull down her fitted baseball tights. He struggled in vain with the material that was like a second skin on the husky little Puerto Rican girl. "Fuck!" he yelled out of frustration. Desperate, he sliced through the pants with his knife. The material gave way, exposing her muscular thighs.

Terrified, Leticia remained very still, her heart threatening to bust through the bone in her chest. Papo's eyes lit up like he'd struck gold. Leticia's bare little vagina seemed to look innocently back into his drug-crazed eyes.

"No!" Leticia pleaded, her body coming alive, ready to fight.

Papo placed one hand over her mouth and laughed loudly as he proceeded to enter her virginal opening. Leticia didn't scream. Instead, she bit the inside of her cheek so hard she could taste the metallic flavor of her own blood. Papo pushed further and further, so entranced in his wickedness that he let the knife fall to the side of their entangled bodies.

Peeking out of the corner of her eye, Leticia fought against the pain stabbing her body and moved her hand toward the weapon. Papo slammed into her torso so hard, her body thrust forward a few inches from the knife. Suddenly, the pain began to move up from her waist to her chest. She felt like her heart was going to explode as her body prepared to go into shock. She tried harder this time to reach the knife, but again was unsuccessful. Just as she was ready to surrender, the fallen pots and pans caught her eye. She felt herself losing consciousness. She began to tremble, and her entire body started to feel numb. Shock was setting in fast.

Papo grunted and made animal-like noises, not paying the little girl any attention.

Leticia reached out and grabbed hold of the handle to the large black cast iron skillet her *abuela* always fried *platanos* in. Using her last bit of strength, she hoisted the makeshift weapon above her assailant's head.

"*Bong!*" The sound of the cast iron connecting with Papo's skull ricocheted off the walls. "Arggh!" he screamed, jumping up.

To Leticia's surprise, he wasn't hurt. The drugs had made him invincible to pain. Unable to move her bloodied legs, she gathered her strength and scrambled for the knife. Papo dived for it at the same time, but Leticia was the victor.

"You killed *Abuela!*" she screamed. As he lunged for her, she jammed the huge butcher knife into Papo's neck. Blood spewed from his neck with each pump of his heart, like a knocked over fire hydrant.

"*Ccuhhhh! Cuhhhhh!*" Papo gurgled his last breath.

Covered in blood, Leticia tried to hoist herself up, but instead, slipped down the wall and passed out.

"Loca! Loca!" Tori called out from the front seat.

"Huh?" Leticia answered, breaking her daze.

"I know you ain't 'sleep. You back in the world now. Your ass better break day for the next two nights," Tori continued, chuckling.

"Nah, I was just thinking," Leticia replied, looking out the window. Although she wanted to cry, the tears wouldn't come.

"Well, we're here," Tori said, biting on her nails.

"Yeah, let's get this shit over with. I got things to do," Chastity said dryly.

Tori looked at the side of Chastity's face and rolled her eyes. She was so tired of her "I'm the boss" attitude. She felt that Chastity had forgotten how they got put on to the game in the first place. It was Tori that had taken a risk and pinched her baby's father, Monty for two ounces of hydro after he got arrested for beating her almost half to death. With two black eyes, Tori had grabbed her newborn baby and the stash, and jetted. Unaware of what to do with it after she took it, she showed the hydroponic homegrown weed to Leticia and Chastity, who at the time, were still involved in petty crimes like taking work out of town on Greyhound, and boosting to get by. When the girls got hold of the weed, they immediately hit the streets and made a name for themselves. At first they were unable to find anyone to buy more weed to re-up, but Chastity kept her ear to the ground, and it wasn't long before she got put on to her supplier. Chastity told her crew that the mystery supplier didn't want to meet or deal with anyone but her, and the girls trusted her.

Tori fell silent after Chastity's comment. She couldn't wait to be alone with Leticia to inform her all about Chastity.

"A'ight, it's on!" Leticia said, cracking her knuckles and opening the SUV door. She knew what was up. They had pulled up on Bushwick Avenue and Furman Street, right in front of a funeral home.

Chastity exited first and the girls followed. She used a lone key to open the door to a small, silver older model Honda Accord. Leticia knew it was old because it had flip-up headlights.

Tori looked around and gave a nod before they all piled into the car. Nobody said a word. It was like old times; no words until shit is said and done.

Leticia had sweat on her forehead and shook her legs back and forth; one part anticipation, one part nerves. She couldn't afford to go back to the joint. But she also knew what had to be done. The rules of the street had to be honored.

Pulling directly in front of their destination, Chastity and Leticia excited the car in a fury, but not before Chastity reached into the small glove compartment and retrieved her

.22 nickel plated Smith & Wesson with its mother of pearl handle.

Tori remained in the car with the engine running, getting out only to slide into the driver's seat. "You got your chirp-chirp on?" she asked Chastity.

"Yeah, but only if the block gets hot," Chastity warned.

"Bang! Bang! Bang!" Leticia used her fist to rap on the familiar metal door. She could hear Shakira's lyrics blaring loudly from inside, but no one answered. She knocked again, harder this time.

"Who?" a female voice yelled from the other side of the door.

"It's me, baby!" Leticia cooed deceitfully.

"Who?" the voice inquired again, sounding confused.

"Diana, open the fucking door!" Leticia yelled, careful not to reveal her name.

"Who is it?" Diana inquired as she looked through the peephole. Seeing that it was Leticia, her eyes grew wide and she looked like a deer caught in headlights.

Pushing forcefully into the apartment, Leticia didn't waste any time. She grabbed Diana, roughly applying pressure to the shocked girl's cheeks. Chastity stepped inside and locked the apartment door. "Why you ain't visit me? I thought I was your girl?" Leticia said, still gripping Diana's face tightly with her fingers.

"Wa-wa-wait, Loca, *mami!*" Diana stuttered, feeling like she was going to faint.

"Wait what, bitch? You a snitch, and in my 'hood, snitches get dealt with!" Chastity spat, moving in on the girl. The only reason Chastity hadn't already taken care of Diana was because Leticia had asked her to wait until she came home. She wanted to exact revenge herself.

"Looks like you were busy," Leticia growled, referring to the candle-lit apartment. "Who the hell you here with?" she grumbled, slapping Diana across the face. It pained Leticia to hit Diana. She was once in love with her. She thought that Diana was going to be "the one" until they got knocked for selling weed to an undercover. Leticia had warned Diana not to tell the narcs anything, but once they were put into separate interrogation rooms, Diana snitched. She told everything, and caused the F.A.B.'s entire petty weed and small-scale cocaine operation to get shut down. Not only was Leticia furious about the two year bid she had to do, but Chastity was still angry over her hustle being blown. It took hard work dodging five-O while she worked to rebuild her operation. Besides, Chastity and Tori had just narrowly missed getting knocked themselves.

"Come on, Loca! I love you, baby!" Diana pleaded.

"Yo, let's murk this bitch! I ain't got time for the dumb shit!" Chastity said, pulling the gun out of her bag. She peeked out of the front window and shut the blinds. She was a little worried that Tori was outside by herself. Tori was always nervous when stuff went down. She wasn't the violent type.

"Nah, shooting her would be too easy," Leticia said through clenched teeth. There was nothing worse than love turned to hate. She grabbed Diana by her hair and twisted her hands around in her long, sandy brown locks.

"Ayi!" Diana shrieked, her nut-brown face turning cranberry red. Her robe had fallen open, exposing the cosmetically perfect breasts that Leticia had paid for.

"Shut the fuck up!" Leticia screamed as she dragged Diana, kicking and screaming towards the bathroom.

"This is taking too long, Loca. C'mon!" Chastity said urgently, tapping her foot.

Leticia ignored her. This was something she had to do. Once in the bathroom, Leticia ripped Diana's robe off. Diana stood shivering, naked and crying, pleading for her life in Spanish.

"You were taking a bubble bath, huh? Sure smells good!"

Leticia sang, her tone becoming increasingly and eerily calm. The entire bathroom smelled of the Bath and Body Works brand, Warm Vanilla Sugar. Candles were lit all around. Leticia remembered when she and Diana used to take candlelit baths together. The thought angered her even more. Leticia's skin was hot and her cheeks flamed over red. She felt outside of herself. "Get in the tub!" Leticia commanded.

"Ple-e-e-ease! Loca, I love you!" Diana pleaded one last time. She knew Loca, therefore, she knew she was going to die. Diana had never anticipated Leticia getting out of prison so early. She was in the back of the courtroom when the judge had said, "Seven to twelve!" and slammed his gavel.

"I said get in the fucking tub!" Leticia roared, her chest heaving in and out. She knew if she stood there looking at Diana any longer, she wouldn't be able to hurt her.

Diana finally relented and stepped one foot at a time into the warm, sudsy water. "Hail Mary, full of grace . . ." she began praying like a good Catholic would during their last rites.

Leticia grabbed Diana by the back of her neck, pulled her tear-soaked face into hers and kissed Diana deeply, sticking her tongue straight down the girl's throat until Diana gagged. Tasting the salt of her tears, Leticia released Diana and balled her fist and punched her across her cheek. The powerful blow sent the busty girl tumbling backwards into the water with a splash.

"What the fuck, Loca?" Chastity asked incredulously as she watched from the doorway.

Leticia looked back, tears rimming her eyes as Diana tried to get her bearings. She'd hit her head on the wall inside the tub, and was dazed and confused. Chastity had her gun in hand, but Leticia walked past her. Chastity looked on, confused.

Leticia calmly walked over to the space saver over the toilet and retrieved a blow dryer. She plugged it into the electrical socket beside the medicine cabinet.

Diana emerged from the water, gasping and wiping her eyes, just in time to see what was coming her way. "No!" she screamed as the blow dryer dangled over her.

"Now you'll know what hell feels like," Leticia said as she let the electrically charged blow dryer drop into the water.

Immediately, the water started to bubble, misty smoke rising from the tub like a witch's cauldron. Sparks flew everywhere. Leticia jumped back, throwing her hands up to shield her face and eyes. Both Leticia and Chastity watched as the electricity caused Diana's body to shake fiercely and white foam to spew from her lips. Leticia watched unfazed as life drained from Diana's body. She retrieved a towel from the round metal holder on the wall and wiped her fingerprints off of the doorknobs and space saver. Throwing the towel at Chastity, she followed suit, wiping anything she remembered touching.

"I still think you should put one in her ass," Chastity said.

"Nah, bullets can be traced," Leticia said, her voice quivering.

"Now that's what you get when you cross the Fly Ass Bitches! The code is death before dishonor!" Leticia proclaimed exciting the crime scene.

"'Member that time we jumped those fake ass CMB girls from Flatbush and dumped one of them in the dumpster?" Leticia joked, still showing no remorse.

Chastity chuckled as they got back in the vehicle.

"What happened? What took ya'll so long?" Tori asked nervously, swinging her head back and forth, looking from Chastity to Leticia.

"Just drive," Chastity instructed, needing some quiet time.

Tori peeled off.

VOLUME 4:
THE CITY OF NEW YORK

After her meeting with Ricky and Bernard, Deidre agreed that maybe the case would be open and shut. Anyone could have kidnapped Amber Reeves, or maybe she was high on drugs and drove off a cliff, or maybe the girl was somewhere skied up and couldn't get home. These were all thoughts that ran through Deidre's mind as she prepared for her new assignment.

Deidre found out that the Reeves had tried tirelessly to keep their little girl away from the lure of drugs. Ironically, Senator Reeves was the driving force in Congress behind the new and improved National Drug Control Policy that had placed a chokehold on major drug outlets across the world. Senator Reeves was also the former Manhattan District Attorney responsible for prosecuting Diego Esperanza, the ruthless leader of the Mexican drug cartel, "Diablo". Reeves hadn't put an end to Esperanza by himself. He'd done it with the help of a driven team of undercover agents from the Bureau, a team consisting of then Field Agents Ricky Blum, Bernard Baker, Ramon Aponte and Daryl Lewis.

As a kid, Deidre had heard stories about the Esperanza

case. She remembered how much time her father had spent away from home, working that case. The case had followed her into adulthood, because even during her undercover training, portions from the Esperanza case were used. Deidre had even heard that Diego Esperanza's son was being groomed all these years to take over his father's cartel. Would the young Carlos Esperanza really have the balls to kidnap the daughter of the man who put his father behind bars for life? It was a possibility that Deidre wouldn't rule out. She also knew that Senator Reeves rode the Esperanza case straight to the Senate.

Arriving in New York was eventful for Deidre. She had missed the crowded streets, tall buildings, and just the excitement of a city that literally never slept.

Before meeting with her team, she needed to go visit the Reeves. They'd been staying in their penthouse suite on Manhattan's Upper West Side. Arriving, Deidre thought she'd need her gun to stave off the throngs of reporters and paparazzi staked outside of the building. She was told that there would be a "controlled release" (the Government's edited release of basic facts) of information to the media. *So how did this circus get assembled?* she asked herself.

Once inside, the heavy air grabbed Diedre by the throat, and she was quickly absorbed by the somber mood that permeated the luxury high-rise apartment. Sitting on a long Victorian style sofa, Senator Reeves held his head in his hands, the hair on the top of his head completely gray. In Deidre's assessment, he appeared as if he'd aged twenty years overnight.

Standing by the floor-length windows with his hands shoved down into the pockets of his Dockers, was the former governor, William Reeves, Amber's grandfather. His eyes were rimmed with red, and sagged at the bottoms.

The women of the family, including Sandra Reeves, flitted around in the kitchen, trying to keep their minds occupied. Deidre couldn't tell what exactly they were doing, but she didn't smell anything good coming from behind the swinging doors.

Sandra Reeves peeked her head out of the doors when she heard the clamoring of Deidre's arrival. "Hello. Another agent to add to the army. You want something to eat or drink?" Mrs. Reeves commented, flashing a bright smile. Her face beamed and didn't show any signs of the stress a mother would display if their only child was missing and feared dead. Deidre made a mental note of it.

"No thanks," Deidre smiled back, hoping her disapproval of the woman's nonchalant attitude didn't show on her face.

The Secret Service and Bureau agents stood guard solemnly with their obligatory Oakley shades covering their eyes, as if a masked gunman would burst through the door at any minute. Several agents waited near the telephone, bulky tracing and recording equipment sitting in wait. There had been only one call to the Reeves, and no one had yet asked for a ransom. That was a bad sign in kidnapping cases. Communication was the only proof of life.

Looking around, a lump grew in Deidre's throat. Her initial intentions were lofty at best. She had come there to tell the Reeves that she was going to find their daughter and save the day. But the drab atmosphere put those thoughts to the back of her mind. Besides, she couldn't tell them that she'd be undercover and risk anyone leaking it.

Senator Reeves thanked her for coming. They were familiar with each other through Ricky. Deidre had met Senator Reeves once during his campaign for Senate. Ricky had been one of the Senator's supporters, and without violating the Hatch Act, Ricky worked tirelessly to make sure the Senator won.

Richard Reeves was a demure man. He carried himself like a true politician, always knowing the right words to say and always flashing a winning smile. Deidre had never seen him without his American flag lapel pin and a red or blue tie on, a true patriot. Senator Reeves was no stranger to politics. His family was just as powerful as the Kennedy's. The Reeves had started their own 21st century Camelot. But like the Kennedy's, the Reeves were not free from skeletons and family secrets.

Amber Reeves was one of their secrets. She'd started using drugs recreationally in junior high school. After her parents divorced, the recreational use turned into a full-blown addiction. The divorce was very hush-hush. In fact, most people didn't know that Sandra Reeves, Senator Reeves' current wife, was not Amber's mother.

Inside the Reeves home, things never went smoothly. The hate between Amber and Sandra was no secret, and neither of them hid their disdain for one another. Family dinners often turned into screaming matches, with Senator Reeves in the middle. In Amber's opinion, her father was always on Sandra's side.

Leaving the Reeves' home, Deidre was back to square one with her thoughts of suspects. Her list, it seemed, would just keep growing. She'd witnessed firsthand how much regard Sandra Reeves had for Amber. Sandra seemed partially jovial, in Deidre's opinion. *Maybe Sandra had gotten rid of the girl once and for all*, Deidre thought.

During her visit, Deidre had walked around in Amber's bedroom, looking for any leads. She found a small diary, and after taking a quick peek, she learned that on the last night Amber was at home, she and Sandra had finally gotten physical and gone to blows. Amber stormed out on her way to the Candy Shop to meet Chazz and the girls.

Deidre hadn't left Chastity Smith, Leticia Ruiz and Tori Banks off her list of suspects either. From what she had been told, these girls were the last ones to see Amber Reeves. One of Amber's friends had revealed to the Bureau that Amber was selling "ice", the street name for meth, to people at school for a crew called the F.A.B. Maybe she owed them money and things turned bad.

Deidre's mind raced with possible suspects. She was going to solve this case. Forget the newspapers. Her name would be set in wood on a door to a large office inside the J. Edgar Hoover Building.

"I got a hundred guns, a hundred clips. Nigga, I'm from New York, New York. I gotta semi-automatic that spits. Next time that you talk, you talk . . ."

Deidre bopped along as she drove over the Brooklyn Bridge. Being back in New York was going to be a trip. She reminded herself to drive through her old Flatbush neighborhood and see how much Church Avenue had changed. From what she'd heard from New York agents, Brooklyn had become the borough of churches and hair salons. Deidre smirked to herself at the joke.

The Mercedes Benz CLS 500 that the Bureau had assigned to her for the assignment drove smoothly. The tires seemed to hug the road, and the leather seats felt soft as a baby's ass. As soon as she'd gotten far enough into New Jersey, she tuned in to the New York radio stations. When she left New York, 98.7 Kiss was the hottest station on the air. All that had changed. Now it was Hot 97, WBLS, and Power 105.1.

All Deidre could think about was her assignment. From what she'd read on the F.A.B., they started off as runaways and petty thieves, boosting, snatching, conning and pickpocketing. Not long after, they got into selling weed, and then graduated to cocaine. After their operation got shut down, they left cocaine alone. Now they were at the top of a new game, shaking shit up. Apparently, the senator's missing daughter was in some way connected to them. The Bureau and NYPD needed evidence. Senator Reeves and Capitol Hill were not going to rest until they got it.

Deidre finally made it onto Adams Street. She looked out the window to her right as she passed the Supreme Court building, and knew that one day she'd be there testifying against these bitches she was about to go up against. If she made the case, that is.

As Diedre approached Atlantic Avenue, the computerized voice on the GPS system instructed her to turn left northwest onto Atlantic Avenue, and continue three miles north. She did as told. Stopping at a light on the corner of Atlantic and Flatbush, she reached over to the passenger seat to retrieve the address. She examined the slip of paper; 710 Hall Street, her new home in New York. Her meeting with her informant and the surveillance team was a few hours away, and she needed to shower and change her clothes.

Suddenly, her cell phone rang. "Hello?" she answered on the second ring.

"It's Denald. We'll meet you on Henry Street by the hospital in two hours," he said.

"A'ight," Deidre replied. She had used her first slang word in years. She smiled.

Deidre pulled up to 710 Hall Street. It was a nice four-story walk up. She needed to meet Amos, the landlord that was going to rent her the apartment. She looked around for a parking spot. One whole side of the block was empty of cars, and the other side had cars parked and double-parked. "Great! Alternate side of the street parking!" she grumbled. Following suit, Deidre double-parked her car in the middle of the block. She retrieved two suitcases, her laptop bag, and another silver metal briefcase from the trunk. Struggling to hold everything, she dropped the metal briefcase. "Oh shit!" she cursed herself, letting everything else fall so she could scoop up the briefcase. She looked around nervously. No one had seen her. Taking a deep breath, she proceeded to her new home. She lifted the gray, brushed-metal doorknocker and rapped three times.

"I'm coming! I'm coming!" a man with a heavy southern accent screamed out from the other side. The man pulled back the door. He was so short Deidre had to catch herself looking around for him.

"I'm DeeDee. I called about the apartment for rent," she introduced herself, looking down.

"Oh, yeah," the man recalled, with a stinky unlit cigar between his lips.

A midget smoking a cigar! I done seen it all, Deidre said to herself.

"Somebody done come here and paid your first month's rent and s'curity," the man said, still not asking Deidre in.

"Yeah, that was my best friend. I'm just moving here from D.C."

"A'ight, well, come on in. My name is Amos," he said, finally moving aside and allowing Deidre in. He turned and led her to the steps. "Yo best friend brang in ya furnitcha too," Amos informed Deidre.

"Yes, I know. I let her monitor the movers for me because I had to tie up some loose ends at home," Deidre explained, thinking quick on her feet.

"So, what brings ya 'round these here parts? I mean, I ain't tryna get in yo business or nothing," Amos commented.

You could've fooled me! " Well, I'm just looking for a change of pace. I hear New York is the place to be, and the city is too expensive to rent," she responded carefully.

"Dee Vee, girrrllll, I'll tell ya. I'm from the South, Alabama to be exact, so this here city life ain't for me," he said, laying on his thick southern drawl.

"DeeDee!" she corrected. She wanted to tell him to get lost. The little man smelled like cigar smoke, dog ass and bologna.

"Here she is, the one bedroom suite," Amos said as he opened the door to Deidre's new digs.

The apartment was quaint, but the hardwood floors were beautiful. She had never seen wine-colored hardwood, and it was so shiny that she could almost see her reflection. The kitchen wasn't eat-in, but it had a small two-burner stove, a small refrigerator, and sink. That was sufficient for Deidre, as she had no desire to cook anyway. The bedroom had huge floor-to-ceiling windows, with large wooden shutters. The Bureau had provided her with black Italian lacquer furniture. The headboard, dresser, and armoire were shiny black and piped in gold, a bit gaudy for her tastes. It was all the seized property of some flamboyant Italian Mafia member or notorious drug dealer.

Deidre was so caught up taking a self-guided tour that she didn't even realize Amos was following her around like a lapdog, and still talking. She looked at her watch. "Shit!" she exclaimed, stopping Amos in his tracks.

"Is there something wrong?" he asked, surprised by her sudden outburst.

"No, it's just that I have to meet a friend in less than thirty minutes, and I need to shower and change," she explained.

"Oh, I get the hint. You want me out," Amos replied with a hint of sadness in his voice. He liked looking at her, especially since he was eye level with her perfectly round backside.

"No, no. I hate to rush you, but I can't keep my friend waiting," Deidre said, escorting him to the door.

After he was gone, she ran back into the bedroom, unlocked the silver briefcase and retrieved her new identification—a driver's license, passport, high school diploma, and birth certificate—all of which read "Deandra Barnes". She placed the driver's license on the bed and dropped the remaining documents into one of the nightstand drawers. She pulled up the black velvet divider inside of the metal brief-case, and made sure her father's silver key was there. She was the only one who knew it even existed.

After her father's death, Deidre and her mother had tried to pick up the pieces of their lives. Cassandra had become distant, indulging heavily in drinking. Deidre had come home from school on numerous occasions to find her mother passed out drunk. One day, she arrived home to find a FedEx delivery guy leaving her porch. "You live here?" he asked.

"Yeah, why?" Deidre responded.

"I got a package for this address, and I see the lady in the house is on the floor. I've been ringing the bell for 15 minutes, but I can't wait any longer. You gonna sign for it?" he asked.

"Yes," Deidre sighed loudly. She could feel the heat of embarrassment settling on her cheeks. She scribbled her mother's name and took the package from the guy. "Thanks," they both said.

Deidre flung her bookbag over one shoulder and held the package under her other arm as she fumbled with her keys. Once inside, she threw her stuff down in the foyer and walked over to the living room. Kicking the empty liquor bottle away, she grabbed her mother under her arms, strug-gling to drag her dead weight to the couch. "Mom!" she screamed, slapping her mother's cheeks.

"M-m-m-m-m," her mother moaned.

Deidre inhaled deeply out of frustration. She walked to a small hall closet and retrieved a blanket to throw over her poor excuse for a mother. She knew her mother would be there for the night.

Curious about the package, Diedre picked it up and went to her room. There was no return address. She shook the box but didn't hear anything sliding inside. "I'm opening it," she mumbled to herself, and proceeded to tear at the purple, orange and white box. It was filled with her father's belongings.

Her first instinct was to throw the box down and run out of the house. She thought that her Uncle Ricky had cleaned her father's locker back when the incident occurred. She probed further. There was a picture of her at six years old, wearing Mickey Mouse ears and standing between her mother and father, smiling brightly. Also in the box was a picture of her father and Ricky standing side by side, smiling like they had no cares in the world.

Deidre flipped through numerous pictures before she felt something fall and hit her foot. It was a small silver key with a tiny piece of white paper taped to it, and written in smudged blue ink was "ANSWERS". Her heart began racing. She had no idea what all of this meant. She surely wasn't going to give the key to her mother to lose. Checking the doorway for her mother, she walked to her white wooden dresser, pulled out the entire bottom drawer, and taped the key to the back of it. Until she could figure out what it meant, it would remain her secret. She never went anywhere without that key.

Deidre picked up two large stacks of crisp one hundred dollar bills and flipped through them like a deck of cards. The strong scent of brand new bills traveled through her nostrils, settling at the back of her throat until she could actually taste it. "Ahhh, the perks of being undercover! I went from an underpaid agent, to a rich ass drug dealer!" Deidre inhaled and sighed, smirked and peeled off five one hundred-dollar bills. She placed the remainder of the money back under the velvet divider in the silver briefcase and locked it.

"Now, let me see which designer outfit I'm going to wear," she mumbled, referring to the clothes she had been issued. She walked to the small closet in the far left-hand corner of the bedroom, dragging the royal blue Samsonite suitcase with her. In the suitcase lay several designer dresses, jeans, shoes, and handbags. "Hm-m-m, never heard of Antik," she said, flipping the tag on a pair of seemingly regular stone washed jeans. "Two-hundred and sixty-five-dollars! Shit, no wonder I've never heard of them!"

Deidre placed the jeans on the bed and continued to unpack. She was amazed at how much money the federal government spent on chasing down criminals. She wondered if, in the end, it was all worth it. She had hung up more than one designer outfit worth thousands of dollars. She shook her head in disbelief. Although most of the items had been seized and confiscated during drug raids or asset forfeiture cases, she was still flabbergasted at the prices.

She had heard that some confidential informants for the government also received nice incentives to snitch. One person who promised to give the Bureau the Cali Cartel on a silver platter was given a million dollars in cash to set up business. He was also provided a Benz and an expensive condominium in Miami. On the flip side, she was glad that she would receive everything she needed to convince the F.A.B. that she was ready to do business with them.

Deidre padded through the apartment, preparing to take a shower so she could meet her team. She had stripped down to her underwear, and slid into her own pink satin kimono bathrobe. No way in hell was she going to wear Bureau issued underwear and pajamas.

Passing one of the large windows, she noticed an NYPD squad car pulled up next to her vehicle. She could see an officer with his ticket book in hand headed towards her car. "Oh, hell no!" she screamed. She had been warned to avoid the local police at all costs. Without thinking, she pulled on a sweater and darted out of her apartment. Flying down the front steps outside, she lost one of her pink fuzzy slippers. "Shit!" she cursed, still running with the cold air stinging the bottom of her left foot. "Wait! Wait! I was just about to move it!" she yelled at the officer as she half-limped, half-ran. She flinched as the cold air slapped at her bare legs, sending an icy chill straight up her spine. She looked like a crazy woman. Passersby stared at her lack of clothing. She would surely catch pneumonia dressed so scantily in the icy New York weather.

The officer standing at the windshield of her vehicle ignored her, and the one in the squad car ogled her half-dressed frame. Panting, she limped over toward the officer, clutching her sweater and robe against the cold. "Please! I'm new . . . to . . . this . . . town," she panted each word out, gasping for breath.

"It's too late. Once I write it, I can't take it back," the officer grumbled, avoiding eye contact—typical police insolence.

Deidre became enraged. She observed the young officer, who looked to be no more than twenty-four years old, and she read his badge. "Anderson" was etched into the small silver plate on his chest. "I can't believe this! The city makes you double-park with that fake ass street cleaning, and then gives you a ticket!" she complained loudly. She suddenly remembered some of the things she hated about her hometown already.

Officer Anderson continued writing without saying a word.

"Ain't nothing but a baby! I can still smell Similac on his fucking breath," Deidre cursed under her breath.

When he was done, the officer ripped off the ticket and went to place it on the windshield, smirking at Deidre. She rolled her eyes and snatched the ticket off of her car. "One-hundred and fifteen-dollars!" she shrieked as she read the white cardboard-like paper. Outraged, she headed back towards the house.

"Hey lady, aren't you gonna move your car?" Officer Anderson asked at Deidre's back.

"Why? You already gave me the fucking ticket!" she replied, retrieving her slipper and continuing into the door.

Officer Anderson's partner, Officer Duke, sat in the squad car completely mesmerized by Deidre's beautiful face and legs. He was smitten, and had to know who she was. Rushing before his partner returned, Duke punched the license plate numbers into the mainframe computer between the driver and passenger seats of the squad car. He quickly read the results—"PROPERTY OF THE U.S. GOVERN-MENT". He knew that meant one of two things: either the beautiful woman was a Fed, or she had purchased a seized vehicle at an auction and didn't get the paperwork straightened out yet. Officer Duke's heart beat fast as his partner moved closer to the car. He hurriedly hit ESC button to erase the information. He glanced out of the passenger side window to the other side of the street, but Deidre had already made her way inside. Had someone made a costly mistake?

After her run-in with the locals, Deidre scrambled to get ready. She took a quick shower, slid on the Antik jeans, a tight fitted micro-fiber shirt that read "J'adore", and a hot pair of dark brown Cowboy boots. She topped off the outfit with a short-cropped chocolate-colored shearling jacket, and brown leather quilted Chanel bag. She scanned her get-up in the long mirror hanging on the back of the bathroom door. Satisfied that she fit the part, she headed out.

Deidre maneuvered her way over to Henry Street, taking in the Brooklyn scenery. The area had definitely changed since she last visited. She had never remembered seeing so many white people in Clinton Hills and Downtown Brooklyn.

Arriving, she noticed the sign for Long Island College Hospital. She drove around the block looking for the blue van, or any sign of Ferguson, Denald, or Buckwalter. With no one in sight, she decided to stop in front of a small playground at the back of the hospital to wait. She watched ambulances pull in and concerned family members bring their sick loved ones to the emergency room. Glancing at her watch, she sighed loudly. "Just like the government! Everything is always hurry up and wait!" she spoke aloud to herself. Suddenly her cell phone vibrated. "Hello," she answered.

"Get out and go into the hospital cafeteria on the first floor," Agent Ferguson instructed.

Deidre had graduated from the FBI academy with Ferguson. They'd always had a secret rivalry going on, which kept both of them on their toes. Having worked together in the past, Deidre had no qualms about Ferguson being her case agent. She thought back to her days in the Academy.

"Huh! Huh!" Deidre panted, her breath the only sound she could hear. She leaned against the tree, hiding. On the opposite side of the field she spotted her target, her enemy. Inching forward, her heart racing, Deidre knew it was do or die.

Ferguson crouched down. She was also behind a tree with no one in sight. Afraid to move to assess her surroundings, Ferguson dropped her firing arm to her side. Suddenly, she heard the ground crunching to her left. "Oh shit!" she whispered, hunkering down, hoping she wouldn't be noticed. The sounds grew closer and closer. Her heart raced; her throat was desert dry. Sweat dripped into her eyes, but she was afraid to move to wipe the beads away.

Deidre squinted her eyes and moved one foot in front of the other slowly.

Ferguson focused her senses, holding onto her gun tightly, trying to make sure she was aware of her surroundings. Looking down, she saw that the crunching noise was coming from a small rabbit. "Whew!" she let out a long sigh of relief, blowing out the breath she'd been holding. Just then, she heard the pop. Paint splattered all over the side of her goggles and helmet. Her nerves caused her to involuntarily vomit.

"Ferguson, once again you failed to take cover! You let the resident animals distract you, and Aponte just killed you! You are dead . . . shot in the fucking head! Scan left, scan right! What is so fucking hard about that?" the instructor castigated, nose to nose with Ferguson.

She heard cackles of laughter coming from the guys in the class as they commended Deidre with pats on the back and ribbings for a job well done. It was the third time Deidre had bested Ferguson in a tactical exercise.

Ferguson snatched off her helmet and goggles and tossed them across the field. *I hate this bitch, but I'll get her back!* she vowed to herself.

Deidre walked over to Ferguson and extended her hand. "All's fair in love and war. I have a lot of respect for you," Deidre said.

Ferguson ignored her hand and walked away. More uproarious laughter followed.

"It's all a mind game, this para-military style they use. My father told me once that they break you down to build you back up," Deidre offered as she joined her predominately male classmates. Ferguson looked on, seething.

"Memories!" Deidre sighed as she circled the block again looking for parking. The pickings were slim; nearly all of the signs read "For Doctors Only". Out of the corner of her eye, she noticed someone waving at her. It was Denald. He was so short and fat, so no one could mistake that frame. He pointed his stubby index finger to a spot in front of the blue van. Deidre pulled the car in front, but when she turned around to walk towards the hospital's entrance, there was no sign of Denald. She did not want to attract any attention to herself, so she didn't look around too hard. *I guess that's a good thing. Shit, if I can't find him, they won't either*, she thought and continued through the automatic revolving doors.

The hospital lobby was bustling with visitors and potential patients. Doctors in scrubs or white jackets flapping behind them flew through the hallways. Deidre seriously wondered why Ferguson would pick such a busy place to meet. On her past assignments, the meetings always took place in hotel rooms or restaurants with private tables.

Deidre greeted a lanky young security guard in a burgundy jacket and gray pants, who was blatantly checking her out. "Good afternoon," she nodded, and he did the same, following her with his eyes. She was about to ask where the cafeteria was when she noticed Ferguson walking toward her. "Hey, what's up?" Deidre greeted with a wide smile.

"Aponte! My nemesis!" Ferguson joked. The two women embraced with a quick hug and pat on the back.

Deidre noticed that Ferguson had put on a few pounds, but she was not fat, more muscular if anything. Her deep chocolate complexion and hazel eyes made her look exotic. Ferguson still wore her hair short, almost like a man's. Sometimes Deidre wondered about the woman's sexual orientation. "You look good. How's city life treating you?" Deidre asked.

Ferguson was a country girl from a small town in Georgia called Valdosta. Living in New York was a huge jump for her. "I love it. This is truly the city that never sleeps," she commented.

"Tell me about it. I just got my first . . ." Deidre began as they approached the cafeteria entrance. Ferguson placed her hand up, cutting her off mid-sentence. Stopping in her tracks, Deidre looked at her confused.

"Listen. The CI (confidential informant) is inside. He

is . . ." Ferguson paused trying to find the words to describe him. Deidre stared at her face looking for answers. "Well, let's just say he is a character. He seems to know a lot about Amber Reeves, and he's good friends with R.J., the brother of the alleged leader of the F.A.B.," Ferguson stated.

"Well, how did you get him to roll?" Deidre asked, concerned.

"We didn't have to, he came to us," Ferguson explained. "What did Biggie Smalls say? 'Money and friends don't mix like two dicks'," Ferguson laughed, looking at Deidre's surprised expression. "What, you thought I didn't listen to hip-hop?" Ferguson asked. "Seriously, it wasn't that hard to get his ass to sing. Where there are friends and money, there is jealousy, and so you got informants. Since his ass is singing, let's just call him 'Billie Holiday'," she continued, chuckling at her own joke. Deidre laughed too as they walked through the swinging doors.

Deidre looked around the large, round institution-style cafeteria trying to figure out which table her informant occupied. The first table held a young guy dressed in what she considered street garb. He wore a beige North Face snorkel, which hung open, exposing his oversized silver chain with the obligatory diamond cross pendent dangling from it. *Maybe that's him*, she thought. But then she noticed several guys rushing towards the guy with cigars in hand, offering their congratulations. Next, she noticed another African-American male sitting alone with his doo rag adorned head in his hands. *This has got to be him*. But Ferguson walked right past him. Ambling forward on Ferguson's heels, Deidre continued to scan her surroundings. She finally spotted a guy in dark shades sitting alone at a table in the very rear of the large room. He didn't have a "street" appearance at all. In fact, he wore a collared striped shirt. He leaned back on the two rear legs of the chair with his arms folded across his chest.

Deidre quickly averted her eyes, and as soon as she did, Ferguson stopped at his table. *That's what you get for stereotyping your own people*, she scolded herself.

"Reemo, this is Agent Aponte, known to you as DeeDee Barnes. Aponte, this is Kareem Porter, better known as Reemo," Ferguson said, introducing them.

"How are you?" Deidre asked, extending her hand. He was nothing like she suspected. Deidre could tell he was short, as his legs dangled from the end of the chair, barely touching the floor. From what she could see aside from the large shades covering his eyes, his cinnamon colored skin was pockmarked, and he had several old healed scars visible–the most distinctive being a dagger-shaped gash above his right eye. He had a long straight nose, and after close observation, round bug eyes. Reemo reminded her of Spike Lee.

"Day-um! You ain't say the *federale* was gonna be banging!" Reemo shrieked.

"Hey, hey!" Ferguson warned, clenching her jaw.

"I'm saying, wasup, Agent Sexy? Reemo quipped.

"I'm fine. Let's talk about the F.A.B.," Deidre said sternly, annoyed already.

"First, let me set the record straight. I ain't no snitch nigga, but a nigga gotta do what a nigga gotta do when his dick is in the dust. Fucking with ya'll crooked-ass feds is what I gotta do," Reemo spat.

Ferguson jumped to her feet like she was about to punch him in his face for that comment. "I'm warning you . . ." she growled.

Reemo's eyebrows rose in surprise, and so did Deidre's. Noticing that she had lost her cool, Ferguson immediately took her seat and let Deidre continue.

Reemo heeded the warning, sensing that he had overstepped his boundaries. "A'ight, here it is . . . boom!" he began, punching his left fist into the palm of his right hand. "Me and that nigga, R.J. been down since elementary school. My moms was fucked up in the game n' shit, so I was always at that nigga's house. His moms was always home cooking, taking us to the movies and all that good shit," Reemo started.

"Does this have to do with the F.A.B.?" Deidre asked, interrupting him.

"Yo, all this shit is relevant, because without us, those bitches wouldn't even exist in the game," he explained.

"Okay, continue," Deidre instructed.

"Anyway, like I was saying, R.J. and his little sister, Chastity had a good life. They pops was some military dude, coming home every so often n' shit. When he came around, Ms. Donna, they moms, was so happy. I can remember that shit clearly. Big R had a real kingly presence and he always taught R.J. to man up. He loved Chastity too. I never knew nothing about having no father, so he kind of took me under his wing. Anyway, when me and R.J. was like twelve, that nigga pops left one day in his uniform and never came back home. Yo, Ms. Donna was sick over that shit. No word from that nigga. She lost mad weight and was forever crying n' shit after that."

"One day, me and R.J. picked up Chazz from school, and we was bullshitting on the way home. When we got to the building, mad red and blue lights was outside n' shit. At first we didn't know they was there for R.J. house. This lady in the building looked at R.J. and said, 'I'm so sorry about your mother, baby,' and we both ran top speed past the cops into the building. The apartment door was swinging wide open with all those fucking blue suits taking pictures, smoking and talking like nothing. But right there in front of us was Ms. Donna, hanging, blue in the face with her pretty eyes bulging out of her head and her face all twisted up," Reemo said, almost whispering. "Word life, that shit hurted even me. My man went crazy, trying to fight five-O," Reemo said, his voice wavering.

Deidre listened intently as Kareem continued.

"R.J. and Chazz got sent to a foster home up in the Bronx. Some Spanish shit. You know they pops was mixed with some kind of Spanish, so them BCW people took that and ran with it. Yo, I missed my man, and we used to meet halfway on the 2 train during school time to hang out. R.J. started fucking up in school off the strength of that shit. He kept running away from the foster home, so they put his ass in a group home. One thing led to another, and me and that nigga started hustling for this cat from Harlem. Yo, we was caking off for two little niggas. R.J. always took care of his sister though. He was always there when she got out of school before she went back to the foster home. Our rise to the top of the game came quick man. We had shit on lock," Reemo proclaimed with feeling, banging his fist on the table. "Then, all that shit blew up when jealous-ass niggas started hating. We got knocked on some ol' setup shit."

"Meanwhile, while R.J. was on the inside. He worried about his sister. She had got used to a certain lifestyle thanks to that nigga. R.J. didn't want his sister in the life n' shit. It really ain't a game for women," Reemo continued, looking from Deidre to Ferguson to gauge their reactions.

"How long did you do?" Deidre asked, wanting him to get on with the story.

"Five strong," he said quickly. "Chazz got kicked out of foster home after foster home. When she got sent to the girls' home, that's where she met Loca and T-baby. All three of them became a crew. They kinda stuck together after that. Those chicks got into the street life even though R.J. forbid his sister from the game. Yo, we heard stories in the joint of how R.J.'s little sister was slanging them thangs crazy. Chazz took care of her brother, but not me. Me and R.J. got separated at intake so it was hard for me. R.J. would make Chazz hit me off every now and then because my moms and my sisters were fucked up." Reemo looked as if he were about to cry over the fact that he had no visitors or regular commissary deposits. "I'm sure you don't know what life is like in the joint when you ain't got no money, no visitors, no mail—yo, you ain't got shit."

"Anyway, R.J. got out before me. That nigga came home to a king's welcome, 'hood style. When I got out, that nigga picked me up, took me shopping, got me a spot to chill, and told me I could work for his sister. See, he ain't getting his hands dirty no more. He don't have to, you feel me?" Reemo looked at Deidre over the rim of his shades. She was hanging onto his every word.

"Tell her what you know about the girl in the picture," Ferguson instructed. Deidre had totally lost sight of that.

"Oh, yeah. Yo, that little white chick was a major asset to the F.A.B. When she first started coming to the Candy Shop to buy her stuff, she drove a Benz and rocked diamonds, but she was a major base head. That chick could sniff a mountain up her nose. Nobody knew she was a senator's daughter. She put Chazz on to the crystal and penny candy game; said she had connections in high places."

"Crystal and penny candy?" Deidre asked, not understanding the reference. She already knew the Candy Shop was a club owned by Chastity and her brother.

"Yeah, meth—street name crystal and all kinds of pills—blue ones, red ones, yellow ones—all those prescriptions shits that white people get high off of, we call them 'penny candy', because they are colorful, cheap, and make you feel good just like penny candies," Reemo explained.

"Ok. I got it, now continue," Deidre said.

"Yeah, so that girl got Chazz a connect and was taking care of the higher clientele, you know, them boys in Harvard, on Wall Street and Capitol Hill. That little white chick was moving major stuff. I'm talking twenty thousand dollars every coupla days. But she was using major, too. Yo, I remember seeing her like three weeks ago, and her Barbie

Doll shape was gone. For real, the bitch looked like Skeletor."

"Then one night, the Candy Shop was popping, asses bopping, titties flying, and we all was in the VIP section, chilling. Well, they was chilling. I was mooching, since a nigga ain't worthy of the top," Reemo griped, clearly jealous of R.J. and the F.A.B. Realizing he was starting to sound whiny, he continued, "Anyway, the white chick came stumbling in. She was all fucked up, screaming and yelling about some money, pointing at Chazz and T-Baby. I mean straight lunching. R.J. jumped up from the table and tried to break up the situation, but she kept on going on and on, making a big scene. All of a sudden, this crazy bitch swatted at Chazz. Security grabbed her and threw her ass straight out the door. That's the last time anybody seen her."

"So, you haven't heard anymore about her since that incident?" Deidre asked. It all didn't make any sense to her. *Why would the F.A.B. sever ties with someone making them a lot of money? How could a senator's daughter be a major drug dealer and no one notice?*

"Nah, I'm telling you she vanished. After that, her pictures started showing up on TV as the senator's daughter," Reemo said.

"Who is the supplier for the F.A.B.?" Deidre asked.

"Yo, that shit is top secret. Only Chazz and R.J. know that. They never take anybody to those top secret meetings," Reemo said bitterly.

"So, how can I get in?" Deidre asked.

"I'ma introduce you as a business partner," Reemo explained. "Tomorrow night they're throwing a welcome home party for Loca at the Candy Shop. You know, the bitch just got out of the joint . . . some bullshit weed charge, not no real time. And that dyke bitch gets a party. When I got out, I got nothing," Reemo complained.

"Okay," Deidre said, eager to leave.

"Meet me there tomorrow afternoon before the party. The Candy Shop is where the old Brooklyn Café used to be," Reemo said.

Ferguson slid a manila envelope across the table. Reemo placed his hand on top of it, and covering it from view, he slid it off the edge of the table and into his jeans

"Yo, I just want ya'll to know that no matter what, R.J. is my nigga from the womb to the tomb. His sister and those other hoes I could do without," Reemo said resentfully before he stood up and walked away from the table.

Deidre didn't trust him. Something in her gut told her he was bad news, but she didn't have much of a choice. He was her way inside the F.A.B. *Find the supplier, and you'll find out what happened to the girl*, she reminded herself.

VOLUME 5:
THE GIRL

The girl could hear her captors moving around upstairs as dust fell through the cracks of the old wooden floor onto her bed. "Ahem! Ahem!" she let out a weak cough as the powdery substance danced in her nostrils and throat. She didn't have enough strength to release a strong cough, nor could she scratch her nose. After she'd tried to escape, they bound her hands. The drug withdrawal had almost killed her when she first arrived. She had been so desperate for drugs that on one of the man's solo visits, she tried to seduce him. When he got close enough to her, she kicked him in the balls and ran. Unfortunately, she wasn't fast or strong enough. He grabbed her by her dusty brown hair and beat her senseless. Before he left, he took what she had offered and tied her securely to the bed.

The girl kept track of the days by making a mark on the wall each time someone came to visit, signifying the number of days that had passed. Maybe they didn't come every day anymore . . . she couldn't tell.

"Dear God," she said a silent prayer that today they'd bring her some food and water. Her captors were a male and female, but sometimes two men came to look in on her. The lady treated her worse than the men. She had no human compassion whatsoever.

The girl squeezed her eyes shut as the footsteps grew louder and louder. She wished herself dead. "Daddy, where are you?" she whispered. She'd long stopped thinking about her mother and father, because the memories drove her insane. Her father was always a loving, compassionate man, and she was the apple of his eye, his Ambie Baby, that's what he used to call her. Tears flooded her dirt-covered face as she listened to her father's voice in her head. She had gone against everything she was raised to be. Her family was the new generation of Kennedy's. The Reeves were starting their own 21st century Camelot. Her grandfather, Governor William Reeves, started the tradition, and her father, the current senator for New York, continued it. Wealthy democrats like the Kennedy's, the Reeves family also had their share of skeletons. She was one of them. Addicted to drugs since the age of thirteen, she had entered into a dark, dangerous world just for the thrill of it.

The sound of the feet ceased; the girl listened intently. Loud moaning ensued. Whenever the man and lady came to visit, they would have sex right before they came to see her.

"Ohh! Ahhh! Yes, yes . . . arggghhhh!" were the usual sounds. The girl knew they were fucking right above her head. The sounds used to arouse her at first, but in her current half-dead state, even if she had a naked man right in front of her right now, she wouldn't be aroused. It seemed like a lifetime before the couple finished. Laughter filtered through the cellar door, as loud footsteps pounded down the stairs. The door creaked open and she opened her gray eyes wide. She wanted to see them, even if they kept their faces covered.

"Your daddy is really worried about you," the man said callously, getting close to the girl's face.

She began to sob loudly. Just thinking about her life—the life she'd thrown away for drugs, her father, the mansion she grew up in—made her sick to her stomach. She wanted to die.

"Here's something for you to eat," the lady said gruffly, placing a ham sandwich, a slice of cheese, and a cup of water on the floor.

"I'm gonna untie one hand so you can eat," the man said. Both covered their faces with masks and wore gloves.

The girl wanted so badly to see a human face. She scanned them up and down, trying to make a mental note of what they wore. Black shirt, blue jeans, black military style boots. Leaning over the side of the bed, with one hand still tied, she weakly grabbed for the food. The lady stepped on her fingers just as she reached her sandwich. "Oww!," the girl screamed in agony.

"How does it feel to have someone step on you? You should know, Miss Rich Bitch!" the lady growled.

"Let her eat. I have to go," the man barked.

"Fuck her!" the lady screamed as she lifted her foot from the girl's hand.

The girl quickly picked up the sandwich and gobbled it down. Her throat was so sore from screaming that the water and food burned going down.

"Good girl!" the man said in an eerily low whisper, his breath burning against her cheek.

"Please, let me go!" the girl sobbed as she looked into his icy blue eyes through his mask. The cold eyes seemed to pierce through her soul.

"I can't do that until your daddy behaves," he informed her.

"You talk too much. Lets go!" the lady interjected.

"Please, wait!" the girl screamed as loud as her sore throat allowed. Her screams were for naught. They slammed the door, leaving her in darkness.

* * *

Sandra Reeves peeked down the long hallway of the high-rise apartment she shared with her husband and Amber. The agents on duty were sitting down, probably asleep since they'd been holding post for days. She inhaled deeply and walked into Amber's bedroom. Entering, she could still smell the girl's strawberry shampoo. The scent seemed fresh like Amber had just washed her hair. Sandra walked over to the closet and pulled back the doors. Everything was the same. Her heart jerked in her chest. She didn't mean what she'd said when she told her stepdaughter, "You'd be better off dead than living like you do now." Sandra was never able to conceive any children of her own, and admitted that she was jealous of how Richard doted on Amber. She rubbed her arms, as the hairs began to stand up.

When Sandra made the telephone call, all she wanted was to scare Amber and get a break maybe. She couldn't help but to think that this might all be her fault. The plan had backfired because her husband was even more withdrawn from her now. Watching him in pain hurt Sandra even more than having the spoiled ass brat around.

She picked up Amber's diary and skimmed the pages. She set her jaw and pursed her lips at what she read: *Drugs, sex, running away*. Amber was a fucking embarrassment and would surely ruin Richard's reputation, Sandra reasoned with herself. It made her feel better, if nothing else.

VOLUME 6:
<u>THE CANDY SHOP</u>

Deidre's stomach did flip-flops. She tied a pink satin scarf to the side of her purse as a signal for her team. After a short walk up to the club's red doors, she looked up at the huge neon sign that read, "THE CANDY SHOP", yanked on the long copper door handles and stepped through the doorway. A burly, six-foot seven-inch, Andre the Giant-looking bouncer stepped out of a small office with a dingy Plexiglas window. Inside the dimly lit foyer, Deidre craned her neck to look up at him.

"The tryout is straight in the back, past the bar!" the bouncer grumbled. Before Deidre could open her mouth, he shoved her in the back with his gorilla hands to move her along.

Deidre wove her way slowly through the club, lost as a puppy. She touched her waist to make sure her cell phone was clipped to her belt; it was her tracking device. She hoped Denald and Buckwalter—her back up—were getting the right signal to track her moves. She observed a small stage in the center of the club. There were mirrors everywhere, and the beautiful hardwood floors looked like no one had ever danced on them. She passed the maze of black marble-topped tables and high-backed chocolate brown suede chairs, and headed towards the bar.

The bartender was a tall, slender man who reminded her of the actor, Omar Epps. His skin was the color of chocolate chips, and his hair was cut military style. She made eye contact with the bartender. Feeling a quick pang of nervousness, she averted her eyes to the black door at the left of the bar. The bartender gave her a quick nod and jerked his head slightly towards the door. Deidre took that as her cue and picked up her pace, not wanting to attract the attention of the surveillance cameras that she noticed in several places above the bar. *Where the fuck is Reemo?* she screamed inside of her head.

Opening the shiny black door, Deidre was immediately assailed by the smell of smoke, sweat, and strong perfume—both cheap and expensive. There was a line of scantily clad women of various ethnicities, body types, and ages. Deidre had no idea what the line was for, but she pushed her way through the door, forcing the line of women to move up so that she could fit at the end. She looked up and down the line. She had never seen so many ass cheeks, thighs and titties in her life.

Deidre's entrance had caused some of the women to turn and glare at her; they did not need any more competition. She, with her beautiful almond shaped eyes, long eyelashes, flawless caramel skin, and athletic body, posed a threat to these women. A few even voiced their disdain, saying things like, "Look at this bitch! Think she's too cute to wear a costume!" and "Who do this outsider think she is, coming up in here?"

Deidre ignored the derogatory comments. She was not there for the same reason as them. She did, however, listen in to try to find out what was going on. She thought she was coming to the club for her first meeting with the F.A.B., but Reemo was nowhere in sight. She listened intently to the jibber-jabber exchanged between some of the women. A tall blonde with small breasts and a very slim frame complained, "This is crazy that we have to try out for the party when we fucking work our asses off here!"

A strip club? Deidre screamed inside of her head. Reemo and her surveillance team had failed to mention that the Candy Shop was a strip club, and the files just said it was a club. It was too late. There was no turning back now. She needed to get inside.

"Next!" Deidre heard a man scream, and the line began to move forward.

The next four girls on the line sauntered through a doorway. Deidre moved up and continued to do so until she was part of the next four to be called. Seething with anger, her heart pounded loudly in her ears. Reemo had set her up! Just when she was about to turn around and leave, she felt pushing and shoving, and then heard Reemo's loud and obnoxious voice.

"Ladies! Oh damn, ladies!" he screamed, grabbing handfuls of ass and tits. Loud groans of disapproval floated down the line. Finally, Reemo noticed Deidre. "DeeDee, I'm sorry I'm late. C'mon, you ain't gotta stand on this ho' stroll," he belted out, garnering more disapproving grumbles.

"Where the fuck have you been?" Deidre whispered angrily.

"Just follow my lead," Reemo said as he pushed through the door.

Sitting on the other side of the door was the alleged leader of the F.A.B. If Deidre remembered correctly, the beautiful girl in the expensive off-white fur vest was

Chastity Smith. Chastity didn't catch Deidre off guard as much as the man sitting on Chastity's right. He was the possessor of those familiar eyes from the picture she couldn't stop staring at the night she got the assignment. It was R.J. Smith, Chastity's brother. Deidre immediately felt sick. Fine beads of sweat lined up at her hairline and she couldn't concentrate. She was fighting what felt like huge bats flitting around in her stomach.

"What up, son?!" Reemo yelled, rushing towards R.J.

"Yo, nigga, what's good?" R.J. replied, never once taking his eyes off of Reemo's company.

Deidre gulped the lump lodged at the back of her throat. She could feel the heat from his eyes on her, and it made her uncomfortable, but in a good way.

"Yo, this is DeeDee, the out-of-town jump-off I was telling you about," Reemo whispered.

Deidre couldn't hear what he was saying. She shifted her weight so that her leg hit up against the weapon she concealed in her boot; reassurance.

"DeeDee, this is my bro, R.J. Bro, this is DeeDee," Reemo said, introducing them.

Deidre couldn't look R.J. in the face. His eyes made her uncomfortable. The chestnut brown cat eyes dug a hole right into her. He was very attractive, with a full beard that connected to a slim trimmed mustache. She referred to that type of beard as the "Ice Cube". R.J.'s soft hair was cut low, but not so low that Deidre wasn't able to see the soft texture of the small curls that hugged his scalp. He extended his hand for a handshake with well-manicured nails and unusually soft hands. *Don't look like he has ever been to prison*, Deidre thought to herself.

"It's nice meeting you, DeeDee. I hear you the one that got my bro on the come up, moving real weight for the team," R.J. said with his low, Barry White voice.

Deidre thought only her daddy could ever sound that sexy. *Stay focused*, she scolded herself. "It's nice to meet you too," she said shyly.

"Yeah, yeah. I just wanted her to meet you n' shit," Reemo said nervously.

Why the fuck is he acting so nervous? Deidre screamed inside her head, slightly panicked but playing it cool.

"So, ya'll found any hot chicks for tonight yet?" Reemo asked, changing the subject.

"Nah yo, same ol' sorry ass stripper chicks. You seen one, you seem 'em all," R.J. commented.

Chastity approached the three of them. "You are so fucking rude!" she screamed at Reemo as she stared Deidre down.

"Nah, lil' sis, I was making my way over to you. Bro got up to holla at me, but you stayed sitting there," Reemo replied. "Chazz, this is DeeDee. DeeDee, this is Chazz," Reemo introduced, not wanting to be accused of being even more impolite.

"W'sup," Deidre said, smiling.

"W'sup," Chastity said in an almost inaudible whisper. She had noticed Deidre as soon as she walked in, and apparently so had R.J.

"Nice to meet you," Deidre said. Chastity ignored her and walked back to her seat behind her Centurion desk. *A hard ass, huh?* Deidre thought. She had never had good experiences with other women, so she didn't have girlfriends. Deidre knew nothing about all-girl shopping sprees, slumber parties, or what it was like to have a best friend to confide in. Chastity's snub was not unusual to her.

"R.J., let's finish this shit. The party is tonight, and Loca deserves some hot bitches at her shit," Chastity said, still eyeing Deidre.

"Yo, Reemo, why don't you and your partner chill for a minute. Let me finish up here and we can go throw some back at the bar," R.J. suggested with a wide smile. He loved Reemo like a brother, but he was more interested in the girl.

"A'ight, cool," Reemo agreed, looking at Deidre for approval.

"What time is the party tonight?" Deidre asked.

"Who invited her?" Chastity asked right back.

"I did," Reemo answered.

Chastity looked at her brother for an explanation. She was very private and didn't take kindly to Reemo inviting any unwelcome outsiders to their private party. She also wasn't feeling Deidre being in her office. Besides Tori and Leticia, Chastity generally hated other females and didn't trust them much at all.

R.J. gave his sister a telling glance that said, just chill. "The party starts at eleven."

"Thanks. Reemo, I'll see you tonight," Deidre said, trying not to sound over-eager. She glanced quickly at Chastity before she turned on her heels and headed for the exit.

"You in the middle, turn around!" Deidre heard Reemo yell at the line of half-naked women patiently waiting to audition. *Fucking clown!* she thought.

Rushing up the street, Deidre spotted an FTD Flowers van and instinctively knew her surveillance team was inside. Heart racing, she climbed into her car and pulled off with her tail close behind.

VOLUME 7: THE DEMONS WITHIN

Leticia examined herself in the long store mirror inside of Burberry. "I don't like it," she griped, making faces at the mirror.

"Huuuhhh!" Tori sighed, frustrated. "We've been to nearly every store in Short Hills Mall. You betta find something," she warned, looking at her watch.

"Yo, for real though, you shoulda took me downtown Brooklyn. All this upper-class shopping ain't for me. I want some Roca-Wear, Sean John and Timbs. Forget Burberry, Gucci, and Christian Dior. These shits is for ya'll girlie girls," Leticia complained.

"Whatever!" Tori laughed. She found Leticia's desire to be a man funny.

"But I'm saying, I do need to hit Gucci again for those chocolate monogram sneakers," Leticia said, chuckling along with her friend.

Tori looked down at her watch for the fiftieth time, anxious to get their shopping trip over with. She had been given specific instructions from Chastity to take Leticia shopping for a hot, high-end outfit for the surprise party planned for Leticia tonight. Tori had no desire to be at the mall, as she was scheduled for a visit with her baby girl in a few hours. Her daughter, Akayla, had been removed from her care after she was arrested for possession of a stolen credit card and grand larceny. She beat the charges, thanks to the high-priced lawyer Chastity hired, but her battle in Family Court had just begun. She was no stranger to hard knocks or the system. Even though she had a black metal box filled with cash in the bottom of her closet, she fully understood that the New York City foster care system could not be bought.

Tori was the seventh child of ten, and often overlooked at home. Her mother ignored a lot of things while she was growing up, including the excessive corporal punishment her father used. Rollow Banks, pastor of the Good Hope Baptist Church, was a man of the cloth that believed that sparing the rod spoiled the child. Pastor Banks was a hero to his storefront church followers, especially the women.

"Sit up straight and don't dirty your clothes before service," Ellsie Banks warned her nine eldest children, who ranged in age from sixteen to seven years old, while they ate breakfast. In the Banks' home, cleanliness was considered next to Godliness. Shortly after breakfast, they all loaded into the family's green 1975 Pontiac station wagon, with its ugly brown oak wood grain doors, to spend the day at church. Pulling up on Pitkin Avenue, all of the children, with the exception of LuLu, the baby who was always on her mother's hip, exited the station wagon in clown car fashion. Tori was last, as usual, which earned her a swat on the back of the head from Pastor Banks.

". . . *Sign me up for the Christian jubilee,*

Just write my name, write my name on the rolls.

I've been changed; I've been changed, since the Lord has lifted me.

I wanna be ready when Jesus comes . . ."

The loud music assailed the children's young ears as they entered the storefront church. Tori immediately raised her hands over her ears in a rude display of disapproval. Tambourines, drums and the old-fashioned organ were thumping with gospel music. Some of the older members had already begun the morning praise portion of the service. Sister Oralie was running up and down the aisle with the Holy Ghost already.

Ellsie marched her children to the front row—the first family row to be exact—and they all slid onto the hard, birch wood bench.

Coral, Tori's oldest sister, removed her dark blue pea coat to reveal her starched white usher's uniform, and quickly took her place at the back of the tiny church to perform her duties. Tori turned around to watch her sister in action. Coral was so pretty in Tori's eyes. Her sister had skin like silk, large round dark brown eyes, the most perfect button nose and straight white teeth. Her hair was down her back, and at sixteen, she possessed the shape of a grown woman. Tori wanted to be an usher. She often wished she were just like Coral. Coral got lots of attention, greeting people with her blinding white gloves and beautiful smile. She was clearly Pastor Banks' favorite child. Tori's father watched Coral with pride. At home, she got whatever she wanted, including her father's undivided attention.

"Psst! Turn around and mind the Lord!" Ellsie whispered harshly at Tori.

The service began as it usually did, with what seemed like a lifetime of standing. Pastor Banks took his place at the pulpit and motioned for everyone to sit down. Tori stared at her father. He was a very handsome man, standing at six-foot three-inches tall, with a broad chest and prominent square shoulders. His skin was similar to Coral's, smooth and creamy and the color of Caribbean sand. His eyes were deep set and dark like coal. When he spoke, he held the entire room captive with his words, all except for his younger children.

Shortly after the service began, Tori started the never-ending fight with her neck to keep her head up, nodding in and out of sleep. At nine years old, she was not interested in redeeming her soul. Nor did she have ten percent to bring into God's storehouse, which her mother and father often used for groceries right after service.

Normally, after service, the Banks children were charged with cleaning up the church. Today, however, Pastor Banks said he was going to drop the children and Ellsie off at home, because he and sister Addie had to visit the sick and shut-in church members at various local hospitals. Ellsie obeyed her husband and loaded the children into the car. She took her place in the front passenger seat to wait on Pastor Banks to drive them home. Sister Addie remained inside the church with Pastor Banks.

"Ma! Ma!" Tori called out from the back of the station wagon.

"What is it?" Ellsie answered, trying to get a glimpse of her husband inside the church, but not daring enough to go back inside.

"I gotta pee-pee!" Tori whined.

"Can't it wait? Your father will be mad if you get out of this car," Ellsie warned.

"No, I really gotta go!" Tori screamed, afraid she would have an accident.

"Go ahead then, and hurry up back!" Ellsie yelled. She didn't care if Tori interrupted anything inside the church anyway. She hated Addie and her Jackée-looking self.

Tori climbed over the other children and exited the car in a hurry. Bursting through the doors, she ran straight down the center aisle toward the small bathroom adjacent to the tiny pulpit. Before she could push the bathroom door open, she heard loud moans coming from behind the pulpit curtain that covered the baptismal pool. Then she heard her father groan like a dying bear. Tori thought her father might be sick or hurt. She rushed to the curtain and yanked it back. "Daddy! Sister Addie!" Tori screamed, shocked at what she found. Her father was standing in front of Sister Addie, who was on her knees with his penis in her mouth. Tori peed all over herself as both scrambled to adjust their clothing.

Her father rushed towards her and grabbed her forcefully by the arm. "If you tell your mother, I will kill you!" he growled with his hot breath blowing on her face.

Tori had seen the devil himself, she was sure of it. When she got back into the car, she was panting and as pale as Casper the Ghost, except she didn't look so friendly.

Coral could see that something was wrong. She leaned over to Tori and whispered, "You better not tell on Daddy!"

That night, the family sat around the dinner table and ate in silence. Tori could hardly eat her food under her father's menacing glares. Her nerves caused her hands to shake and her fork to drop on the floor. Bending over discretely to pick up her utensil, her hand hit the edge of her plate and sent her entire dinner crashing to the floor.

Pastor Banks jumped to his feet in one swift motion. Everything stopped and everyone stared, not knowing what to expect. Tori's father took this opportunity to show Tori what he would do to her if she ever told her mother what she had witnessed. "The Lord doesn't tolerate disobedience and wastefulness! You didn't want that food!" he boomed, yanking Tori out of her chair.

Terrified, the entire family looked on in shock. Ellsie furrowed her eyebrows with worry, knowing first-hand what her husband was capable of. Pastor Banks dragged Tori to the bedroom she shared with her sisters.

"Take off your dress!" he demanded.

"Please, Daddy! I'm sorry! I didn't mean to drop it!" Tori pleaded as she watched her father pull out the short black cow whip.

Pastor Banks lifted his arm in fury and the cow whip crashed against Tori's hand and forearm, which she had raised in self-defense. The bone in her pinky finger made a loud crunch as it shattered under her skin.

"Aggghhhhhh!" Tori released a blood-curdling scream, which did not seem to dissuade her father from his assault. Pastor Banks was a man possessed. Up and down he went with the cow whip, its small beaded leather ripping into Tori's delicate skin until she bled.

At first Ellsie tried to tune out the sound of her child screaming for dear life. When she stopped making noises, Ellsie became worried. With LuLu in her arms, she rushed into the girls' room. Tori lay perfectly still, stiff with shock as her father continued whipping. "Rollow, that's enough!" Ellsie screamed out of fear for her child's life.

Pastor Banks turned around swiftly, dripping with sweat and eyes squinting with pure menace. He looked like the devil himself. "Shut your mouth, woman! The Lord said the wife is her husband's servant!" he misquoted the Bible as he lashed Ellsie across her face.

Shocked, Ellsie stumbled backwards, fighting to get her balance. Enraged, he hit her again. By now, all of the children were standing in the doorway crying for their daddy to stop. Pastor Banks cracked his whip against his wife's frame, but this time the whip tragically caught baby LuLu around her neck. Blood gushed from the baby's soft, sienna-colored skin. Ellsie's baby began to convulse in her arms. "Noooo!" she screamed as the baby flopped from her grasp and hit the hard tiled floor.

Time stood still. Tori's body lay bloodied and in shock

just feet away from her lifeless baby sister. Cries of pain and anguish echoed throughout the house. Everyone was screaming and jumping up and down, except for Tori and Lulu.

Ellsie dropped to her knees. "Lord what have I done?" she screamed in agony.

Tori closed her eyes, breathing in snot and blood, the sight of her dead sister forever etched in her brain. She never saw her father again after that, and her mother had to be committed to a psychiatric ward. The remaining nine children were separated and placed in foster care.

"Tori! T-baby!" Leticia called out, confused as her friend ran through a red light without even blinking.

"Yeah girl, I'm a'ight," Tori assured. Any time she thought about that fateful Sunday and the days, months, and years that followed, she got the chills. Her father's violence and the scars, both emotional and physical, could not be erased. That's why she hated to be around fighting, violence, and bloodshed. Witnessing death was something she never wanted to do again.

"I got my sneakers. Are you getting the bag you looked at?" Leticia asked.

"No, I just want to get out of here. I gotta go see KayKay. If I'm late, that bitch of a foster care worker will surely tell Judge Henly on my next court date," Tori explained.

"Damn, man! They still bugging off that? Can't they see you are a good mother? Shit, everybody makes mistakes!" Leticia spat. She despised the foster care system.

"My bitch of a sister, Coral don't make it no better. She always got something to tell the court. Yo, it's like she got somebody telling her all of my business," Tori complained.

"She just wanna keep your baby because she can't have none," Leticia said.

"I know, but I can't help wondering how this bitch be finding out information," Tori said, concerned.

"Yo, the streets is always talking," Leticia replied.

The ride back to Brooklyn in Tori's 2004 Mercedes Benz ML55 truck was quiet, aside from the *Game* CD that bumped.

"*. . . Hate it or love it, the underdog's on top,*
And I'm gone shine, homie, until my heart stop.
So envy me, I'm rap's MVP . . ."

Leticia and Tori had a lot on their minds as they bopped to the music in silence.

"Ms. Banks, you're late again," Ms. Dudley, the foster care worker said pointedly.

"I'm sorry, I got stuck in traffic," Tori explained, huffing and puffing from running up the block.

Coral was sitting in the family visit area at the Little Flower Foster Care Agency, with Akayla in her lap. Tori's heart raced as she wiped snot from her nose and approached the two. "Hey, baby girl!" Tori sang, extending her arms towards her two-and-a-half-year-old daughter. The baby was dressed in a yellow Roca Wear baby sweat suit, with her thick hair pulled into two Afro-puffs.

"No!" the little girl said, grabbing Coral around her neck.

"What's the matter? It's your mommy!" Tori said, the glee in her voice fading.

"No-o-o-o-o!" the little girl screamed and squirmed as Tori tried to grab her. "Mommy!" Akayla screamed with tears running down her honey-colored chubby cheeks as she looked to Coral for help.

Tori's heart was broken and tears immediately poured from her eyes.

"C'mon, baby, visit with your Mommy," Coral said, trying to persuade her niece to go to her biological mother.

"You Mommy!" the baby said, still holding onto her aunt.

"Are you teaching her to call you Mommy now?" Tori asked angrily.

"She chooses to call me Mommy, and if you . . ." Coral began, but was cut off.

"She is a fucking baby! She can't choose to call you shit! You are trying to steal my baby, that's why you keep telling the court that I'm a drug dealer!" Tori yelled, her tears mixing with her makeup.

"I don't have to listen to this!" Coral grumbled, holding onto the baby while she reached for the baby's coat.

"Fuck you, Coral! You always had it out for me since the thing with Daddy! Why don't you and your pastor husband have a fucking baby of your own! You can't judge me. Only God can judge me!" Tori screamed and cried at the same time. She was aching inside.

"No, you need to be smart and stop putting your so-called friends before your own child!" Coral spat before she stood up to leave.

"You bitch!" Tori yelled, starting at Coral as the foster care worker held her arms.

The baby was even more frightened now, and the security guards rushed to the area where the family sat.

Tori bent down and kissed her screaming daughter on the forehead. "Mommy loves you anyway," she said through racking sobs. She could not control her grief. Tori knew that she would give up everything she had if she could just have her daughter back.

As soon she made it out of the foster care agency's doors, she leaned up against the aluminum siding on the building. Her tears flowed and she felt like dying. Fumbling with her pocketbook, she dug out a clear pill bottle. Her hands were shaking as she pulled the green stopper out and tapped three small pills into the palm of her hand. Looking around to make sure no one saw her, she threw the pills into her mouth and swallowed. She had just violated the first commandment of hustlers—never get high on your own supply. Tori waited a few minutes for the pills to take effect. Finally, she began to feel at ease. Wiping her eyes and nose with the backs of her hands, she managed to temporarily squash her pain.

VOLUME 8:
THE PARTY

R.J. took a long pull off his blunt. Inhaling deeply, he swore he could feel the drugs, like small hands massaging his lungs. His lungs agreed with him as he started coughing so hard that tears ran out of his eyes. "Yeah, that's how you tell that good shit!" he said to himself. He took a couple more tokes off the blunt, getting his mood right.

Looking down at the gift box at his feet again, he felt differently. The weed had calmed him down enough to accept it. Inside the white Saks Fifth Avenue box was a beautiful Ed Hardy velvet blazer, a pair of Evisu jeans, and a Gucci fedora, all gifts from his little sister. The card on the box read, "To my Big Brother: Your outfit for tonight. Luv, your baby sis, Chazz." R.J. read the card over and over, and then let out a short grunt. "Ain't this a bitch? My baby sister, the kingpin, sending me something to wear!" He snorted, giving the box a short kick. R.J.'s pride made it hard for him to accept the way his sister doled out money to him.

He fully understood that as a condition of his parole, he shouldn't be engaging in any criminal activity, but Chastity took that to the hilt. He didn't take the way she treated him out of her love and concern that he never return to prison. Instead, he looked at it like she wanted to be the boss of him. He loved his sister dearly, but the situation was killing him inside.

R.J. looked around his apartment. Everything in it had been purchased for him by his sister. He had to admit that he'd taught her well, but it still made him feel like less of a man.

His buzz was beginning to wear off as he gazed at a picture of his mother and father. "Fucking punk ass!" he mumbled, referring to his father, a man he once revered. "You left like a bitch, and she took the fucking easy way out, leaving us here like stray dogs!" he growled, talking to the picture like his parents were right in front of him. R.J. felt like crying. He'd failed his mother and his sister. He was supposed to be the man. His father left him in charge. *I'm not a man . . . I ain't shit!* he thought to himself. "Arrgh!" he belted out, punching himself in the chest several times with all his might. He had to pull it together. "I'm the fucking man! I am the fucking man!" he screamed, hitting himself again as hard as he could. He tossed the picture across the room. "I am the fucking man!" he assured himself once more.

Leticia rolled her eyes into the back of her head. "Aw . . . shit! That's what I'm talking about!" she whispered as the beautiful girl between her legs went to work on her clitoris. Leticia grabbed the girl's hair and pushed her head forcefully toward her slimy wet vagina. *"Slurp! Slurp! Slurp!"* She hadn't had good head in two years, even though she got her fill of pussy while she was locked up. In her opinion, it was better when you didn't have to sneak around. "Arrgghh!" she growled as she climaxed, sounding like a real man in ecstasy. "Shit! You got a magic tongue!" she gasped, sitting up. "Get up!" Leticia commanded, and the girl did as she was told. Leticia pushed the girl on the bed, grabbed her strap-on dildo, and proceeded to mount the girl doggie style, just as a man would.

Loud banging on the door interrupted the hot sex session. "Fuck!" Leticia yelled, unable to ignore the persistent knocks. Pulling on her baggy jeans and a wife beater, she rushed to the door. "Who?" she screamed.

"It's me, Chazz!" Chastity yelled back.

"I'm busy!" Leticia screamed, still not opening the door. She was too horny to care.

"Yo, open the door!" Chastity demanded, banging, for added emphasis.

Relenting, Leticia unlocked the door and opened it.

"Your ass is supposed to be getting ready for our night out," Chastity complained, noticing Leticia's appearance.

"Can't we do it another time?" Leticia asked.

"Listen, ho! Whoever you got up in here can fucking spread. We got plans," Chastity said, referring to the fake dinner plans Leticia thought they had. Leticia didn't know anything about the Candy Shop or the party they had planned for her.

"Baby, come back to bed," the girl cooed, coming into the living room doorway.

"I gotta cut it short. I got business to take care of," Leticia said regretfully, thinking about how freaky she was about to get.

"I'm going downstairs to the car. Hurry the fuck up! We got reservations!" Chastity announced.

"Ahhh, shut the fuck up and go wait!" Leticia responded mockingly. They were like true sisters; argue, fight, and then make up.

Tori lay in a fetal position in her bed, a picture of Akayla against her chest. She looked over at the cable box and knew it was time to get up for the party. She was in no mood. Dealing with Chastity had become a chore.

Rolling over, she reached onto her nightstand and grabbed a small plastic baggy of colorful pills. She had taken the pills from the bags she was supposed to deliver to Heldy, a Nigerian soothsayer uptown. The last time Tori went to deliver to Heldy, the toothless old lady had warned her, "You friend's will betray ya! They will toss you away like garbage! There is an enemy amongst them!" Tori cursed Heldy out and told her that if she didn't have anything to tell her about getting Akayla back, to stop fucking playing that voodoo shit with her. Just for that, Tori withheld part of Heldy's package. She told herself that it served the old African bitch right.

Tori grabbed the pills and seriously considered taking all of them. But the thought of her daughter being raised by her fanatically religious, hypocritical sister quickly helped her change her mind. She decided instead to take two, which would definitely get her through the party with ease. "Mm-m-m!" she moaned as the drugs took effect.

Springing to life like a cartoon character, "Pa-a-a-rtay!" she sang while clapping. "Now, what am I gonna wear?" she spoke to herself aloud. Her mood went from night to day just like that.

Deidre sat at one of the tables toward the front of the Candy Shop so she could have a good view of the entire place. She was trained never to sit with her back towards the door. She was amazed at how many people were there waiting for the guest of honor. In Deidre's opinion, the auditions earlier that day had definitely paid off. Beautiful girls were everywhere. Some danced on the stage, some danced alone in cages suspended from the ceiling, and some even did the *Coyote Ugly* on the bar. Deidre knew now for sure why they called the club the Candy Shop. She'd observed more than one beautiful piece of eye-candy make drug transactions. Just like Reemo said, the Candy Shop served their customers well, and drug candy was being sold like it was real candy.

Deidre fit right in with the seemingly well-dressed crowd. Just looking at her, no one would ever guess she was a federal agent in her beautiful black Nicole Miller dress that opened all the way down to her ass crack, with a spider web-shaped sequin design covering her back. The knee-high, slim fitting leather high heeled boots gave the dress that extra oomph she was looking for.

Damn, this Loca chick must be special to them, Deidre thought to herself as she sipped slowly on her first drink, a Cosmopolitan, patiently awaiting a glimpse of the F.A.B. She was anxious to meet the rest of them after all she'd read about them. She felt like a star-struck teen waiting for her idol backstage at a concert.

Deidre had long since stopped listening to Reemo, who accompanied her there as he rambled on with street tales for days. According to him, he was more dangerous than Al Capone, Pablo Escobar and Scarface put together. *Ri-i-i-ight!* She looked down at her watch just as the club erupted into a frenzy.

"Surprise!" the crowd yelled.

Let the party begin! Deidre thought to herself. Everyone had surrounded the F.A.B., so she couldn't get a good look at them until they made their way past her table in route to the VIP table, where more half-naked girls awaited the guest of honor. *Yep! Those were definitely the same females from the pictures in the criminal file folders.*

"It's your night, Loca! The world is yours! Welcome home!" the DJ screamed into the microphone.

Deidre was so caught up in the festivities she didn't even notice R.J. strolling in her direction.

"Wasup, bro!" R.J. yelled, standing between Deidre and Reemo.

"Wasup, my nig!" Reemo stood up, giving R.J. the customary one hand slap and shoulder bump. "You remember DeeDee, right?" Reemo asked.

"How could I forget her?" R.J. commented, damn near undressing Deidre with his eyes. "Whatchu drinking?" R.J. asked her.

"I'm good," Deidre said. Undercover, she was not eating or drinking shit from anyone.

"Nah, only the best for any friends of my bro," R.J. said while simultaneously motioning for one of the topless girls to take care of the table. After whispering something to the girl, within minutes, there was a huge bottle of Vive Clicquot on the table.

"See, that's my man right there!" Reemo smiled, but was steaming inside.

"Come on and join us at the VIP table," R.J. said, grabbing the midnight blue bottle of expensive champagne from the table.

Deidre and Reemo followed R.J. to a huge table at the rear of the club. The VIP table was beautifully decorated with gold and white place settings, beautiful gold silverware, gold bottles of Cristal champagne at every seat, and several gorgeous gold vases with white roses as centerpieces. A huge cake sat at one end of the table with the words "Welcome Home, Loca! The World is yours!" written on top. Deidre had never seen anything so beautiful. The table looked like it had been set for a wedding.

Everyone turned to look at them as they approached the table. Deidre's eyes immediately went to Chastity. Chastity wore a low-cut shirt that exposed her entire chest bone, her breasts covered only by thin drapes of material. Her entire chiseled back was exposed, leading down to her close-fitting rhinestone jeans, which showed off her perfect shape. Her hair was beautiful and thick, arranged with loose curls accenting her face. Chastity's jewelry was sick; the solitaire canary diamond on her left middle finger could be seen even in the dark club. *I didn't realize how pretty she was*, Deidre thought as R.J. and Reemo left her standing there.

"Baby sis, you remember DeeDee from earlier, right?" R.J. asked, pulling Chastity over to Deidre.

"Yeah, wasup," Chastity said. Her mood seemed more relaxed than earlier that day. Deidre just nodded her head.

"Let me introduce you to the guest of honor," R.J. commented, moving Deidre around the table.

Reemo looked on, incensed. He wanted everyone to know Deidre was with him, but he could tell R.J. was really feeling her.

"Loca, wasup, *mami*!" R.J. yelled, approaching Leticia, who had two half-naked women on her lap.

"Ooooh, shit, big bro! What the deal is, *pa*!" Leticia sang, jumping up to greet R.J. This was her first time seeing him since she'd been home. Everyone purposely stayed away so that her homecoming party would be more special.

Tori approached as they embraced. "R.J., what's good?" Tori yelled over the music, grabbing R.J. for a hug also.

Deidre just looked on, but she caught a few disapproving glances from both Leticia and Tori.

"Oh, yo, let me introduce ya'll both to DeeDee. She's a friend of Reemo's and a new business partner," R.J. said, turning to face Deidre. Deidre observed the pretty girl in front of her from head to toe.

Leticia had finally settled on a pair of Sean John slacks from the new Sean John store on 5th Avenue, and a shirt to match. Her braids were freshly done and spinning. Alan Iverson ain't have nothing on her!

"Fuck Reemo!" Leticia spat. "I hate that hater-ass nigga! Any friend of his ain't a friend of mine!" she continued, looking down the end of the table at an unsuspecting Reemo, who was chatting it up with other party guests.

Deidre was shocked. That comment had completely caught her off guard, and she immediately became a little nervous. Reemo had failed to tell her that the girls hated his guts, and that the only thing that kept him around was R.J.'s loyalty to him.

"Don't mind her. What's your name again?" Tori said into Deidre's ear.

"DeeDee," she replied.

"I'm Tori. Nice to meet you," she said, extending her hand.

Whew! Deidre thought to herself. *At least one of them is approachable.* She thought Tori was cute, with her stilettos on to add height to her stocky frame. Tori's Mohawk hairstyle gave her plain chubby face a little pizzazz, and the sparkly gold fitted dress she wore accented her hips and helped hide her square backside. Deidre had to hand it to the F.A.B.; they all knew how to rock the right outfit.

She finally took a seat at the VIP table, with Reemo to her left and R.J. to her right. Expensive bottles, half-naked women, fine-ass men, and diamonds seemed to be a regular part of their lifestyle. Until tonight, Deidre had thought it unrealistic to believe that a couple of young girls from the ghettos of New York could be living this fabulously. If she didn't see it with her own eyes, she would have never believed it. But street riches came at a price—a very high price. There was no way these females were making that kind of money without any glitches.

"*. . . A Ferrari, a Jaguar switching four lanes with the top down,*

Screaming out, money ain't a thang!

Bubble hard in the double R, flashing the rings with the windows down,

Screaming out, money ain't a thang . . ."

Jay-Z and Jermaine Dupri had the club thumping, and it was the right song for the moment. Everyone was flossing, and Deidre could definitely tell for the F.A.B. that money wasn't a thang!

Deidre lifted her third glass of champagne, watching all of the bodies move in sync with the music. As she scanned the partygoers, she thought she was hallucinating when she noticed three men in ski masks exiting the restroom area and rapidly heading in her direction. The world seemed to stop for a minute. Three shots rang out, and then screams. Two more shots put things back into perspective for her.

"Fuck F.A.B.!" Deidre heard one of the guys yell as the barrel of an Uzi was pointed at the table.

"Everybody, get on the floor! Put all the money and jewels on the floor, now!" another gunman yelled.

All Deidre could hear were screams. The club was clearing out, and half-naked women ran in every direction. She felt sick. She was under and alone, with no inside contact or backup, and no wire to alert her team about what was going on. In order to preserve her cover, she had to come to the party alone. She had been instructed by Ferguson to attend the party unarmed out of fear that the club's bouncers would notice she had a weapon. Luckily, she disobeyed that order.

As she lay on the floor, Deidre noticed R.J. slowly reaching under his shirt for his weapon. Reemo followed suit, but wasn't so lucky. He decided to play cowboy, standing up and aiming his gun at the assailants. Before he could get a shot off, one of the masked gunmen's shots caught Reemo in his chest, sending him flying into the wall. As his wounded body slid down, he left a trail of blood on the wall, which was also spattered all over Deidre's face and clothes.

"Now, nobody else try nothing fucking funny!" the shooter demanded.

Deidre closed her eyes. She couldn't tell where the girls were. Reemo gasped for breath. She needed to make a split-second decision as the triggerman who had shot Reemo walked around the table collecting money and jewelry. She reached over slowly and picked up Reemo's black and chrome Kimber .45. Just as she got hold of the gun, she came eye to foot with one of the gunmen, who stood above R.J. The gunman held his gun to R.J.'s head, stating, "A man that runs with all women is a bitch!"

R.J. lay stock still, looking death in the eyes as the gunman cocked his weapon. Deidre unloaded Reemo's clip into the gunman's center mass (chest and abdomen area) in a matter of seconds. R.J. rolled to the left and just missed having his head blown off. Deidre's shots had caused the gunman's body to shake, and his finger involuntarily pulled the trigger. R.J. had moved just in time.

R.J. picked up his gun and caught one of the other gunmen in the knees, but not before he saw his sister being hit in the face with the butt of a gun by the third triggerman. Deidre noticed Leticia struggling with the guy who had hit Chastity. Tori was under the table, crying and covering her ears as she stared at Reemo's bloody body.

Deidre hoisted herself up, and with one knee down and one knee up, she retrieved her weapon from the side of her boot. *"Bang! Bang!"* She let off two rounds at the man who had Leticia in a headlock, but none of the shots hit the intended target.

The gunman swiftly turned his weapon towards R.J. *"Tat-tat-tat-tat!"* the semi-automatic shots rattled off, one after another. R.J. dove for cover, and just as he did, *"Bang!"* The gunman holding Leticia slid to the floor. Deidre had shot him once, right between the eyes.

R.J. threw his weapon down and rushed to his sister's side. Deidre was right on his heels. With Reemo's weapon clutched in her right hand, she bent down and picked up R.J.'s weapon from the floor. They all exchanged a telling glance as Deidre put both weapons in her bag.

It seemed like an eternity, but the whole altercation hadn't lasted more than three minutes. A shaken Deidre listened to the wail of sirens in the distance.

VOLUME 9:
THE TRUST FACTOR

Deidre's mind whizzed a mile a minute as she rushed out the back door of the Candy Shop. Soaked in Reemo's blood, she concealed the two guns used to kill the robbers. Leery, she looked up and down the block. With her heart pounding, she jumped into her car, hitting the radio power button twice and flashing her high beams to open the hidden compartment behind the GPS screen. She immediately threw the guns into the space, quickly closed it, and took a deep breath before she pulled out of the parking spot.

Two more police cars flew by as she approached the corner of Flatbush Avenue, adding to the gang of blue and white vehicles parked outside the club. The EMT's were already inside trying desperately to revive Reemo.

Deidre's hands shook as she navigated her vehicle down several side streets before arriving at the apartment. Her mind raced in many directions, but her first concern was making the murder weapons disappear. The correct protocol was for her to keep the weapons as evidence against R.J. and Reemo, which would be used against them in court once she made her case. R.J., Reemo, and the F.A.B. would just think she made the weapons disappear, which is exactly what she wanted them to think.

She felt confident that her actions in the club had sealed her fate with the F.A.B. Saving R.J. and Chastity's life was sure to garner her some trust points from the crew. What she was afraid of were the questions that might follow, like, *"Where did you learn to shoot like that?"* and *"Why did you save the lives of people you don't know?"* Those girls were far from dumb. She just hoped that they didn't figure her for a cop or an undercover.

After finding a parking spot, Deidre rushed into the house.

Amos listened intently as Deidre's feet thundered up the stairs. He looked over at his cable box and read the time. Three-ten a.m. Making a mental note, he picked up the telephone and dialed a familiar number.

Once inside, Deidre locked the door and rested her back briefly against the cold metal before she slid down to the floor. She'd just experienced her first brush with death, and it wasn't a very good feeling. Not to mention, the combination of alcohol and adrenaline pulsing through her veins left her feeling nauseous as hell. Crawling over to the bed, she barely made it to the high mattress. *I just gotta lie down for a minute*, she told herself.

The loud sound of the phone ringing invaded Deidre's ears. "Ahhh!" she winced, grabbing for the receiver. Her head was pounding. "Hello," she whispered.

"We need to meet. Did you see the news today?" It was Ferguson, and she did not sound happy.

Deidre struggled to open her eyes, as pain shot through her cranium. Sitting up, she realized that she still had her clothes on from the night before. Blood had soaked through the expensive black fabric of her dress and caked her skin an awful rust color. She felt disgusting, and the smell of Reemo's dried up blood was making her gag.

After assuring Ferguson that she would meet her in Canarsie at the Arch Diner, Deidre turned on the television to see what Ferguson was talking about. Flipping through the channels, she finally found an all-day news broadcast on NY-1. As she pulled her dress over her head, she heard the reporter speaking about the incident. She quickly raised the volume, listening intently:

"... *A brazen robbery at the cabaret-style gentlemen's club, the Candy Shop, located just feet from the MetroTech business center in downtown Brooklyn, left five people dead, including two of the gunmen. One person was also critically injured. Police say the club closed its doors to the public for a private celebration for one of the club's investors, when three gunmen sneaked inside posing as food caterers. Police say the gunmen had hidden their weapons earlier that day while delivering food, in order to avoid the club's security checks. One of the people killed was off-duty police officer, Andre Henderson, who was moonlighting as the club's bouncer. Police have confirmed that they have one of the gunmen in custody . . .*"

Deidre couldn't believe that the bouncer she once called Andre the Giant was really Andre the cop. She turned off the television and immediately began wondering about R.J. and the girls. Before she left the Candy Shop, she'd scribbled her number on a crumpled napkin and handed it to Leticia. She told Leticia to call her after all the police activity was over. Leticia whispered a low, "Thank you!" to her before taking the paper and putting it in her pocket. Deidre seriously hoped they would take her up on her offer.

* * *

After the shooting, the entire F.A.B. was transported to Brooklyn Hospital.

Chastity was given a cold compress for her eye, and was assured by the doctors that she would not be permanently scarred. She'd taken a pretty hard blow from the butt of a gun and her face was now colored green, blue and purple.

Tori was treated for post-traumatic stress because she refused to talk. She just shook her head from left to right, and rocked back and forth for several hours after the incident. Although she had arranged for many murders, she never took part in them. Just the sight of blood made her cringe.

It was no time before the DT's showed up, cheap polyester trench coats flapping behind them. It was also no time before they got shut down. The F.A.B. wasn't talking. It was a robbery. That was their story and they were sticking to it. Even if the F.A.B. had a responsible party in mind, they wouldn't tell fucking Jake anything. They despised cops, except for the ones on their payroll.

After leaving the hospital, they all decided to stick together. Not only were they spooked, but they needed to figure out who was responsible for the incident. Their number one concern was with how the gunmen got into their club with weapons.

"I'm telling ya'll, it was fucking Reemo!" Leticia screamed, pacing the floor.

"Nah, yo. I'm telling you that nigga may be a little retarded, but he ain't grimy," R.J. argued.

"You don't know who set that up," Tori commented.

"Fuck who did it! We all in a jam now. The Candy Shop was the entire business after Amber got ghost," Chastity explained. "Those chicks was bumping all our shit within hours, but now with the club being a crime scene, the block is hot. I gotta hit my connect off, so we all gonna have to get our hands dirty," she announced, looking from face to face with her one good eye.

"I'm down for whatever, but I'm telling you, Reemo set that shit up!" Leticia screamed.

"We need to call his out-of-town partner. Reemo has made big returns, thanks to her," R.J. said. He couldn't stop thinking about DeeDee.

"Yo, she was gangsta last night too! That bitch blazed like a dude!" Leticia said, excited. She liked the way DeeDee looked too.

"Or like a fucking cop," Chastity mumbled.

"I don't think she's a cop. Like I said, I seen first-hand the kind of return she is bringing in off that crystal," R.J. informed them. Reemo had come back with two huge returns, and R.J. knew he couldn't have done it by himself. Reemo wasn't smart enough to make his money double that fast.

"She gave me her number," Leticia said. The entire room was silent for a minute. Everyone's mind was racing with ideas.

"Call her," Chastity instructed.

Deidre's meeting with Ferguson wasn't as bad as she thought it would be. She was told that she would no longer have a twenty-four hour tail; it was too risky. After last night, Deidre's cover would've easily been blown had there been any undercovers inside the club with her. Now that Deidre was almost in, she would be on her own for the most part. It was the safest way, according to Ricky and Ferguson. She didn't have a choice. Ferguson told her she needed to wear a wire whenever doing business with the F.A.B. Deidre agreed. Both women arranged to meet under the Williamsburg Bridge once a week for updates. Deidre would call for surveillance, as needed. She would be fully undercover and all alone—unless she called in for backup.

Deidre left the meeting feeling indifferent. She didn't

know what to make of all of the unorthodox occurrences on the case, and again, she ignored her instincts.

Back in her car, she noticed that she had a missed call. She immediately called the number back.

"Yo!" the person on the other end answered.

"Somebody call me from this number?" Deidre asked.

"Yeah, it's Loca," Leticia announced.

"Oh, wasup? Ya'll a'ight?" Deidre asked.

"Yo, we never talk on the jack. How long you in town for?" Leticia asked.

"I'll be here for a minute," Deidre said calmly.

"A'ight, we wanna meet with you tomorrow. I'll hit you back with a time and place," Leticia said, and hung up the phone.

Deidre's heart thumped out of nervousness and excitement. Tomorrow sounded good to her.

VOLUME 10:
THE FIRST MEETING

Deidre sat across the table from the F.A.B. inside Caliente's in the Village. For some strange reason, she wasn't nervous.

"Where you from, DeeDee?" Chastity asked, looking Deidre straight in the eyes.

"D.C.," Deidre responded, taking a forkful of her shrimp and Alfredo pasta.

"Murder Capital, huh?" Leticia commented, picking up her oversized daiquiri.

"That's what they say," Deidre said nonchalantly.

"You like go-go music?" Chastity asked.

"Yeah, that's my shit!" Deidre replied, holding Chastity's gaze.

"That shit sound like somebody banging pots and pans to me," Leticia added. Everyone laughed. They finished their meal with light conversation and lots of laughter. Deidre was in; she was sure of it.

Deidre and the F.A.B. left the restaurant in good spirits. The laughter and camaraderie made her feel like she'd known the girls for years. Her guard down, she headed towards Chastity's ride. "So, wasup? Ya'll gonna let me deal without Reemo or what?" Deidre asked. She didn't feel it was too soon. Besides, they all knew this meeting was about business.

"Be easy, ma! We got you!" Leticia assured, patting Deidre on the shoulder.

All four girls piled into Chastity's Range. Tori sat in the front while Leticia and Deidre got in the back. Chastity peeked at Leticia through the rear view mirror. The previously light mood suddenly turned dark. Leticia slid across the seat, getting very close to Deidre. "Yo, DeeDee, I heard you a fucking cop," Leticia growled, placing the barrel of a snub nose .40 caliber Glock to Deidre's temple.

Deidre gulped down the lump in her throat. She sat stock-still. *I knew these bitches were up to something!* she thought to herself. "Yo, I don't know whatchu talkin' about," Deidre said calmly, trying to watch what she said.

"You fucking heard me! I heard you was a fucking cop!" Leticia barked again.

"Loca, whatchu doin'?" Tori yelled nervously from the front seat. No one had told her about the plan.

"Shut up and mind your business!" Chastity screamed at Tori. At that, Tori rolled her eyes, crossed her arms and turned around. She wanted to slap the shit out of Chastity. *I'm really sick of this bitch*, she seethed.

"I'm not a fuckin' cop. You need to get that gun outta my face!" Deidre said, playing tough, when really she was shook as adrenaline burned in her veins. She had no idea who she was messing with. Looking into Leticia's cat green eyes, she swore she could see fire.

"A'ight, I'll take it outta your face," Leticia snarled, moving the gun from Deidre's temple to her eye socket. "Now, take your bag off your arm and pass it to Tori," she instructed, her hot breath poisoning Deidre's breathing air.

Deidre obeyed the order. Sweat glistened on her forehead and dripped down her back to her ass crack, and her chest heaved in and out as the cold steel pressed against her skin.

Leticia ran her hand up and down Deidre's chest, feeling for a wire. Then she made Deidre take off her shoes. Leticia enjoyed watching the fear in Deidre's eyes. It made her feel powerful.

The car continued to move, but Deidre felt like her heart was going to stop. Peering out of the windshield, she couldn't pinpoint their location. She hoped that Ferguson had allowed her surveillance team to tail her on this first meeting, like she'd requested.

Leticia continued to hold the weapon on Deidre as Chastity rummaged through Deidre's purse. Taking out her driver's license, Chastity read aloud, "Deandra Barnes . . . hm-m-m-m. When is your birthday, *Deandra Barnes*?" Chastity asked nastily.

"What?" Deidre snapped.

"Bitch, you heard her! When the fuck is your birthday?" Leticia barked.

Deidre had heard Chastity but she was buying time. "February 11. Ya'll bitches is bugging! Let me the fuck out of this car!" Deidre yelled, still playing hard.

"Sit still before you get it!" Chastity commanded, scanning Deidre's driver's license in the darkness of the car. "Yo, I'm keeping this. T-baby, tomorrow you need to call Quita and tell her to work her magic," Chastity instructed as she slid Deidre's fake license into her bag.

Deidre was startled by the recent turn of events. *These bitches are no joke*, she thought to herself.

Quita, one of Tori's younger sisters, worked for the DMV and could run the license in the system to check out her story.

"A'ight, ain't nothin' in here," Chastity said, tossing Deidre's pocketbook into the back seat. "Let's rock. Where ya'll wanna go now?" she continued, making an abrupt U-turn.

Leticia removed the gun from Deidre's face. "I knew you wasn't a cop. You cool as ice. No hard feelings, you understand n' shit, right?" Leticia said, patting Deidre on her shoulders.

"Just don't ever fucking refer to me as a fucking cop again!" Deidre screamed, straightening out her crumpled clothes. Everyone started laughing. Inhaling deeply, Deidre felt a sense of relief. She was finally in.

They drove around for another two hours before they agreed to call it a night. Deidre was tired, but she knew she had to do whatever it took to stay in good graces. Chastity drove her back to her car, which she had parked in the Village. They agreed to meet tomorrow to discuss business. Deidre had to admit that the girls were very thorough. They didn't just trust anybody.

Pulling up on her block, she looked around before she got out of the car. Confident she was safe, she exited and headed into her apartment building. All she could think of on her way up the steps was getting some rest. Unlocking the door, she threw her keys on the floor and immediately began to strip. Almost out of her clothes, she flicked on her bedroom light. "Ahhhhh!" she screamed, spotting another person in her room. Holding her chest, she gathered enough air to wolf out her question. "What the fuck are you doing in here?"

"What? You're not happy to see me?" Ricky crooned.

"Why would you come here? You trying to blow my cover?" Deidre asked, annoyed and concerned.

"Trust me, no one saw me come in. I had Ferguson make me a key," he said, walking over to Deidre and touching her hair. Flinching, she moved away from him. "I missed you," he whispered, knowing that his words held a lot of power. "I just had to have you," he continued, nibbling on her ear.

"Why? So your crazy-ass wife could follow you here and let this entire block know I'm a fucking home wrecking FBI agent?" Deidre remarked, walking over to the windows to close all of the shutters.

"That wasn't my fault. Besides, I've already apologized," Ricky huffed.

"You shouldn't be here, Ricky. I think we're done," she replied, closing her eyes and trying to stay strong.

"Not until I say so. I love you, Deidre. Your father wanted me to take care of you," Ricky remarked, moving close to her again and pressing his body against her back. He knew exactly what to say and do to make her capitulate.

Her head told her no, but her heart said yes, yes, yes! She turned around and threw her arms around his neck, just as she'd done so many times as a child. "I missed you too," she cried into the pale skin of his neck. Deidre was starving for Ricky's attention and affection since the incident with Lorna. She refused to admit it to herself, but subconsciously she felt she was nothing without a man's love.

Ricky closed his eyes and smirked behind her back. Running his hands down her spine to her ass, he gripped her bottom tightly. As she kissed him and caressed him, his eyes meticulously scanned the room.

VOLUME 11:
THE DECEITFUL ONES

Ricky left Deidre's apartment, satisfied that he still had her under his spell. He noticed several missed calls on his private cell phone. He pressed "talk" to return the last call. "Hello?" the voice on the other end greeted. It was Bernard.

"What's the problem?" Ricky asked impatiently, frustrated by the number of times Bernard had called him.

"Listen, I spoke with the team, and Aponte is moving through these obstacles with no problem. I told you she is capable," Bernard said.

"Listen, let me handle her. How do you niggers say it? 'Let me lay the pipe and keep my bitch in check'," Ricky said mockingly, as if he were an old school rapper.

"What did you say?" Baker growled through the receiver.

"Oh, are you mad because I said 'nigger'? Huh, Bernard? Agent fucking Baker?" Ricky whined in a woman's voice. "Shut the fuck up!" Ricky barked, squinting his icy blue eyes into slits. "Now you listen to me! You let me handle Aponte. You just hush your fucking mouth and do as I say. I need to get what is owed to me. Remember, Bernard, you got kids to feed just like me. You wanted to play this game, now play! I can ruin you. Who do you think they'll believe? Me, or your black ass?"

Ricky's chilled voice backed Bernard down. He looked at the phone as his dark face filled with blood causing it to take on an almost purple hue. He wiped sweat from his head as his stomach churned with fear. Ricky was a powerful and very dangerous man.

Ricky had taken a special trip to New York. He had some things to get straightened out. He arrived at the pre-arranged meeting place and banged on the door. "Hey, baby!" were the words he was greeted by. He was not moved by the sexy siren standing in front of him. He was too infuriated to care.

Storming into the hotel room, he began his tirade. "You mean to tell me those fucking losers you hired couldn't kill one measly piece of shit informant!" Ricky screamed.

"Well, they didn't expect super-agent to step in. Didn't anybody ever teach that bitch to play her position when she's undercover?" Ferguson replied.

"Aponte is the least of our troubles. That fucking informant is gonna blow this shit if he makes it," Ricky said, gritting his teeth.

"Why don't you just kill Aponte yourself?" Ferguson asked.

"Mind your business when it comes to me and Aponte!" Ricky barked, taking his overcoat off.

"Well, this whole elaborate plan might backfire. Besides, I'm tired of holding this Reeves bitch hostage," Ferguson complained, folding her arms across her chest.

"Yeah, well, her stupid-ass father should have refused to sign that drug control policy. Senator Reeves reneged on our deal, and now I got the fucking entire Mexican cartel breathing down my throat. That law could ruin us. So I've got to teach the little senator a lesson. I thought getting his

slut-bag daughter addicted was going to be enough of a signal, but that bastard didn't budge," Ricky vented, getting
close to Ferguson.

"Well, what now?" Ferguson asked, taking a few steps
backward.

"What now? *What now?*" Ricky growled, descending on
her like an eagle swooping down to grab a mouse. He
grabbed her shirt with both hands and ripped it open, sending the buttons flying all over the room. Ferguson's chest
swelled and her eyes bulged open. Her heart raced, not
from fear, but excitement. Breathing like an animal in heat,
Ricky buried his face in her breasts. Taking a mouth full of
her almost-black areolas in his mouth, he bit down on Ferguson's sensitive flesh like a rabid dog.

"Aggghhhh!" she screamed, urging him on. He bit her
breasts unmercifully as she dug her nails into his shoulders.
"Fuck me!" she panted, barely getting the words out.

Ricky lifted his head from her chest, looked into her
slanted eyes, and slapped her with all of his might across her
face.

"Fuck you!" she screamed, blood trickling from her lips.

"Yeah, that's what I want to hear," he chuckled. "Your
pussy is not better than Aponte's," Ricky said cruelly, getting Ferguson's attention. He knew how much Ferguson
hated Deidre.

"Oh yeah?" Ferguson commented, sliding from under
Ricky's grasp and dropping to her knees. "But I can suck
your dick better than she can," she murmured, flashing a
wicked smile before wrapping her full lips around Ricky's
pale pulsing tool.

"You need to kill that informant. I don't care how you do
it," Ricky growled as Ferguson looked up into his eyes and
continued slurping. "Mm-m-m-m!" he moaned. He felt like
the most powerful man in the world. Things were going
splendidly, and just like he'd planned.

* * *

"Ten, twenty, thirty, forty, fifty. A'ight, it's all here," Officer Duke confirmed, slamming the leather briefcase closed.

"What, nigga, you thought I was gonna try to gyp you?" Chastity asked indignantly, rolling her eyes.

"C'mon, baby, business is business . . . pleasure is pleasure," Officer Duke whispered, moving his six-foot, five-inch muscular body closer to her.

"Oh, I thought so! Not only do I pay you cash, I give you my priceless pussy. You know how many men wanna be in your shoes?" Chastity said, pushing her breasts in his face.

"Your eye is looking much better," he said, changing the subject.

"Did you find out what I asked you about?" Chastity asked, licking her lips seductively. She was a pro at getting what she wanted through manipulation.

"Yeah, the dudes that tried to rob ya'll are from Baltimore. One just got out of a federal prison, and the two others have been in and out," Officer Duke offered.

"What about the name I gave you?" Chastity inquired, reaching out to touch his manhood.

"Nah, I didn't find shit on any Deandra Barnes. She ain't never been processed through the system—clean as a whistle," Officer Duke replied, breathing hard.

"A'ight, thanks," Chastity said, removing her hand and walking away. She was very into teasing.

"Nah baby, you ain't getting off that easy. Now bend your ass over!" Officer Duke commanded, licking his plump lips. He wasn't going to be toyed with. He grabbed Chastity roughly and flipped up her skirt, swiping his erect penis over her perfectly shaped bare ass, moving it up and down until he found her moist vaginal opening. "No panties on? You were ready for this, huh?" he asked, pushing all nine inches of his dark meat into her flesh.

"Mm-m-m-m!" Chastity moaned and laughed at the

same time. When she turned her face away, her smile faded. Officer Duke continued to ram her pelvis, servicing her hot box as usual, but she wasn't into it.

"Arrggh!" Officer Duke moaned in pleasure, grabbing her hair and yanking her head back as he bent over her back trying to reach her mouth to give her a deep French kiss.

Chastity turned her face away. She wasn't kissing him anymore. Something was different about their lovemaking. It had become routine and mundane. She sensed that there was someone else, and she planned on finding out who that was. She said a silent prayer that she wouldn't have to kill him for cheating on her, or kill the bitch for that matter.

As usual, Officer Duke sexed Chastity to sleep. Sliding on his clothes, he tipped out of her house without waking her . . . or so he thought.

"Spread your legs apart!" the police officer screamed.

"Officer, I didn't do anything!" Tori complained, scrunching up her face in response to being manhandled.

"Shut the fuck up and spread 'em!" the officer yelled, grabbing both of Tori's arms forcefully so he could handcuff her.

"Ouch!" she screamed, as he roughly placed the cold metal shackles on her wrists, rendering her helpless.

"That shit hurts so good, don't it," the officer whispered in her ear as he traced his tongue down her neck.

"Hell yeah!" she moaned as he took advantage of her while she was helpless.

"Get on your knees and suck it!" the officer commanded, releasing his throbbing tool from its polyester captivity.

Struggling to stay balanced with her arms behind her back, Tori waddled a little and dropped to her knees. "Yes, Officer Duke," she cooed as he forced all nine inches of his stiff rod into her pouting lips.

"Mm-m-m-m!" he grunted as he proceeded to ram Tori's

face, gagging her in the process. *I get two friends in one night, and fifty G's,* Officer Duke smirked to himself. "You got what we talked about?" he grunted, as he rammed in and out.

"Uh huh!" Tori moaned through sucks.

"Good girl. I get good head and free drugs. I ain't never leaving your ass, baby," Officer Duke commented.

Tori was so happy to be getting attention from him that she'd started stealing and making side deals with him.

Officer Duke thought he was the man.

Chastity sat on the motorcycle a few feet away from Tori's building. Breathing hard and biting her bottom lip, she contemplated busting all of the windows out of Officer Duke's black Lexus LS-400, the car he'd probably purchased with the money she paid him. Chastity had followed him after he collected his payment, fucked her brains out, and left her in bed. Suspicious of where he was going, she'd jumped on R.J.'s motorcycle and secretly followed Officer Duke. She had warned Tori never to mix business with pleasure, especially with someone who was bringing Chastity pleasure! Officer Duke had been on their payroll since he graduated from the Police Academy one year back.

Chastity was furious when she saw him exit his car and enter Tori's building. Still giving Tori the benefit of the doubt, she watched the window, hoping she wouldn't see him. Well, she did. Officer Duke closed Tori's curtains. Not only did Tori disobey what she was told, she was also fucking Chastity's first love.

Bladen Duke was one of the first and only men Chastity had let into her heart romantically. She'd never trusted any man aside from her brother. Things didn't work out with Chastity and Bladen of course, because he couldn't handle her bossy attitude and the fact that she liked to wear the pants in their relationship. After they broke up, they remained friends, having sex almost every time they were together. It was a homie/lover/business associate/friend relationship, but in Chastity's mind, he would always be her man, which meant he was off limits to Tori. Tori had violated a cardinal rule amongst women. If your friend slept with him and you know about it, then you can't. Officer Duke was playing both friends.

Biting down on her bottom lip even harder now, Chastity's eyes filled with tears, and she didn't cry easily. Deciding to keep this bit of information to herself for a while, she plotted her revenge.

Putting her plan into action, she picked up her cell phone and dialed a number she'd been dialing very often lately. "Hello, Coral? Yeah, it's Chastity. You should tell the foster care worker to give your sister a drug test. Yup!" Chastity said into the receiver. *Bitch ain't never gettin' that fucking baby back!* Chastity said to herself as she revved the bike and pulled away from the curb.

Two days had passed since their dinner, and Deidre hadn't heard back from the F.A.B. She decided to go visit Reemo, who was still fighting for his life in the hospital. She got dressed and headed to Brooklyn Hospital.

When she arrived at the Intensive Care Unit, she looked for room 808. Locating the room, she walked slowly inside. All she found was an orderly cleaning up, and winding up the wires to the heart monitors and preparing the bed for a new patient. A sense of panic grabbed Deidre tightly around the neck. "Where is the patient that was here?" Deidre asked.

The orderly stared blankly at Deidre, with no response.

"I said, where is the patient that was here?" she screamed, her voice trembling.

"No speak English," the small Latina replied, looking at Deidre like she was crazy.

Deidre rushed out of the room towards the nurse's sta-

tion. She wanted answers. Before she could make it, someone grabbed her arm. "What the . . ." she whirled around,
her heart racing.

"He's gone," R.J. commented in a low voice.

"I was just here two days ago. They said he was doing
better," Deidre said, feeling sick to her stomach. Although
Reemo was an arrogant asshole, from what she'd learned,
he never really got a break in life. She felt bad for him.

"I know. I was shocked myself. He didn't deserve this
shit," R.J. commented, lowering his head.

Deidre took a good look at R.J.'s face, noting his red eyes.
Even though he'd been crying, he still looked damn good.
He wore a black leather Pelle Pelle jacket, a pair of Evisu
jeans, and beef and broccoli Timbs . . . simple, yet sexy. R.J.
never rocked a lot of jewelry. He showed wealth in other
ways, like his well-manicured hands, always freshly cut hair,
and the plain solid gold Presidential Rolex he rocked.

"No, he didn't deserve this," Deidre agreed, tears rimming her eyes.

"Yo, that was my nigga from the womb to the tomb!" R.J.
lamented.

Deidre felt like crying. She loved to see a man show his
sensitive side, while remaining rugged and manly. "What
happened?" she asked, breaking an eerie silence that settled
around them.

"Don't know. The nurse said some lady came to visit him
early this morning, and right after the lady left, Reemo went
into cardiac arrest. His lungs collapsed and they couldn't
save him," R.J. explained, rubbing his chin.

"Damn! I'm sorry for your loss," Deidre lamented, rubbing her hand over his arm for comfort.

"It's a'ight. He was a soldier," R.J. replied, his voice grat-
ing on the words. "You wanna get lunch?" he asked Deidre
as they headed for the elevators.

"That's cool," she replied, butterflies fluttering in her stomach. She was attracted to something about him.

R.J. watched Deidre's perfect hourglass shape move in her fitted jeans. He loved women that could wear jeans and still look like they were ready to go into a classy restaurant. Besides, what man could resist a woman who rocked a hot pair of Manolo's?

They walked over to a small café on Dekalb Avenue. Deidre was nervous at first, but after a few minutes, she felt unbelievably comfortable with R.J. They quickly exchanged personal information.

"Tell me about yourself," R.J. said, sipping his Mojito.

"I grew up in D.C., knocking around from foster home to foster home after my father committed suicide," Deidre lied. She knew using foster care would give them some common ground.

"Word? My moms committed suicide too," R.J. shared.

"My father was my whole world. He never got over my mother's death. She died during childbirth," Deidre continued, mendaciously.

"My moms was torn up after my faggot-ass pops left. You know, the same ghetto story. Mom's raising kids alone after the pops up and left. Only thing is, my pops wasn't no slouch, addict, or nothing like that. He was a military man with strong values, but I knew he was into some shady shit. After he left, I found a lot of money stashed in our apartment. I still think that nigga got killed or something. I just can't see him leaving us. Losing my moms was even worse, she was my world. You know, no matter what a mother does, you only get one," R.J. preached.

"I never wanted to believe that my father killed himself. When I heard it, I didn't believe it and I still don't. He would've never left me all alone. Maybe we were meant to meet," Deidre said, this time speaking the truth.

"For real," R.J. mumbled while crunching on his chicken fingers.

A few minutes of silence passed.

"How'd you get into the game?" R.J. asked the million-dollar question.

Deidre almost choked on her iced tea. That information wasn't included in her script. "I started off running numbers for this old lady that lived next door to one of my foster parents. I met a man about a horse, and the rest is history. I don't like to talk about it," Deidre fabricated on the spot.

"I like that," R.J. said. He knew she was legit, because real hustlers never tell how they got put on. He was smitten.

"What does R.J. stand for?" Deidre asked, figuring since he wanted to get personal, she would do the same.

"Nah, I never tell anyone my real name. Too much baggage attached to that name. So just call me R.J.," he said, slightly annoyed.

Deidre scolded herself silently. *Damn! You asked too much too soon.*

During the entire time, Deidre did not look R.J. directly in his face, partly out of guilt, because of who she really was, but mostly because she'd finally figured out the uncanny resemblance. Maybe God was trying to tell her something. They say girls usually seek out men that remind them of their fathers.

R.J. looked at his watch. "DeeDee, I gotta go. I got a very important meeting," he said.

Here's my number," she blurted out, scribbling the number down before her brain could really register what she was doing or may be getting into.

"Ah, I was gonna ask for that," R.J. said, flashing a smile. He grabbed the paper with the priceless digits. Surveying it, he thought how old school it was to get a phone number on paper. "Whoa, whoa! Don't insult me! Put your money away," he said, holding up his hand as Deidre pulled out her cash. R.J. paid the check, walked Deidre to her car and was gone.

That night after his meeting, R.J. called Deidre, and they spent three hours talking. He couldn't get her out of his mind.

Deidre couldn't stop thinking about him either. More importantly, she couldn't stop thinking about what he'd said about mothers. She realized that the lie she told about her mother dying was sometimes what she wished for. She had not spoken to her mother at all in the weeks she'd been in New York. Guilt trampled on her mood. She decided to leave the city and go home to see her mother.

R.J. climbed into the back of the black Lincoln Town car that had been waiting for him.

"What's the status?" his partner asked, exhaling a ring of cigar smoke into R.J.'s breathing air.

"I'm almost where I want to be," R.J. replied, waving the smoke from his face.

"And what about your sister and her little crew?" the man asked, this time blowing his smoke towards the ceiling of the car.

"My sister will do whatever I say. She only thinks she's in control . . . for now," R.J. remarked.

"Well in that case, I think this belongs to you," the man said, shoving a black leather briefcase across the seat in R.J.'s direction. R.J. opened the briefcase, examined the contents and looked over at the man. "I guess so," he commented, opening the car door and exiting.

VOLUME 12:
THE VISIT HOME

Deidre drove from New York to Fairfax, Virginia in record time. Four hours straight, and she was there. She wanted to surprise her mother, therefore she didn't call ahead. Pulling into the cul-de-sac, she looked at the house where she'd grown up. Nothing had changed. All of the lights were on. "Maybe she is sober. Lights on . . . good sign," Deidre whispered to herself, putting her car in park. She fished her old house keys out of her purse, ambled up the front steps and unlocked the door. "What the . . . ?" she grumbled as she crossed the threshold. The sound of loud noises attacked her ears.

"Mom?" Deidre screamed out, moving closer to the noise, that she now recognized. "Mom?" she called again. Still no answer. Walking slowly, she heard her favorite childhood song resounding throughout the house:

"*. . . Your Daddy's home. Your Daddy's home.*
Your Daddy's home to sta-a-a-a-y . . ."

Deidre began to regret coming home already. That song brought back memories . . . sad memories. "What're you doing?" Deidre screamed over the music, finally locating her mother sitting alone in front of the television with her "Easy Jesus" in her lap.

Cassandra stretched her red rimmed eyes in surprise and looked up at her daughter. "What're you doing here?" she mumbled, wiping drool from her lips with the back of her hand. She was dressed in a nightgown, which was stained in the front, her hair was sticking up all over her head, a clear sign that she had not bathed or combed her hair, and Deidre could smell the stench of alcohol from a distance. Her mother was on a binge again. Deidre wondered how many years it would take for her mother to get over the past.

"You remember this birthday party?" Cassandra screamed over the loud music, jutting her hand forward and spilling some of her drink.

Crinkling her face, Deidre searched in vain for the remote. "How can you hear yourself think?" she screamed.

"Your father had just come back from one of his so-called business trips, and you were so gotdamn happy to see him," her mother slurred, tears now streaming her cheeks. "You were always so happy to see him. Oh yes, your Daddy could do no wrong," Cassandra continued, taking a swig of her libation.

Deidre walked over to the television, refusing to look at the tape of her and her father. She turned it off. Turning back towards her mother, she felt relieved that she'd chosen to visit Cassandra. Her mother was clearly in no condition to be alone. Kneeling in front of her, Deidre removed the liquor from her grasp.

"What are you doing? I'm not bothering anybody with my drink. It's just a lil' bit," Cassandra mumbled, rolling her eyes at the same time.

"Mom, you can't keep doing this to yourself," Deidre whispered, grabbing her mother and hugging her. Deidre shut her eyes, straining to fight back tears.

"Me? Doing it to myself? No! He did this to us! You are

selfish just like him!" Cassandra screamed through tears, shoving her daughter away.

"Okay. You're not in your right mind. Let's go lay down," Deidre consoled, grabbing her mother by the arm, trying to get her to stand up.

"Don't touch me!" Cassandra garbled her words, snatching back her arm.

"Huh," Deidre sighed. She wanted to run out of the door and return to New York. Right then, she admitted to herself that she felt more comfortable around the F.A.B. and R.J. than she did around her own mother.

"Ha-ha-ha-ha!" Cassandra suddenly let out a scary cacophonous laugh. A startled Deidre looked at her mother, confused. "Did you know that your father was an adulterous slut? Did you know that his woman never stopped calling me? Up until the day your father died, she called and called!" Cassandra bellowed, pointed an accusing finger in Deidre's direction.

"Mom, please let's not talk about this now. I came off assignment for one night to see you. I've missed you," Deidre pleaded, again attempting to get her mother out of the chair.

"No! You listen to me. What I have to say is important," Cassandra announced, attempting to stand up on her own, only to fall back down in the chair.

Deidre inhaled, exasperated, and walked to the couch, leaving Cassandra alone.

"Your father cheated on me every day of our marriage. That woman, she was beautiful. She had long hair and a beautiful body. She was young and gave him what I couldn't. I met her. So young and dumb, that home wrecking bitch! Why would a man leave his wife for her? It didn't matter if she was pregnant, or if she had had fifty children. Your father would've never left me for her. But he left her brokenhearted. He didn't know that I spoke to her. I visited with her. I never wanted her to see you, and I never wanted you to see them!" Cassandra wailed. She was overcome with racking sobs.

Deidre just listened to her mother ramble. It was hard to hear. She didn't want to believe a word her mother was saying. Her father was her hero. *Not my father! He loved us . . . both of us! She's crazy!* Deidre thought to herself, in full denial. She rested her head on the back of the couch, closing her eyes in anguish. Her mother ranted until she wore herself out.

Deidre jumped out of her sleep. Looking around frantically, trying to get her bearings, she finally remembered where she was—on her mother's couch. Sitting up, she scanned the room. Her mother was not there. Deidre quickly remembered the painful night she'd endured and was overcome by an urgency to leave.

"Good morning!" Cassandra chimed, coming from the kitchen with a smile on her face like nothing ever happened.

"Morning," Deidre mumbled. She was not in the mood for this Dr. Jeckyl and Mr. Hyde routine her mother performed so often. Her mother's behavior took her back to a place in her childhood that was very painful. All she wanted to do was leave.

"You want breakfast?" Cassandra asked.

"No, that's okay. I have to get back on assignment," Deidre replied, standing up and straightening her rumpled clothes.

"Look, about last night . . ." Cassandra started.

"Mom look. I just came to see how you were doing. Don't worry about it. I'm used to it," Deidre said with an attitude.

"Baby, I'm in pain everyday. With you gone, I'm lonely," Cassandra explained, choking back tears.

"You don't have to explain," Deidre whispered. She walked over to her mother and kissed her on the forehead, just like her father used to do. "I love you. I'll call you." Deidre said, walking straight to the front door. She left her mother standing alone, also just like her father used to do. In her car she broke down in tears. Looking out the windshield at her mother's house, she prepared to pull out.

Her undercover cell phone rang. Deidre pulled herself together and picked it up. "Hello . . . ? What's up, Chazz . . . ? I'm on my way back to the city . . . What ya'll gettin' into tonight . . . ?" Deidre said into the receiver, her heart racing. "Nah, I'm a'ight. Just got a cold. I'll see ya'll when I get there," she replied to Chastity. Deidre disconnected the line, threw her car in reverse and headed back to New York.

VOLUME 13: THE WARNING

It felt like days, but actually months had passed. The last remnants of the blustery New York winter cleared up, and the first signs of spring in Brooklyn became apparent. The first thing Deidre noticed was how many people came outside as soon as the days got warm. She hardly saw anyone on the streets during the winter when she first arrived in Brooklyn. Now, she had to damn near dodge human bodies just walking down the sidewalk. All of the motorcycles that revved up and down her block at night were also a telltale sign that the weather had broken.

She had become closer with the F.A.B. and R.J. It had taken some time, but she'd finally broken the wall that stood between her and them. Every day she documented everything she did with them—shopping, eating out, drug deals—everything. But, she still hadn't found out anything about Amber Reeves.

Deidre stared at her computer contemplating what to write. The night before, Chastity had revealed to her that the F.A.B. was in the process of constructing their own meth lab in upstate New York. "I'm trying to cut out the fucking middleman," Chastity had said. She hadn't told Leticia and Tori yet. "Loca is my girl, but the bitch got a big mouth, and Tori ain't about her business these days. DeeDee, I'm kinda trusting you these days, and a bitch like me don't fuck with no other bitches," Chastity had told Deidre.

Deidre thought about forgetting the entire conversation and letting it go. She had seen firsthand the real side of Chazz, Loca and Tori, and they were normal girls trying to survive and move past their pasts, just like her. *Maybe this one thing can pass*, Deidre thought to herself. *Ferguson wouldn't know unless I told her.*

Deidre didn't even realize that the lines between her being a drug dealer and a Fed were beginning to become blurry.

"*Bang! Bang!*" The door to Deidre's apartment rattled. Startled, she raised her eyebrows and looked up from her computer screen. On display were all of the things that revealed that she was an agent, including her wire and gun. She furrowed her eyebrows and moved cautiously towards the door. "Who is it?" she screamed from inside, hand on her gun.

"Dragonetti Flowers!" the male voice announced. Deidre slowly opened the apartment door, standing behind it so she could peak out slightly. "Flowers for DeeDee," the young white boy announced.

Deidre stepped around the door to accept the package. Twenty-four fully opened red roses were thrust into her hands. She gasped at their beauty. "Thank you!" she said, digging in her pocket and handing the boy a five-dollar tip. The bouquet was so large it almost blocked her view entirely. Placing them on the coffee table, she hastily picked up the card.

"*Seems like we were meant to meet. You may be the love I never knew—R.J.*"

Deidre read the card several times before she placed it up against her chest. "If you only knew who I was!" she mumbled as she walked over to her nightstand and picked up her cell phone.

"Yo!" R.J. said, picking up.

"Thank you for the beautiful flowers," Deidre said in a low sexy whisper.

"Beautiful flowers for a beautiful woman," R.J. replied.

"You shouldn't have, really," she said modestly.

"Stick with me and there is more where that came from. I gotta go, ma. I'm taking care of business," he said mysteriously, and was gone.

Deidre clipped the phone shut and sighed. Suddenly it dawned on her. *How did he know my address?* She hadn't told any of them that she was staying in Brooklyn. They always thought she stayed in a hotel, and actually had a pad in her hometown of D.C. That lie worked when Deidre needed to disappear when she had to meet with Ferguson. The girls just always thought she was back in D.C. Deidre always prayed that no one would ask to accompany her home. Receiving the flowers threw her off course, and her heart began to thump . . . hard.

"Tsk-tsk, Ricky! I can't believe you. You disappoint me," the skinny Mexican man said in a heavy Spanish accent.

"I just need more time. Reeves surprised me too when he signed the drug control policy," Ricky said nervously.

As powerful as Ricky was, Carlos Esperanza had become the most notorious drug kingpin in the world. He even had the Colombians beat. The Mexicans had the crystal meth game on lock, and they planned on keeping it that way.

Carlos didn't like Ricky. In his assessment, his father, Diego had been taken away from him as a child at the hands of Senator Reeves, when Reeves was District Attorney. Carlos had no childhood visits with his father behind bars. He'd been groomed all of his life to get retribution for Diego. Ricky owed a debt to Diego, and Carlos was going to collect. He expected to be repaid when, as agreed, Senator Reeves kept the new drug control policy from becoming law. As far as Carlos was concerned, Reeves and Ricky had reneged on a deal that was made years before he was even old enough to drive. The younger Esperanza was more ruthless than his father, and he intended to let Ricky know it.

"You now owe me twenty-million instead of the seven you lost when your partner stole from my father," Carlos informed Ricky, cracking his knuckles.

"C'mon, man. I took care of Ramon as soon as he did that. I thought I had settled that score. It was years ago. I've been bringing you almost a million a week since then," Ricky said, pleading his case.

"I don't give a fuck! Senator Reeves fucked up my business, and you took money and product from me with the promise you would fix it! You haven't delivered!" Carlos scolded, breathing hotly in Ricky's face. It made his dick hard to see this old man sweating under the pressure.

"Just give me more time!" Ricky implored. He hated this little snot nose, wetback bastard!

"I thought you said you knew where Ramon's children were, and that you would take care of them. In my culture, revenge is the settler of all disputes. You don't just kill a man, you kill his entire family," Carlos said flatly. "Don't you think my father deserves revenge?" he asked, his accent making Ricky sick to his stomach.

"I need them right now. They are going to provide a way for me to pay you back. I think one of them may have the money," Ricky said.

"Yes. Isn't one of them a fucking federal cockroach just like you?" Carlos asked.

"Yes, she is a federal agent, and I'm using her to get to the other two," Ricky answered.

"So you don't know which of Ramon's children has the money, huh?" Carlos inquired, running his hand through his long, greasy jet-black hair.

"No. Ramon had two families, and I have grown close to all of his children in one way or another. I'm using them against each other to find out where the money is. I promise, I'll have your money back!" Ricky swore, feeling even his balls sweat.

"How many fucking years will it take, Ricky? I'm not happy with you, and neither is my father," Carlos stated threateningly.

Ricky looked on with fear dancing in his eyes.

"Well, you only have a short time before I kill you and *your* whole family. I want my money!" Carlos demanded. Snapping his fingers in the direction of a tall man standing guard at his office door, the man came forward with a large suitcase, which he handed to Ricky. "This will be your last supply until I get all of my money," Carlos informed, turning his swivel chair around, giving Ricky his back.

Ricky picked up the suitcase and backed out of the door, his body drenched in sweat. As soon as he stepped into the penthouse elevator, he upchucked his stomach contents. This shit was out of hand. It was nothing like when he first got into the game. He learned that there was a whole new breed of criminals taking over. He was going to have to step up the heat on Deidre and the F.A.B., but first he needed to exact revenge on Senator Reeves.

"Hello," Senator Reeves breathed into the phone, groggy from the sedatives his doctor had prescribed since Amber went missing. He bolted upright at the sound of the voice.

"Did you sign the contract yet?" the voice at the other end asked.

"I can't right now. The FBI wants to keep all media away right now. It would be very suspicious if I cut a deal with

20/20 or *Dateline* for my story," Senator Reeves whispered, his head beginning to spin. A plan that he thought would be well-hatched had cracked.

"Well then, you better find the money then. You better start making phone calls for Congressional earmarks, or sell your ass if you have to!" the voice barked.

"Please, just release her! We can find another way!" Senator Reeves whispered, moving close to the door to make sure all of the law enforcement officials that had taken up residence in his apartment thought he was still asleep. He had offered up his daughter as a sacrificial lamb because he wasn't man enough to face his own demons.

"There is no other way now. It's too fucking late. When you signed the National Drug Control Policy and agreed to this plan, you signed your daughter's death warrant! You wanted to get rid of the embarrassment anyway, didn't you! Well consider it gone!" the voice growled, disconnecting the line.

Senator Reeves dropped to his knees. What had he done? He wept for his daughter, his career, and for the shame he would surely bring to his family if his secret ever got out.

"Life is a mystery. Every time I am alone, I hear you call my name, and it feels like home," Amber Reeves recited the Madonna lyrics in a weak raspy voice. She hadn't had a visit from the lady or man in a few days. In order to keep herself from losing her sanity, she sang songs all day and all night until she fell asleep. Hearing footsteps, she didn't know whether to be excited or scared. Amber wanted them to just kill her and get it over with. The door creaked open and the bright light that came in temporarily blinded her.

"Sit up!" the female demanded from behind the bright light.

Amber struggled to get up, but the one hand that was cuffed to the bed made it hard for her to sit all the way up.

Not to mention she was very weak. She used her free hand to shield her eyes as she tried to get a good look at her assailants.

"Put your fucking hands down and sit up!" the lady demanded again.

Amber did as she was told.

"Now speak to your daddy. Tell him you are about to die, and that only he can save you," the evil, faceless woman instructed.

"Daddy, please save me! I'm begging you, Daddy! Pul-e-e-ese! They will kill me! Give them what they want!" Amber screamed into the light, her entire body trembling. Her weakened state made it hard for her to even get enough air into her lungs to scream out the words.

"Okay, now shut up!" the man commanded.

Amber didn't know he was there. With his usual black mask on, he rushed over to her side. She couldn't see anything but spots because she'd looked into the light so long. She didn't see what he was holding. Suddenly, she felt him grab her free hand, and she immediately tried to pull it away.

"Keep the fuck still! Do it now!" he screamed, instructing another man to move.

Amber could see the sweat on the second man's shiny black bald head. She locked eyes with him, still struggling to free her hand from his grip, but it was too late. "Bernard! No! Arrgh!" she let out a deafening scream as the man chopped off her index and middle fingers on her right hand. Blood squirted everywhere. "Aghhh!" Amber continued to scream, biting down on her tongue so hard that blood filled her mouth.

"This is going to be a message for your daddy. His time has run out," the man said, leaving the girl to bleed to death.

Bernard ran out of the room, almost knocking over the

video equipment. "She saw my fucking face, and she screamed my name on the tape!" he said, panting and out of breath.

"She's going to die, so what do you care? If you're good, we'll edit out your name, but only if you help me finish this job," Ricky said with no remorse at all.

The media cameras camped in front of the Reeves' estate made it hard for the FedEx delivery guy to walk up the driveway. Before he could make it through the sea of reporters, he was stopped by a man dressed in a suit, dark glasses and a clear coiled wire in his ear. "Can I help you sir?" the Secret Service agent asked.

"Um . . . um . . . I got a package for Senator R-R-Reeves," the meek delivery boy stuttered.

"I'll take it," the agent replied, grabbing the box.

Senator Reeves was informed of the arrival of the package, but was not allowed to open it. The Secret Service agents that guarded his house twenty-four seven opened it instead. The three agents covered their noses when they finally tore open the box, revealing two rotting human fingers. After lab tests were performed, Senator Reeves was informed that the two fingers in the box indeed belonged to his daughter, Amber. Mrs. Reeves fainted. There was also a note inside, and he knew just who it was from.

It was no time before the story hit the media. More pressure came from above for Deidre to find the girl, or at least her body.

"Bernard!" a female voice boomed. Bernard ignored his wife and stared at himself in the large vanity mirror in his luxury bathroom. He raised his service weapon to his head and squeezed his eyes shut. *"Bang! Bang! Bang!"* The loud knocks on the door startled him and interrupted his action.

"Bernard, baby, your breakfast is getting cold. C'mon and eat," his wife yelled through the door.

Bernard looked down at his hands that were shaking uncontrollably. He could still see the girl's blood all over them. Tears fell from his eyes like large raindrops, soaking his silk tie.

"Bernard Baker, do you hear me talking to you?" his wife yelled again, playfully.

Bernard placed his gun in his waist holster and wiped his face dry. He didn't have the heart to kill himself in his own home. He knew his wife and kids would never be able to get over it if he did it that way. He'd done enough damage. "I'm coming, baby," he replied, adjusting his clothes.

His wife was the only thing saving him at this point. His involvement with Ricky Blum was causing him to lose his mind. He was also worried about Deidre. Bernard realized that he was partly responsible for her being in danger. Money had changed his life for the worst, and he didn't like it. Bernard felt that there was one thing he had to do before he officially got out of the game. He looked at himself in the mirror one more time. *It's your job to save Aponte's life*, he murmured to himself, walking towards the bathroom door.

"It's about time you came out. You take longer than me to get ready," his wife joked, grabbing him for a hug.

Bernard returned her embrace, closing his eyes, hiding the tears that threatened to fall from the corners.

VOLUME 14:
THE SNITCH

"A'ight, DeeDee. It's time to do business again," Chastity said. Tori and Leticia looked on.

Deidre pulled out a small black bag and handed it to Chastity, who, in turn, handed it over to Leticia. Tori rolled her eyes at being left out. "It's all here," Leticia said a few minutes later.

"Tori, pass DeeDee the stuff," Chastity commanded. She still wasn't taking any chances yet. If anything were being taped, they wouldn't have DeeDee making any deals directly. That was how mistrustful Chastity really was. Just DeeDee's mere presence at the deal made her just as guilty. Tori huffed and puffed as she obeyed Chastity's command.

Deidre opened the small duffel bag and peered inside at the tiny bags filled with pills and crystal meth. Her thighs trembled against the wire taped to her leg. Now that she had procured several pieces of evidence against the F.A.B., she still needed to find out about the girl. "Thanks. This looks good," Deidre said as she re-zipped the bag.

"*Looks* good? That's the shit right there!" Leticia said, bopping her head.

"DeeDee, do me a favor. Test that meth out," Chastity said calmly, biting on her pinky nail.

"What?" Deidre asked, her eyes growing wide. They'd never asked her to use the product before. She instantly became sick to her stomach.

"You never verify if our shit is legit. Why is that?" Chastity asked, raising her eyebrows.

Deidre instantly knew what she was getting at. "Yo, Chazz, I been dealing with ya'll for a minute. I mean, there is some kind of trust between us, right?" Deidre replied, trying to think of a way to get out of the situation. Getting high undercover was a sure way to get pulled off the case. She didn't want to do that; not before she found Amber Reeves and made a name for herself.

"Just try it. We want you to know what you gettin'," Loca said, standing up in front of Deidre.

"I never get high on my own supply," Deidre remarked, looking at all three girls.

"Here. This is my supply," Chastity came back, shoving a small piece of foil filled with methamphetamine towards Deidre. "Tori, tell her how it's done," Chastity smirked derisively and looked over at Tori.

Deidre's heart raced and her palms dripped with sweat. She balled up her toes inside her shoes, hoping she could find a way out of the situation.

"What, bitch?" Tori screamed, her eyes hooding over.

Suddenly laughter filled the room. Chastity and Leticia couldn't hold back their enjoyment. Tori stood up and stormed out of the room.

"What the fuck is up with this ho'?" Leticia asked, looking over at Chastity, feigning confusion.

"Ask her. Tell 'em why you mad, son. Tell em' why you mad," Chastity said mockingly, sounding like the mad rapper. Everyone laughed, including Deidre.

"I used to love those skits; *'Tell 'em why you mad, son!'* "
Leticia repeated.

Deidre was happy to see that almost everyone was in a
good mood. They had all quickly forgotten about Deidre
"testing" out the product. While the girls were distracted,
she dumped the drugs onto the floor and mixed them into
the carpet with her shoe. No one even noticed. Since the
mood was so light, she decided it was time to broach the
subject about Amber Reeves.

"Yo, did ya'll hear about that New York senator's daughter?" she asked. The room fell silent.

"Nah. What about her?" Chastity asked seriously, looking over at Leticia as if to say, *"Keep your mouth shut!"*

"She went missing a while back. Now somebody sent two
of her fingers to the Senator," Deidre recited as planned.

"Word? That's some real gangsta shit! That bastard-ass
senator is probably crooked as a motherfucker, that's why,"
Leticia commented.

Chastity remained silent. She gave Deidre a strange look
and kept staring at her.

Deidre immediately grew uncomfortable. "A'ight, well, I
gotta go. I'll holla," she said, standing up to leave. She didn't
want to stick around and seem desperate.

"DeeDee, I been meaning to talk to you about something," Chastity said dryly, leaning forward in her chair.

"Wasup?" Deidre replied, her mouth pasty. *Damn, I hope
she doesn't ask me to get high again*, she thought to herself.

"I think you've proven yourself. You bring back good returns. I wanna go into business together," Chastity offered,
getting straight to the point.

Deidre smiled inside, but kept a poker face on. They
trusted her. "Under what terms?" she asked.

"You work for me, I'll give you sixty percent off whatever
you bring in. You won't have to get any product from me
anymore," Chastity laid her offer out.

Leticia raised her eyebrows but remained silent. *Is she serious? Sixty percent is more than me and Tori get, and we're her partners*, Leticia thought to herself, tapping her foot under the table.

"Let me get rid of this supply, talk to my boys down south and get back to you," Deidre replied, playing hard to get. Seeming too eager was a sure way to make them suspicious.

"A'ight. Do what you gotta do, but this offer ain't gonna be around forever," Chastity said.

As soon as she made it to her car, she called Ferguson. "I did it! I made the deal on wire, and I got them to offer me a job inside of their clique!" Deidre relayed, excitedly. ". . . No, still nothing about the girl," Deidre said, her mood changing.

Ferguson agreed to meet her at their usual spot to retrieve the evidence.

"So, Aponte, you're doing well," Ferguson commented, taking the drugs from Deidre.

"Yeah, they trust me now," Deidre said, proud of her accomplishments.

"You need to dig deeper. You need to pressure them into letting you know who they get their drugs from," Ferguson urged, seemingly unpleased with Deidre's progress.

"That's impossible. The other girls don't even know. Only Chastity and her brother go to those meetings. If I ask them that, I'll blow my cover for sure," Deidre griped.

"Do it," Ferguson said calmly, standing on her words.

"Did you hear what the fuck I said! I could get killed! Besides, I need to find out about Amber Reeves!" Deidre said heatedly.

"These orders came from headquarters. You need to get in deeper," Ferguson continued, unmoved by Deidre's words.

"Fuck headquarters!" Deidre screamed, storming off. She was going to do things her way.

"Aponte, I'm serious! You need to go deeper!" Ferguson shouted at Deidre's back.

Deidre made more deals with the F.A.B., which proved lucrative for the girls, and she finally agreed to work for them. They were really feeling Deidre at this point. She had not found any signs that they had anything to do with Amber's disappearance. She had been with them almost every day since she'd gone under. In fact, she had become really close with all of them in one way or another—especially Chastity and R.J. Deidre began to regard them as family. She'd missed more than one meeting with Ferguson, and most days she didn't wear her wire or document her dealings with the F.A.B. In her mind, most of the time she was a part of the F.A.B. and not the FBI

"What about this one?" Chastity asked, turning to Deidre.

"Yeah, that one is hot," Deidre commented about the Louis Vuitton duffel bag.

"A'ight, I'll take three," Chastity told the lady inside the Louis Vuitton store. The lady arched her eyebrows and opened her eyes wide in surprise. "That's right, I said three: one for me, and one for each of my girls," Chastity demanded ostentatiously.

"What about Tori?" Leticia asked.

"She ain't here, so she don't get shit!" Chastity spat. She hadn't let anyone know what she knew about Tori and Officer Duke. She had her own plans for the deceitful couple.

"Yo, Chazz, you know she had to go to Family Court today. Why you bugging?" Leticia asked, confused. Leticia was also growing tired of Chastity's omnipotent behavior.

"Too bad!" Chastity said coldly.

Deidre just remained silent. She didn't know what to make of Chastity's behavior towards Tori.

"Let's go to Neiman's now," Chastity sang, beaming a bright smile. When she was angry or upset, shopping was the only cure. Besides, she never let anyone see her sweat.

The girls shopped until they were ready to drop.

Deidre went home with a Louie duffel bag, six pairs of high-end shoes, a platinum and sapphire David Yurman cuff bracelet, and enough crystal meth to put Chastity behind bars for life.

"Your Honor, I think it is preposterous that you're asking my client to take a drug test when she has never had any drug allegations against her!" Tori's lawyer sputtered indignantly.

"Your Honor, there have been several allegations of drug use, and it is also alleged that the mother sells drugs as well," the state's attorney interjected.

"Coral, you bitch! I know this is all your fault!" Tori screamed, her body trembling. She looked horrible. Her weave tracks needed to be redone, her nails were in serious need of a refill, and her eyes were bloodshot from staying up the entire night getting high. She had recently graduated from pills to snorting meth, and it showed. If it weren't for the expensive clothes she rocked, she would've looked just like a street junkie.

"Order!" the judge yelled, banging her gavel. "Ms. Banks, you will submit to a drug test immediately! This court is adjourned!"

Tori's legs felt weak as she left the courthouse. She knew that if she took a drug test, she would never get Akayla back. She had racked her brain trying to figure out how Coral and the foster care worker were finding out her every move. Her mind raced with ways to get her baby back. At first, she contemplated waiting for Coral outside the court, jumping her, taking Akayla and going on the run. But Coral was hardly ever alone, so that wouldn't work. Suddenly, something popped into Tori's muddled head; the NYPD detective that had approached her a few weeks earlier . . .

"Mommy loves her baby," Tori said, struggling to hold on to her wriggling baby girl. The baby clearly didn't want her to touch her, but Tori wasn't giving up that easy. Deidre sat on the couch inside the foster care agency looking on sadly. Tori had called Deidre that morning and asked her to come along on the visit for moral support. That's how close Deidre had gotten to the F.A.B.

"Okay, Ms. Banks the visitation is up," the foster care worker announced.

"Just give me a few more minutes," Tori implored.

"We've gotta go. You'll see her in two weeks," Coral said dryly.

Tori didn't respond. She had been warned that if she ever caused a scene at the agency again, her visits would be suspended.

"Bye, baby! I'm your Mommy, and you will know it," Tori said, kissing Akayla on the head.

The baby screamed and held her arms out for Coral, which broke Tori's heart. Tori began sobbing. Even Deidre was on the verge of tears. Without looking back, they both rushed out of the agency doors.

"Ms. Banks?" a short bald white man called out.

Tori and Deidre turned around in response. The man was dressed in a white T-shirt, old faded jeans and dirty sneakers—NYPD street gear. He also had a red wristband on his left wrist, which must've been the color of the day.

"Who are you?" Tori inquired, wiping her face.

"My name is John. I want to talk to you about your baby," the man said, extending his hand for a shake.

"What? Who the fuck are you?" Tori screamed suspiciously. Deidre moved closer to Tori.

"I am someone who can help you. I know what Coral has been doing to you," the man said, appealing to Tori's emotions.

"Look, she ain't in no condition to be fucked with," Deidre said, taking up for her friend. She knew right away the man was a cop. She could immediately spot when white cops tried to dress down like they were part of the civilian population. They always gave themselves away by wearing dirty ass sneakers. Besides that, the man was wearing a wristband signaling the color of the day so other cops would recognize him if need be.

"Tori, I can help you get that beautiful baby back. Let me talk to you alone without your mouthpiece," the man continued indignantly, ignoring Deidre.

Deidre shifted her weight from one foot to the other impatiently. She didn't want the local cops anywhere near the F.A.B. while she was under with them.

"DeeDee, go wait for me at the car. Let me see what he is talking about," Tori instructed, her mind on Akayla.

"Tori, think about this. He don't know you!" Deidre barked, trying to appeal to Tori's logical mind.

"Look, just go wait in the car!" Tori snarled right back, shooing Deidre away.

Deidre was surprised at how easily the man had influenced Tori. Nonetheless, she obeyed Tori's wishes, sulking away and heading towards the car.

"Tori, I'm John. I wanna offer you some help. But I need your help," the man began, finally having Tori to himself.

He laid out his offer, and Tori lost it. "Fuck you! I ain't no snitch, you fucking pig! How dare you!" Tori screamed after she heard his offer.

"Suit yourself. It's your baby we're talking about here.

This is my card just in case you change your mind," the man said, sliding his card into Tori's bag before she stormed off.

Returning to the car, Tori didn't tell Deidre what had happened, nor did Deidre ask.

Tori never told Chastity and Leticia about John Schmidt, the detective who offered to help her get Akayla back if she turned on her crew. Initially, Tori had told him to go fuck himself, but after what had just happened in court, the offer didn't seem so bad. She was desperate to touch her baby girl. Akayla was all she had left in the world besides her girls, and she was sick of Chastity treating her like a red-headed stepchild. She felt she should be the one going to the meetings with the connect, and more importantly, she felt she should be part owner of the Candy Shop as well. Chastity had taken sixty percent of everything sold at the Candy Shop, but it was Tori who introduced Chastity to Amber Reeves in the first place.

Tori bit into her bottom lip and gritted her teeth. "Fucking bitch! It's all her fault I don't have my baby!" she grumbled under her breath as she left the Family Court building.

After leaving the courthouse, Tori stood in front of the Marriott in downtown Brooklyn, opened her purse, unfolded a small foil package, and quickly and furtively inhaled the powdery substance. She knew that her drug habit was getting progressively worse, but it was all she could do to ease the pain she felt. Digging further into her handbag, she pulled out the detective's card, and dialed on her cell phone.

"Hello, is Detective Schmidt there?" Tori inquired. Without waiting for an affirmative response, she continued on. "This is Tori Banks. I'm ready to do business," she said through tears. She didn't even think twice before placing the call. The drugs had her mind, and Akayla had her heart. Nothing else mattered. Just like that, she became a snitch.

VOLUME 15:
THE RE-OPENING

Deidre posed in front of the full-length mirror hanging on the back of her bathroom door. "Hm-m-m-m, not bad if I say so myself," she commented to herself aloud about the black and purple John Galiano dress Chastity had purchased for her earlier that day. Although everyone made their own money, Chastity seemed to take pride in buying them all outfits for special events. Deidre peeped Chastity's control issues, but took the gifts in lieu of refusing them so she wouldn't be perceived as disrespectful. Sliding the dress down over her hips, she took it off.

"Next!" she said, looking over at her bed, which was full of clothes.

"*B-z-z-z-z! Ri-i-n-n-ng!*" Both of Deidre's cell phones began ringing simultaneously. She'd assigned each a different ringer so she would know when to be "Deidre" or "DeeDee" when she answered each one. "Shit!" she mumbled, racing over to the nightstand. This had never happened to her before. Instinctively, she picked up her undercover phone first and looked at the caller I.D. It was R.J. Before answering it, she peered down at her private cell phone. It was Ricky.

"Hello!" Deidre picked up the call that she regarded as most important.

"Hey, beautiful, how long before you're ready to go?" R.J. asked in his deep baritone.

A huge smile spread across Deidre's face. *This dude was fucking getting in my head in the worst way*, she thought to herself. "Give me about an hour. I'm driving, so I'll meet you there," Deidre said, still smiling.

"Are you smiling?" R.J. asked, knowing the answer.

"Not at all!" Deidre lied, trying in vain to straighten her face.

"Yeah, right! I know everything!" he laughed.

"I will see you at the party," Deidre chuckled, hanging up the phone.

The time Deidre spent with R.J. made her happier than she'd ever been. He made her forget that she was an agent every time.

She walked over to the bed, picked up her wire and placed it in the nightstand drawer. "Won't be needing that!" she whispered as she pushed the drawer shut.

It was the grand re-opening of the Candy Shop. The line outside extended from the front doors to around the block, and down another block. Hundreds of people turned out.

The club had received a beautiful make over. Chastity changed the color of the entire interior to bright candy apple red, including the hard wood floors. The stage had five shiny poles instead of one, and there was a huge mural of the F.A.B. painted on the back wall. Chastity's face was the largest in the painting, with smaller depictions of Tori and Leticia at each side of her. When the spotlight hit the stage, everyone could see the dancers, but they could also see the beautiful faces of the F.A.B. There were eight cages suspended from the ceilings throughout the club, each holding a beautiful girl dancing inside.

All of the patrons were in awe at how beautiful everything turned out. They all had the same jaw dropping reaction when entering the arched doorway. From the cheers resounding through the crowd, it was clear that everyone was enjoying themselves.

". . . *I'll take you to the Candy Shop,*
Give you one taste of what I got.
Keep going 'til you hit the spot,
Whoa! . . ."

The Fifty Cent and Olivia lyrics had the crowd jumping. It was the perfect song for the night. The party was in full swing. All of the club's working girls were making money hand over fist, and "candy" sales were tipping the scales. Chastity had done well for herself, once again.

Deidre finished her apple martini and looked out into the atmosphere from the bar. She saw R.J. approaching out of the corner of her eye, but decided to ignore him and play it cool.

R.J. rushed up to her, gave her a once over and grabbed her hand. "Yo, dance with me!" he screamed into Deidre's ear.

"A'ight," she agreed. She would do anything to get near him.

Scrambling to find an empty spot on the dance floor, they pressed against each other and danced close, even to the fast songs. Deidre felt R.J.'s nature rise every time she swiped her body up against his. A month after their first date, and several hundred dollars worth of flowers later, Deidre felt herself crossing a dangerous line. One of the cardinal rules for an undercover is: "Never fall in love".

This life is better than being an agent on any day, Deidre thought to herself. She was enjoying her new lifestyle more than she expected. Carefree living, tax-free money, shopping, and no problems—what a life! She was feeling closer than ever to the F.A.B. Chastity trusted her and had put her in charge of collecting money from all of the new dancer/pushers that worked at the Candy Shop.

"Excuse me, can I cut in?" Chastity yelled over the music, placing her body between her brother and Deidre. Although she liked Deidre, Chastity was still territorial when it came to R.J.

"Sure," Deidre conceded, stepping aside.

R.J. laughed as he reached over and grabbed Deidre's hand, pulling her back towards him. Chastity danced in front of her brother while Deidre danced behind him. They all laughed. It was like they'd known each other all of their lives.

"Hey, I wanna talk to everybody about something," Chastity announced to R.J. and Deidre.

"When? Now?" Deidre asked, still moving in sync with the music.

"Yeah, in my office," Chastity said, stopping her motion.

"A'ight, c'mon," R.J. said. They all walked single file off the dance floor.

R.J. never let go of Deidre's hand. Along the way, they grabbed Tori and Leticia.

Everyone made themselves comfortable in Chastity's newly remodeled office. She sat at a long brown and red-speckled lacquer table located in the center of the office, with ten leather swivel chairs around it. *Nothing but the best*, Deidre thought to herself. Chastity whispered something to R.J., and he excused himself. Deidre followed him with her eyes until he was out the door.

"Yo, Chazz, what is this shit about? I got bitches all over me out there," Leticia complained, sweat glistening all over her face.

"Just relax!" Chastity demanded.

Tori was silent. Deidre noticed that she seemed unusually distant and didn't look too hot either. Tori had a simple pony-tail in her hair and wore no makeup. She had huge bags under her eyes, like she hadn't slept in years. Deidre found it especially strange that on a night like this, Tori wouldn't be dressed to kill, as usual. Instead, she wore a fuchsia Juicy Couture sweat suit with a matching bag. Cute, but not appropriate for the occasion.

After everyone was seated, Chastity began. "Ladies, we have finally arrived at the big time," she said, raising her shot glass of Patron. "I must admit, three girls from the 'hood have changed the way shit is done. Nobody can touch the F.A.B. crew," she continued. All of the ladies looked on reverently.

"First, to my main bitch, T-baby. W go back like babies on pacifiers. You have proved to me that you got my back. Death before dishonor! To you, my nigga! Loca, you know how I feel about a bitch. You down for whatever, and I got the utmost respect for your gangsta. I know you always got my back. Ya'll bitches is the truth!" Chastity proclaimed, raising her glass in tribute. The ladies followed suit. Giving Tori a shout-out had burned Chastity, but she had to keep fronting for now.

"And last but not least, DeeDee. I don't usually trust out-side bitches. When I first met you that night, I was like, yo, who is this country bumpkin' bitch, kickin' in the door wavin' the four-four? But you can bang with the best of them. You are officially a part of F.A.B., and that shit is from the heart. Not to mention that you might be my sister-in-law in a minute!" Chastity continued, chuckling and again raising her glass in tribute. She walked over to a blushing, guilt-ridden Deidre and put her hands on her shoulders. "As a matter of fact, we're graduating yo' ass today. Everybody, raise your glasses to the new Sergeant of our crew! To DeeDee, the bitch from that backwards ass D.C. with more

New York heart than some niggas! Cheers!" Chastity shouted enthusiastically, clinking her glass against Deidre's and Tori's. Chastity wanted Tori to be jealous.

"That's wasup! Who the fuck are we?" Chastity cheered like an athletic team coach.

"F.A.B.!" they all yelled in unison.

Deidre gulped her Patron, squinting her eyes from the tangy taste, and feeling right at home. She was with her newfound crew—her girls—the Fly Ass Bitches. At that moment, there was no place she'd rather be.

"A'ight, fuck the bullshit! There's money to be made!" Tori proclaimed, jumping up from her seat. She was seething inside. If she would have stayed another minute, she felt like she might pull out on Chastity and shoot the bitch right in her smart-ass mouth.

"Yeah, I'm going back to my private party," Leticia chimed in, following Tori out of the door.

As Deidre got up to follow Tori and Leticia out of Chastity's office, Chastity whispered to her, "Yo, DeeDee, let me holla at you for a minute."

"Wasup?" Deidre asked, turning back.

"Keep an eye on her. I think she's stealing from me and shit," Chastity said, pointing towards the door.

"Who?" Deidre asked incredulously.

"Tori, that's who. I think her paper been short for a minute. For real, I think she's stealing. Plus, I heard through the grapevine she might be tootin' n' shit," Chastity announced seriously.

"Nah, I don't think she would do some shit like that," Deidre replied, shaking her head in disbelief.

"I'm just saying, I will have the bitch killed if she fucks with my paper, that's all," Chastity replied flatly, laying the foundation.

"It won't come to that, I'm sure. But I'll keep an eye on her," Deidre assured.

Diedre was in a rush to find out where R.J. disappeared to. She had to admit to herself that she was feeling him hard, and the liquor she had consumed made her horny as hell.

As she bumped her way through the crowd, she ran head-first into someone. "Oops! Excuse me!" Deidre said, looking up into the man's face.

"You're excused, beautiful," Officer Duke said, looking down at her.

"Thanks," Deidre said, rushing off.

Officer Duke turned around and followed her with his eyes. *Damn, she looks very familiar. Where do I know that beautiful-ass face from?* he asked himself, but his thoughts were immediately interrupted.

"Whatchu doin' in here?" Chastity asked, aggravated.

"Day-u-u-u-u-um! You lookin' fuckin' right tonight!" Officer Duke exclaimed. He surveyed Chastity from head to toe. The white Michael Kors baby doll dress she rocked, with the white Guiseppe Zanotti stilettos made her look like an angel. Not to mention all the diamond accessories that sparkled on various parts of her body.

"I asked you a question," Chastity continued, ignoring his bullshit compliment.

"Can't I celebrate with my baby and business partner?" he asked, reaching for her manicured hands.

Chastity rolled her eyes. She wanted to punch him in his lying-ass face. "I gotta go," she said dismissively. "Where you goin'?" Officer Duke asked, grabbing her arm. Just as he did, Tori approached the two.

"Hey, Duke. Long time no see," Tori sang, flashing a fake smile. Officer Duke ignored her.

"Yo, Chastity. Let me holla at you," Officer Duke said, almost pleading.

"Nah, baby. I gotta go. I got a business to run," Chastity smirked, looking Tori dead in her eyes. "Oh, T-baby, why don't you entertain Duke, since you haven't seen him in so long," she said sarcastically, sauntering away.

"What the fuck did you tell her? You dirty bitch!" Officer Duke growled in Tori's ear.

"I didn't tell her . . ." Tori began, but he stormed off before she could finish her sentence. She felt like shit. Nothing seemed to be going her way. Tori looked out into the club and everyone was enjoying themselves. Chastity, Deidre, and R.J. were having fun together, and Leticia was surrounded by about five girls who worked in the club. Nobody seemed to care about her or how she was feeling. Officer Duke was riding Chastity's ass like a pimple.

Tori gulped down the remaining bits of her drink and slammed the glass on the tabletop. "Fuck all of them!" she slurred as she headed for the door. She had a meeting with Detective Schmidt planned for early next morning, and she couldn't afford to miss it.

VOLUME 16:
THE LOVE I NEVER KNEW

The party ended, the club had cleared out, and everyone was heading home. Chastity, R.J. Deidre, and Leticia were the only people remaining in the Candy Shop.

Deidre was bent. She had let herself drink to the point of no return, another no-no for an undercover. She watched in a daze as the others counted up all of the proceeds from the night. Even in her inebriated state, she could tell that there was over five-hundred-thousand-dollars on the table. The sound of the money counter reminded her of a movie or some shit.

"DeeDee, I'm taking you home with me. You can't drive right now," R.J. announced, grabbing her hand to help her up.

"Word, DeeDee, your ass is smashed!" Leticia joked.

"Shut up, Loca! You can't talk!" Deidre slurred, pointing a crooked finger at Leticia.

"Bitch, at least I can stand up on my own!" Leticia quipped as she turned her head and licked the cheek of the young girl she had on her lap.

"Ee-e-e-w-w-w!" the rest of them bellowed in unison, and then everyone busted out laughing.

Chastity was trying to prolong things, because she knew she was going home by herself tonight. Her stalling plan didn't work for long. She could see the anticipation in her brother's eyes. She wanted the best for R.J., so she finally gave up. "A'ight, ya'll can go. We're done here," she announced.

Deidre opened her eyes, squinting to get focus. Her head was throbbing, and the room was spinning. She looked around, dazed for a few seconds. She finally realized she was in R.J.'s house. She lay on his off-white soft suede sofa as he prepared coffee to sober her up. She let her eyes wander from the huge 52" plasma on the wall to the expensive paintings hanging around the living room. She immediately noticed a large family portrait hanging up. It was of R.J., Chastity and their mother . . . his father was not in it. *She was beautiful,* Deidre thought to herself of R.J.'s mother. She looked like an Asian model; slanted eyes, beautiful butter colored skin and silky jet-black hair that extended past her waist. Now Deidre knew where Chastity got her beautiful features from.

"A'ight, I'm back," R.J. said as he handed Deidre her mug.

"Your mother was beautiful," Deidre said softly.

"Thanks," R.J. replied, sliding closer to her

She took a small sip from her mug and looked over at R.J. They both knew the deal. They felt the same way for each other.

R.J. grabbed Deidre's drink and set it atop a *Sports Illustrated* that lay on the coffee table. He turned back towards her and took hold of her, pulling her into him.

Her heart melted. His scent was intoxicating. She inhaled deeply and closed her eyes. She wanted him. She couldn't control the feelings, although she knew it was wrong and could get her into a lot of trouble.

"I want you!" R.J. whispered in her ear.

"What about Chastity?" Deidre whispered back.

"She wants us to be together," R.J. assured, placing his mouth on top of hers.

Deidre returned the favor, and slipped her tongue between his plump lips. Before she knew it, she was in her underwear. Lucky for her she had opted not to wear her wire. She watched in anticipation as R.J. removed his clothes, exposing his sexy muscular chest, washboard abs and powerful legs. Her head instantly felt better. She definitely had all her wits about her at that point.

R.J. lifted her like a doll from the sofa in one scoop and carried her up the stairs toward his bedroom. Deidre was breathing hard as her pussy began getting moist. She held onto his neck and buried her face in his skin, like a damsel being rescued.

The bedroom was pitch black, and all she could see was R.J.'s silhouette as she tried to adjust her eyes in the darkness. Suddenly, he got on the bed and began kissing her neck, slowly moving his hands down her stomach, past her freshly shaved triangle, and finding her soaking wet pussy, he began fingering her. Both of them were breathing heavily. Deidre moaned loudly. She wanted to see him. Opening her eyes she blinked fiercely trying to force them to adjust. Finally, her eyes adjusted to the darkness.

R.J. leaned up over her. "I'm feeling you so much," he whispered, parting her legs with his knee. He grabbed his rock hard dick and prepared to enter her.

"Ohhhh!" she let out a long sigh and looked up into R.J.'s face. *Oh shit!* Deidre thought, and suddenly she felt her stomach knot and she felt sick. Placing her hands on his chest, and with all her might, she frantically pushed R.J. away and jumped out of the bed with her chest heaving.

"What's the matter?" he yelled, eyes wide with shock and sweat dripping from his face.

"I can't do this!" Deidre wolfed, trying to cover herself. She was spooked. She could've sworn she'd seen her father in the bed with her.

"It's okay. I understand," R.J. assured, confused and clearly disappointed. He knew it would happen; he didn't need to rush her.

Deidre was embarrassed as she hurried to put her clothes on. She was sober enough to think about Ricky; her father; the Bureau and most of all her assignment. *What the hell am I doing?* She wondered seriously. She was falling, and falling fast.

"Why don't you just stay the night?" R.J. asked, not wanting her to leave. "We don't have to do anything," he assured.

Deidre looked at him again. He really did look just like her father, and it bothered the shit out of her. But she felt such a strong love for him too. It was like he was the love she never knew. She hadn't dated, nor had many boyfriends. Ricky was all she'd ever known.

"Please, don't go," R.J. said, walking over to where she stood and grabbing her face. Tears rimmed her eyes. "What's the matter?" he asked, confused as hell.

"I can't love you. I don't even know you," Deidre whispered. She wanted to tell him the truth so bad.

"Love knows best. We were meant to be," R.J. assured as he began undressing her again.

Deidre was weak for men. She couldn't control her feelings. *Fuck Agent Aponte! Right now, I'm DeeDee Barnes,* she said to herself, and she finally gave in.

Once again, Deidre found herself lying with R.J. He entered her gently, her moisture saturating his love muscle and pubis. She closed her eyes and let her emotions carry her away, and he did the same. Their bodies moved in sync for the next hour, and the lovemaking was more powerful than anything either of them had ever experienced. *He is the one!* Deidre said to herself as she folded her legs around his and placed her head on his chest. Listening to his heartbeat, she was fully disillusioned, and for the moment, once again she'd forgotten that she was an FBI agent.

VOLUME 17:
THE RAID

The summer was in full swing in New York. It was ninety degrees outside and the Mr. Softee ice cream trucks could be heard blaring those annoying songs on every other block. The street corners were alive with hustlers and gold diggers, and more importantly, the Candy Shop was back in its full swing of business. The F.A.B. was making money hand over fist, and Deidre was under a lot of pressure from the Bureau to go deeper and deeper.

Deidre walked through the dressing room in the basement of the Candy Shop collecting the money that the dancers had made for the night. That used to be Tori's job, but lately she had been making herself scarce around the crew.

As Deidre approached a dancer that called herself Mystique, she noticed a picture that caught her attention. She did a double take and walked back over to Mystique's booth. "Who is this?" she inquired, pointing at the picture.

Mystique looked at Deidre through her gray contact lenses and fake eyelashes, and with an attitude asked, "Why you wanna know?"

"I think I know her," Deidre said.

"You don't know her, you just seen her on TV like e'r-body else," Mystique said dismissively, pouting her dark brown painted lips. The big-breasted girl looked like something out of the circus. Her pale skin, those gray contacts, dark lips and black inch-long nail tips made her resemble a side show attraction.

"Seen her on TV?" Deidre asked, playing dumb.

"Yeah, she's senator Reeves' daughter," Mystique said, lowering her eyes.

"How do you know her then?" Deidre asked, pressing the girl for information.

"What? You think I ain't good enough to know a senator's daughter?" Mystique asked indignantly.

"Nah, I'm not saying that at all. Just asking," Deidre assured. She had to play nice to get the information she wanted.

"Well, her name is Amber. She was my best friend, and now she's gone," Mystique said sadly.

"Where did she go?" Deidre kept pressing forward with her questions.

"That fucking black ass guy picked her up after she had a fight with Chastity, and I never seen her again. I begged her not to go. He looked crazy, and I could tell he was gonna do something to her because he was mad nervous," Mystique informed, lighting a cigarette.

"What guy? You seen him before?" Deidre asked. She was getting excited about the information she was getting. She didn't realize she might be overstepping her boundaries.

"Yeah, he was the one who got Amber hooked on that shit. He is from D.C., some fed nigga that she was fucking with. She met him at her father's confirmation ceremony," Mystique continued.

Deidre's mind started racing. *A fed?* she thought to herself. "What did he look like?" Deidre asked.

"Look, what the fuck, are you a cop?" Mystique asked, growing suspicious of Deidre's constant questions.

"No, I'm just concerned about your friend. I mean she might be dead," Deidre blurted, trying to appeal to Mystique's conscience.

"Don't say that!" Mystique yelled, bursting into tears. "Amber was so good to me. When I didn't have shit to eat, she fed me. People criticized her for being a friend with a lowlife like me. She never judged me. From the time I met her, I told her to stop using that shit. Her father did this to her. That bastard knew that she was selling drugs for the F.A.B. He was making money off of it. So was the black bald headed guy, and the other white fed motherfucker!" Mystique shared as she wiped smudged mascara off her cheeks.

"What . . . ?" Deidre began, but before she could get the words out, she heard a loud crash. Startled, she and Mystique both spun around at the same time.

"Oh shit!" Mystique yelled.

Deidre opened her eyes wide when she saw them.

"Police! Don't fucking move!"

Deidre had a gun pointed right in her face. Girls were screaming and running in all directions until the cops threw in a can of tear gas. "Ahem! Ahem!" Deidre started coughing as one of the cops grabbed her roughly and threw her up against the wall. She was escorted upstairs.

"What the fuck is ya'll doing! Get the fuck off of me!" Leticia screamed.

Deidre could hear Leticia tussling with the police as she was led outside with everyone else.

"Yo, DeeDee! This is some bullshit! Remember, its death before dishonor! Don't say shit to these pigs!" Leticia yelled out to her.

Chastity kept her head up and her mouth shut. She was too cool to fight or yell, but inside she was fuming.

The Candy Shop was raided, and the NYPD totally trashed the newly renovated club. They took a sledgehammer to the cherry wood bar, and all of the tables were smashed into pieces. The shiny glass liquor cabinets were pried open and all of the expensive bottles of champagne were confiscated. The cops also found the safe hidden in the floor in Chastity's office, which was also emptied of its contents.

Deidre sat in a cell at central booking with Leticia and Chastity. Nobody said a word. All she could think about was her cover being blown. Fucking with the locals was a sure way to do that. After seven hours of sitting on the cold hard benches inside the small crowded cell, they finally heard something.

"DeeDee Barnes!" a tall court officer yelled out. Deidre stood up and walked towards the door of the cell. "Going to see the judge," he said to her. She looked back and Leticia and Chastity, who both looked on, perplexed.

"What about us?" Leticia yelled as she watched Deidre being led out.

Deidre turned her head quickly, hearing Leticia's question. She never turned around to look back again; she was afraid that the worried look on her face would give her away. *What the fuck is the Bureau trying to do . . . get me killed?* she thought to herself.

Without so much as a word to Deidre, the judge immediately let her go, but Chastity and Leticia remained locked up. She was relieved to get out, but worried as she left the jail. She immediately jumped on the telephone and called R.J. She needed to let him know what was going on.

"Hello!" R.J. picked up.

"It's me. They . . ."Deidre began.

"Yo, be easy on the phone. Meet me at my house," R.J. said, cutting her off mid-sentence.

Deidre agreed. She hung up from him and immediately dialed Ferguson. "What the fuck are ya'll doing? Why didn't ya'll just let me stay with the rest of the girls?" Deidre asked, pissed off.

"I warned you about those fucking local cops. We need to meet, *now!*" Ferguson yelled.

Deidre hung up. She had no intention of meeting with Ferguson. She headed straight for R.J.'s house.

"What was going on when this happened?" R.J. asked as he paced the floor.

"Nothing unusual. I was doing the collections, and Chazz was upstairs getting ready for the night," Deidre explained.

"Where was Loca and T-baby?"

"Loca was upstairs with Chazz, and T-baby was nowhere to be found," Deidre informed. It immediately struck her as strange that Tori wasn't at the club. She started thinking back to the night of the re-opening and how bad Tori looked.

"Somebody dropped dime," R.J. said, rubbing his chin, deep in thought.

"But who?" Deidre asked. She knew for sure that this raid had nothing to do with her case.

"I don't know, but we'll find out," R.J. said. He moved towards Deidre and kissed her cheek gently. "Are you okay?" he asked, rubbing her bruised cheek.

"Yeah, I'm fine. What about Chazz and Loca?" Deidre inquired, anxiously biting her bottom lip.

"I'm waiting for the judge to set bail for them. I hope they don't jam Loca. She just got home," R.J. replied.

"Damn!" Deidre sighed, staring blankly. All sorts of things ran through her mind. Most of all, she was worried about her girls.

R.J. startled her when he began kissing her neck. Deidre felt herself getting hot, but she couldn't concentrate. The girls were the only real friends she'd ever had, and she was stabbing them in the back every day in the name of the government. She felt like crying. She turned into R.J. and laid her head on his chest. She listened to his heartbeat and felt comfort. He kissed her again, and this time she returned the favor.

R.J. grabbed her face and looked into her eyes and said, "I think we were meant to be."

"You say that a lot," Deidre replied, avoiding direct eye contact. Sometimes those words made her uncomfortable.

"I mean it," he whispered, kissing her again. This time he slid his hand under her shirt and caressed her already erect nipples.

"Mm-m-m-m!" she moaned.

R.J. continued his quest, and proceeded to unbutton her pants. Deidre didn't fight against what she was feeling, and grabbed R.J.'s manhood. "Yeah!" he groaned, biting her left ear. "Ohhh," she cooed. R.J. had her out of her clothes in no time. He kissed her bellybutton as he cupped her perfect ass cheeks.

Deidre placed her hands on top of his head and pushed his head down toward her throbbing hot box. Before she could react, R.J. plunged his tongue into her flesh, parting her labia. He repeated the motion several times, driving Deidre insane. "Ohhhh!" she yelled out, pushing toward his tongue.

R.J. continued to lap up her juices like a hungry dog, and the more he licked, the louder she moaned. When he was done, he brought his wet face into hers and kissed her deeply again.

Deidre licked all of her own juices off of his lips. "Let me taste you," she whispered, trying to sit up.

"No, I want to feel you," he groaned, easing her back down and placing his manhood deep inside of her.

"Ahhhhh!" she screamed out in ecstasy. R.J. continued to pump up and down, picking up speed. Deidre could feel her thighs trembling, and before she knew it, she exploded. "Aggghhh!" she screamed again, grabbing the skin on R.J.'s back. She was in love, she was sure of it.

After making love, they lay still in each other's arms.

"R.J.," Deidre whispered.

"Yes, love?" he replied.

"How did you know my address when you first sent me flowers?" she asked.

"I'm like God. I know everything," he replied with a chuckle.

"I'm serious," she said, leaning up on one arm as she looked in his face.

"I'm serious too. I know everything about you."

"Like what?" she asked, nervously.

"Like the fact that you are in love with me," R.J. replied, looking her directly in her eyes.

She fell silent and laid back down.

Tori watched the news broadcast about the raid, and she didn't feel a thing. "Good for those bitches!" she mumbled as she shoveled a heap of crystal meth into her left nostril. Snitching was easy. All she had to do was give the detectives the information they requested, and wait for them to contact her about Akayla. Detective Schmidt told her that he would even drive Akayla home if everything worked out right. Tori believed him. In her junked up state, she would have sold her organs on the black market, so she damn sure didn't give a damn about selling out the only people that had been there for her since she was a kid.

* * *

Chastity and Leticia were released the next day. All the raid had turned up was about sixty illegal prescription pills, which the cops couldn't pin to anybody since there were like twelve dancers there when they came in. Everybody claimed a certain amount of the money that was found, being mindful to keep their claims right under ten-thousand-dollars.

The detectives were pissed, therefore they stole the rest of the money and things that were seized.

Detective Schmidt and his squad were sure they had fool-proof information that the Candy Shop would be loaded with illegal pills and crystal meth. Unfortunately for them, their snitch was wrong.

VOLUME 18:
THE TURNING POINT

Deidre was exhausted from her hot night with R.J. She wanted to go home, shower, change, and go check on Chastity and Leticia. Ricky, Ferguson and headquarters never crossed her muddled mind.

Deidre parked her car, and just as she did, her private cell phone began vibrating. She looked down into the cup holder and picked up her phone—it was her mother. "Hello, Mom," Deidre answered, waiting to hear if her mother was loaded or not.

"Deidre . . . I need to see you right away," her mother slurred into the phone.

"What's the matter?" Deidre asked, rolling her eyes as she walked towards her apartment building.

"I had a dream someone was trying to kill you!" Cassandra cried.

"No one's trying to kill me, Mom. I can't come to Virginia right now. I promise I'll try for next week," Deidre placated. She was disgusted with her mother, as usual.

"No, baby girl, they are going to kill you! The FBI is

going to kill you like they did your father!" Cassandra wailed, garbling her words.

"You need to go lie down and dry out. I'll call you back and check on you later," Deidre said, sickened and slightly embarrassed by her mother's outburst. She disconnected the line and shut her phone off.

She had finally made it inside. *Fucking crazy!* she thought as she began removing her clothes.

Officer Duke pulled his car onto Hall Street right behind Deidre's. As she parked, he watched her. "That's where I know her from! That's the bitch from the ticket!" he said out loud to himself. He immediately dialed Chastity's number. "Yo, I need to talk to you about that new bitch ya'll running with," he said into the receiver, pulling off. Although he was on her shit list, Chastity agreed to meet him at his apartment, spurred by his offer of information on DeeDee.

Officer Duke was happy to tell Chastity that when Deidre was given a ticket and he ran her plate, the car came back as "Property of the U.S. Government", which meant that either Deidre was a fed, or she bought the car at a federal auction and never got the paperwork straightened out. He also told her what he'd found out about who had dropped a dime before the raid.

Infuriated, Chastity hid her feelings. She had another mission in mind. "Thank you, baby. I'm sorry for the way I've been treating you. It's just that I love you so much, I get jealous when I can't have you all the time," she said deceitfully, sliding close to Officer Duke.

"You're welcome. I told you I'd do anything for you, and I forgive you for acting like a bitch," he replied, touching her hair gently.

"You know I want you. I missed you," she said softly.

He let a huge grin spread across his face. "I missed you too. What you got for me?" he asked, tugging on her belt.

"Wait, be patient. Since I knew you were going to hook me up with some good information, I got a surprise for you. Lemme go to the bathroom first," Chastity said seductively, licking her lips and switching her full hips.

"That's wasup!" Officer Duke beamed, excited.

Chastity sashayed out of the bedroom, went into the bathroom and changed into a sheer, Italian lace La Perla bra and panty set. She checked herself in the mirror, inhaled, and placed her hands behind her back as she exited the bathroom.

"Close your eyes!" she yelled down the hallway of Officer Duke's apartment before she reached the bedroom.

Officer Duke was butt ass naked sprawled out on his bed. "Hell yeah!" he yelled back, thrilled.

"Don't open those eyes," Chastity warned as she walked into the room and crawled onto the bed.

"Ohhh, baby!" Officer Duke whispered, inhaling her Gucci Envy perfume. Anticipation had the hairs on his arms and legs standing up and goose bumps covered his entire body.

"Don't open your eyes yet," Chastity demanded setting herself up. She started her deed by licking his stomach, making her way up his chest to his neck, then his mouth.

"Ahhh," he let out a soft moan.

"Open your mouth for me, baby," Chastity murmured. Officer Duke complied. "Eat this, you lying, sneaky bitch!" she growled, placing the barrel of a .40 caliber Glock into his mouth.

Shocked, Officer Duke tried to jump up, but his teeth hit the metal of the gun just as she pulled the trigger. *"Boom!"* Blood splattered all over her, the wall and the pillow.

Chastity jumped as the blood and brain matter spattered all over her face, chest and hair. She was spooked. Murder wasn't her thing; she usually let Leticia take care of those things. Shaking, she took the sheet, wiped her prints off the gun, and placed Officer Duke's hands around it. Racing into the bathroom, she hastily cleaned herself up. The smell of fresh blood and shit was enmeshed in her nostrils. When she shot him, his bowels and bladder also released all over her and the bed. With her heart racing, she gathered her things and quickly left his apartment. She left the rental car that she'd paid someone to rent for her right in front of his building.

"Taxi!" she called out, and she was gone.

One traitor down, one to go!

Chastity returned to her house. Rubbing her hands together to mask the trembling, she tried her best to appear cool. She took a long hot shower and washed her hair at least six times. She needed time to gather her thoughts. Once she was satisfied that she'd beaten her battle with the tremors, she called Deidre.

"Yo, DeeDee, I need you to meet me at my house right away," she said, with urgency lacing her words.

"Now?" Deidre asked. She had finally decided to meet with Ferguson. After missing several scheduled meetings, she couldn't really afford to miss another one.

"Yes, it has to be now," Chastity replied, pacing the floor.

"A'ight, I'll see you in a few minutes," Deidre conceded. *What's this all about?* She thought. Nonetheless, she slid on her jeans and prepared to get ready.

Chastity hung up and dialed Leticia's cell phone. "Yeah, Loca, it's me, Chazz. She's on her way, so hurry up and get here," she said anxiously.

Leticia agreed immediately, and picked up her cell phone to call Tori. "Yo, T-baby, where you been?" she asked.

"I've been stressed over this case. I'm just chillin'," Tori lied, looking down at her drugs.

"Well, something came up. You heard about the Candy Shop?" Leticia asked, already knowing the answer.

"Yeah. I was on my way there when I heard," Tori continued with her lies.

"Well, we need to meet right now," Leticia demanded.

Tori rolled her eyes and looked at herself in the mirror. "I'll be there," she said.

As Deidre rushed to get dressed, she looked down at her cell phone and noticed ten missed calls. Ferguson was blowing her phone up, but Deidre felt torn. Her first priority had become the F.A.B., and not the FBI

She picked up her gun from her nightstand and looked down at her wire. She contemplated wiring up, but the sound of Chastity's voice made her feel uneasy, therefore she decided against wearing it. Grabbing her bag, she raced out of the door.

Amos peeked out of his front window, and with phone in hand, he dialed the number. "Yeah, she just left," he said into the receiver.

Deidre pulled up to Chastity's house, and the girls were already sitting in Chastity's vehicle. An ill feeling permeated Deidre's stomach. She swallowed hard, put a half smile on her face, and knocked on the dark tinted window. Leticia opened the door and let her into the back seat.

"What's up?" Deidre asked, slightly winded. Nobody responded as Chastity pulled out.

"... *Why is rattin' at an all time high?*

Why are you even alive?

Why they kill Tupac n' Chris?

Why at the bar you ain't take straight shots instead of poppin' Crist?

Why? Why?

All that I been given is this thing that I've been living.

They got me in the system.

Why they gotta do me like that . . ."

The Jadakiss lyrics were blasting from the speakers, and no one in the car said a word. Deidre stared out of the back passenger window. She could see the Brooklyn Bridge in the distance as the car moved closer and closer to it. Chastity, Leticia, and Tori were all unusually and unnervingly silent. She decided to test the waters and she spoke.

"Yo, that's my joint! Turn it up!" she yelled to no one in particular.

"Yeah, turn it up Chazz! Those lyrics are real!" Leticia agreed, eyeing the side of Deidre's face from the corner of her eye. She watched Deidre for the entire ride.

Suddenly, the car came to a jolting stop. Deidre peered out of the windshield. It was dark, and the block they were on was desolate. They were right under the bridge. She looked across the street at a tan and green building with a huge sign that read "The Watchtower". She made a mental note just in case. Her stomach churned, causing her to feel like taking a shit right there on the spot. Something just didn't feel right. Bursting with questions, she decided to remain silent; asking a question at this point could prove deadly.

"Get out," Chastity instructed. Everyone exited the car almost simultaneously. Chastity left the car running.

Deidre picked up on it and the hairs on the back of her neck stood up. She felt like throwing up. She could definitely feel tension. Usually being out with the girls was easy, but something was definitely different.

Leticia walked around the back of the vehicle and went into the trunk. Deidre couldn't see what she was doing. Tori looked nervous, as usual, and she paced back and forth, chewing on her trembling bottom lip. Chastity stood stoic. That was her usual. She never showed emotion.

Deidre wanted desperately to look around. She had a feeling that she had been outed. She was afraid to move. She didn't want to bring any suspicion to herself. She shoved her hands deep into the pockets of her jeans—she didn't want the girls to see them tremble. Her heart beat painfully against her sternum. She realized that she was in dangerous company.

"Ga'head, start walking," Leticia said, breaking the silence.

Tori's eyes grew wide. "What's going on?" she asked, the words spilling from her lips in rapid succession. No one answered. Deidre knew that whatever was about to go down it wasn't going to be pretty.

Chastity led the way, Tori followed, and Deidre was next. Deidre could hear Leticia's Nike Air Max crunching the ground behind her.

After about two minutes of walking, Chastity stopped abruptly and turned around. "A'ight, let's get down to the shit," she growled, moving a piece of her perfectly straight auburn hair from her eyes.

"Yeah, DeeDee," Leticia continued with a screw face.

"Yo, wasup?" Deidre asked, truly confused.

"You know what the fuck is up," Leticia replied, moving close to Deidre's face—so close that Deidre could smell Remy on her breath.

"Nah, I'm lost." Deidre said, trying her best to play it cool, her stomach contents threatening to leap up into her esophagus.

"Basically, bitch, we wanna know what fucking academy you completed. Was it the Feds or NYPD?" Chastity retorted, moving in behind Deidre. There was nowhere to go.

"What the fuck are ya'll talking about? Not this bullshit again! As much as I been doing in the fucking streets, ya'll accusing me of being a cop again?" Deidre yelled. It was either play the big bad bitch role, or die, and she knew it.

"Ma-a-a-aybe sh-sh-sh she's telling the truth, Chazz. C'mon, it's DeeDee, our friend," Tori stuttered as she nervously moved back and forth. Her nose was running nonstop. This wasn't her type of thing. Besides, she was feeling guilty about what she had done.

"Shut the fuck up, T-baby!" Chastity yelled.

In one sudden motion, Leticia grabbed Deidre's shirt and ripped it open, exposing her breasts. Deidre had no time to react and her mouth fell open. "Yo, strip!" Leticia barked.

Deidre put up a defensive stance and yelled, "Fuck you! I don't need this shit! Ya'll bitches is crazy!" At that moment she realized she was still an FBI Agent and not really a part of the F.A.B. It was up to her to get out of this situation alive. Ferguson and Ricky couldn't save her ass now.

"She said strip!" Chastity whispered gruffly in Deidre's ear.

Deidre could feel the heat from Chastity's breath moving eerily down her neck. The next thing she felt was the cold steel as the barrel of a gun she couldn't see was placed right against her cerebellum. She slowly began removing her clothes. As soon as she pulled her jeans down, her gun fell from her waistband.

"Looks like a fucking service weapon to me," Leticia said, grabbing Deidre's .357 Sig Sauer from the ground to examine it.

"I bought that shit on the street!" Deidre said with an attitude.

"I don't see no wire. I'ma kill you anyway," Chastity growled, leveling her gun at Deidre's half-naked body.

"Aggghhhh! Please, Chazz! Wait!" Tori screamed, jumping up and down.

Deidre knew that Tori might be her only hope.

Leticia grabbed Tori by her hair and slapped her so hard that blood spurted out of her mouth. "Shut the fuck up!" Leticia shouted, tossing Tori to the ground. She raised her leg and stomped on Tori's hand, and then kicked her in the chin. Tori shrieked in pain, dizzy from the blows. Leticia continued to brutally assault Tori, while Chastity stared at Deidre, trying to gage her reaction. Nothing.

Deidre remained silent. She knew this was a part of their

test. The first rule an undercover learns is never come to the aid of a victim in the presence of the crew. Criminals know that a cop's first instinct is to help. Deidre knew helping Tori was a sure way to blow her cover.

Finally, Chastity interrupted Leticia's vicious attack. "Enough, Loca!"

Leticia immediately stopped wailing on Tori. Sweating and breathing hard, she looked like a demon possessed.

"Now, back to you," Leticia wolfed, smearing Tori's blood on Deidre's face.

Deidre turned her head. Between her nerves and the smell of the blood, she felt vomit creeping up her throat.

Tori lay moaning on the ground, holding her face.

"Yo! Loca, Chazz, I've been nothing but loyal. Wasup with this shit?" Deidre asked, still playing the angry role.

"Bitch, you don't know nothing about death before dishonor! Now, what fucking academy did you go through?" Chastity asked as she pulled back the hammer on the chrome snub nose .38 revolver special.

Deidre swallowed hard. This was not how she pictured herself dying. Six years of service to the federal government, and she was about to die on a dirty, desolate block in Brooklyn, New York, all alone. "Yo, I'm standing here, half-naked with no wire! I'm telling you, I'm not a fucking cop!" Deidre screamed. It was her last ditch effort to save her life.

"A'ight, if you're not a fed or a cop, then I got a job for you," Chastity said, calmly lowering her weapon.

"Anything!" Deidre pleaded.

"You need to kill for the F.A.B. It's death before dishonor," Leticia cut in, stepping into Deidre's personal space menacingly.

"Whatever you want me to do," Deidre replied. She would really do anything to stay alive.

"Remember I told you that I never trust outside bitches?" Chastity asked, pursing her lips.

"Yeah," Deidre responded.

"Well, sometimes inside bitches can't be trusted either," Chastity said, turning her sights on Tori.

"You see this snitch right here? She ain't got no loyalty or honor!" Leticia screamed through clenched teeth, tears streaming her face as she walked over and grabbed Tori up off of the ground by her hair.

"Aggghhhh!" Tori screamed, placing her hands on top of Leticia's, trying to keep Leticia from ripping her hair out.

"Wait. What's going on?" Deidre asked, looking around.

"Basically, we are killing two birds with one stone. If you ain't a cop, then you will kill this snitch bitch right here. If you refuse, then you and the snitch gonna die," Chastity announced.

"*What?*" Deidre asked, buying time.

"Tell her, T-baby. Tell DeeDee what you did," Leticia snarled, wiping away tears.

"Ple-e-e-ease! What about Akayla?" Tori pleaded through blood and tears.

"Bitch! You think I didn't know you was fucking Duke? Yeah, I knew. You think I didn't know you were stealing drugs and money from me, and that you was getting high? That's why I was telling Coral your business. Bitch, you ain't fit to be a mother. You ain't fit to be a person! You're weak, fat, ugly, and stupid!" Chastity yelled, spitting in Tori's face.

"Ohhhh God!" Tori screamed like someone gut punched her. Her heart was breaking. She couldn't believe her ears. Chastity knew all along that she was betraying her crew.

"Your man, Duke, also found out that it was you that had the Candy Shop raided! After all me and Loca did for your sorry ass over the years! We took you from nothing!" Chastity screamed.

"Chazz, please don't do this! I'm sorry! I was trying to get

Akayla back! I need you and Loca! Ple-e-e-ease give me an-other chance!" Tori groveled.

"Shut the fuck up! You wasn't thinking about us when you fucking snitched!" Leticia screamed, punching Tori in her stomach.

"And you, DeeDee. Where'd you get that car from?" Chastity asked, looking at Deidre evilly.

Deidre was thrown off guard for a second. "Umm, my car?" she responded.

"Yeah, bitch, your car!" Chastity yelled.

"I had one of my runners in D.C. get it at a seizure auction," Deidre replied, thinking quickly on her feet. *Why are they asking about my car?* she thought to herself.

"Yo, this is taking too long. Let's get this shit over with," Leticia cut in.

"Ple-e-e-ease!" Tori squealed. She knew her girls well enough to know what her fate was going to be.

"Here," Chastity said, handing Deidre the gun. "Mirk this bitch or get mirked," she demanded.

Deidre's heart beat so hard, she felt like she would pass out. She placed her sweaty palms around the handle of the gun. *Its do or die,* she said to herself. She immediately thought about her mother. She knew that Cassandra would have nothing to live for if she died. She thought about Ricky and R.J. Deidre wondered if R.J. knew about this all along. Tears welled up in her eyes and her lips quivered. She was in too deep. She had put herself in this position.

"Kill her *now!*" Leticia screamed, snapping Deidre out of her trance.

"No-o-o-o! Ple-e-e-ease!" Tori screamed, placing her hands together to beg for her life.

Deidre raised the gun and pointed it at Tori. Her hands shook uncontrollably, and she held her breath.

"Ple-e-e-ease, DeeDee! DeeDee, don't do it!" Tori begged

for mercy at the top of her lungs. There was no one else around to hear her.

Deidre grit her teeth and fought back tears. She couldn't stand to look at Tori.

"Do it or die!" Chastity screamed.

"Death before dishonor!" Deidre screamed, closed her eyes and pulled the trigger.

"*Bang!*" One shot hit Tori dead in the center of her chest. Her body instantly crumpled to the ground like a deflated air balloon.

Leticia turned away, and punched at the air as tears soaked her face. As hard as she was, she was heartbroken over Tori's murder.

Deidre threw the gun down, turned her face away, bent over and threw up. Her heart raced, and her entire body was soaked with sweat.

Chastity just stood there looking down at Tori's lifeless body. "Death before dishonor. DeeDee, my nigga, I knew you wasn't a cop," she said, bursting out laughing.

Deidre stood up and rushed to put her clothes back on. After gathering herself mentally, she started walking back towards Chastity's vehicle.

Leticia stood over Tori's body, sobbing like a baby. "C'mon," Chastity demanded.

"We can't just leave her here like this!" Leticia yelled.

"The bitch was a snitch. Let's go!" Chastity screamed, with no emotion behind her words.

Deidre looked at Chastity, and out of nowhere, she took off running. She ran and ran, until she couldn't run anymore. She needed to get away . . . she wanted out.

VOLUME 19:
THE FEDS

Deidre sprawled across the king size bed in Suite 211, at the Crowne Plaza Suites, staring blankly at the ceiling.

After the murder, she went to her apartment, gathered a few things—most importantly, her father's key and some cash. Each time she closed her eyes, she envisioned Tori's face. She thought back on all of the days she had accompanied Tori to her visits with Akayla. She also thought about R.J. non-stop, and several times she picked up her cell phone to call him, but stopped herself.

She thought about Ricky, Ferguson, and Bernard. She knew for a fact that they would have the undercover recovery team out searching for her. She hadn't returned any of their calls to her cell phone, nor had she returned any of her mother's phone calls to her private cell phone. Deidre was one of the feds, and that reality hit her as soon as she pulled the trigger and committed a senseless murder. She wasn't ever really a part of the F.A.B., she just thought she was.

She reached over and grabbed the bottle of Grey Goose vodka from the nightstand and took it to the head. The drink went down smoothly, but burned at the end, and she beat her chest to help ease the burn. Feeling relaxed, she eased herself back on the soft pillows.

"*Knock! Knock!*" Deidre looked over at the door, and then looked down at her gun. She ignored the knocks.

"Housekeeping!" a female voice called out.

"Go away!" Deidre slurred. She waited a few minutes, and when she was sure the housekeeper was, gone she dragged her feet over to the door, gun in hand, opened it slightly, and retrieved the daily newspaper from the floor. The front-page headline read:

"Police Officer Found Dead in Brooklyn Apartment"

There was a huge picture of Officer Duke on the front page. Deidre turned to page five of the paper to read the full story. She looked at the familiar face of the officer, and remembered seeing him a few times at the Candy Shop. On the page next to his story was an article about Tori's murder. The last line of the article read that a partial print was found on the murder weapon.

Deidre threw the paper across the room. She couldn't read anymore.

"What the fuck do you mean you can't find her?" Ricky screamed, his pale face turning beet-burgundy.

"She was supposed to meet with Ferguson, but she never showed up," Bernard replied nervously.

"You and fucking Ferguson better find her, or else!" Ricky threatened.

Bernard touched the gun in his pocket. He wanted so badly to take it out and shoot Ricky right in his face. Instead, he turned on his heels and walked out of Ricky's office.

Bernard hadn't been the same since the murder of Amber Reeves. The nightmares were uncontrollable. Every time he closed his eyes, he saw the girl's face when he cut her fingers off; the severe pain etched in every crease of her skin. Now he was afraid that Ricky was going to finally give up on finding the missing money and just kill Deidre.

Bernard had contemplated suicide several times. He was into the crooked federal fold too deep, and there was only one way out now. All of the murders were mounting, and he just couldn't take it anymore. First, he needed to save Deidre.

Bernard settled into his car and retrieved his secret cell phone. He dialed Deidre's private cell phone number, knowing that she wouldn't recognize the number.

Deidre looked down at her private cell phone. She had never seen the number before. The first thing that came to mind was that her mother had gotten drunk, fell out somewhere, and someone was contacting her to come pick Cassandra up. It wouldn't have been the first time. Reluctantly, Deidre picked up the line. "Hello," she whispered.

"Aponte, it's me. Don't hang up!" Bernard rushed the words out.

"What do you want?" Deidre asked. She knew she was in trouble.

"I don't want to talk to you about your disappearing. There is something going on. I need to meet with you right away," Bernard said.

"I don't fucking trust you. What do you know?" Deidre asked, paranoid about Tori's murder.

"It's about your father," Bernard blurted out. He knew that would get Deidre's attention.

"What about my father?" Deidre asked, softening her tone.

"He didn't commit suicide. Those girls didn't kidnap Amber Reeves, and you were set up to go undercover so you could be murdered," Bernard rushed the words out of his mouth.

Deidre was silent. She couldn't believe what she was hearing. She agreed to meet Bernard in New Jersey.

The small Italian restaurant was nearly empty, except for a couple sitting in a far off corner at a small round table.

R.J. adjusted his dark blue Yankees cap, and swaggered in the direction of his dinner guest. "What's up?" he asked, extending his hand for a pound.

"You weren't supposed to sleep with her," Ricky said, ignoring R.J.'s requested for a pound.

"Ay, I'm a man. She's a beautiful woman," R.J. replied, with a smirk.

"You weren't supposed to fucking sleep with her!" Ricky growled, lighting his customary cigar.

"Look, you told me to make it all seem real, and that is what I did. Shit, I sacrificed my best friend for this shit," R.J. said, taking a seat.

"And now you're gonna throw your own sister to the wolves? You sure you still want to go through with this? I mean, Chastity is your sister," Ricky reminded him.

"Look, I'm supposed to be the head nigga in charge, not my fucking baby sister!" R.J. growled, leaning close to the table so that the patrons in the restaurant wouldn't hear him.

"You fell in love, didn't you," Ricky changed the subject.

"I can't love," R.J. replied, averting his eyes away from Ricky's.

"You know somebody has to take care of Deidre, and it can't be me," Ricky warned.

"I can do it. I'm a man. My father didn't raise no punks," R.J. said arrogantly, pointing to his chest.

"Okay, Ramon, Junior. I like your style," Ricky commented, sipping his gin and tonic.

"Didn't I tell you never to call me that?" R.J. griped. He

hated to be reminded that he was named after his father. He was still angry with this father for walking out.

"I just like to fuck with you. I think that's a nice name. You should really look into your Dominican roots," Ricky responded, chuckling evilly.

R.J. had no idea that Ricky knew all about his father. He also didn't know that Ricky had tortured and killed his mother because she wouldn't give him the money Ramon Sr. had left behind.

"So, when is it going down?" R.J. asked.

"The next meeting. As soon as the drop is made, we will have the heat on Chastity, and she will go down. We've got enough on her to put her away for life without ever implicating you," Ricky informed.

"What about the dyke?" R.J. asked.

"She's going to resist arrest—if you know what I mean—and we'll take care of her," Ricky replied. "But you still need to keep up your end of the bargain," he reminded R.J.

"Oh, no doubt. I'll find out where that sexy ass Agent Aponte is hiding out, and it's done. She's in love with me," R.J. replied, flashing a winning smile.

"Good. You get what you want, and I get what I want," Ricky reiterated. He was really upset by R.J.'s last comment. He felt that Deidre wasn't ever supposed to love another man. Nonetheless, money came before anything, so Ricky shook R.J.'s hand, sealing their deal, and they both continued to eat their authentic Italian meal.

Bernard looked over his shoulders nervously as he waited for Deidre to arrive. They agreed to meet behind McGuire Air Force Base in Trenton, New Jersey.

Deidre drove slowly, looking around for any signs of other cars. She'd already spotted Bernard's vehicle. As she approached, her sweaty hands slipped around the steering wheel. As soon as she came to a stop, Bernard quickly jumped into the passenger seat of her car. Deidre jumped fiercely, almost coming out of her seat. "Fuck! You scared me!" she yelled, with her voice cracking.

"I'm sorry. I had to move quickly. Keep driving until I say stop," Bernard huffed. He was just as nervous as she was.

Deidre used one hand to feel her gun, which was tucked under her left thigh. "So, what's this all about, Bernard?" she asked, anxious to get to the point of their meeting.

"Stop here," Bernard instructed. Deidre complied. "Turn off all the lights," he said, and she did as she was told. "Aponte, I've known you since you were a little girl. I just want you to know that I would've never done anything to hurt you. I respected your father a lot," he began.

"What are you talking about, Bernard?" Deidre asked seriously.

"Your father, Ricky, Lewis and I were into some things you wouldn't understand. We got in over our heads, and money started coming in all directions. Ricky slowly started taking over things . . ." Bernard began, but Deidre cut him off.

"Wait! Are you trying to tell me my father was a dirty agent?" she asked, biting into the side of her cheek. She was tired of people demeaning her father's memory.

"I know you may not believe it, but we were all a part of it. Aponte, the money came so easily!" Bernard replied regretfully.

"No. No. I don't believe you," Deidre said, shaking her head from side to side.

"I know it's hard to believe, but just listen," Bernard continued. "We got in over our heads, and everybody started pocketing money on the side. It was supposed to be one time, but Ricky kept going further and further. Ramon, Lewis, and myself wanted out, but Ricky wouldn't hear of it. So, your father and Lewis decided to take matters into their own hands, and that's when things got ugly," Bernard stated. He was going to finally provide Deidre with the truth about her father's death . . .

"Listen man, I'm getting out now before it's too late. Diego is expecting too much from us," Ramon complained.

"I agree," Bernard said.

"Me too," Lewis agreed.

"No one is getting out of shit! This is millions of dollars we're talking about here!" Ricky screamed.

"It's also years behind bars. I just moved my family. I had to leave my other life behind. I can't do it, man," Ramon replied, throwing his hands up.

"Fuck that! You can't get out now!" Ricky growled, pushing Ramon in the chest.

"Hey, man!" Bernard interjected.

Ricky punched Bernard in the face. He was like a man possessed.

"Rick, man, you're losing it over this shit," Lewis said calmly, trying to appeal to Ricky.

"I said no one is getting out until I say so!" Ricky said through clenched teeth.

"We're all grown men. I am out of it!" Ramon retorted, walking toward the door.

"Where's your half of the money?" Ricky said, rushing after him.

"That's my money. I worked for it," Ramon replied, turning on his heels.

"It's my money!" Ricky barked, drawing his weapon.

Everyone stopped dead in their tracks.

"Hey, Rick man, you're going too far. We want out, and that's that," Lewis said, trying to back Ricky down.

Bernard remained silent. He didn't even have a weapon on him. They were only supposed to meet to discuss the last deal they were going to make with the Mexicans.

"Shut up!" Ricky screamed, pointing the gun at Lewis. "Walk over there next to your punk ass gringo friend," he demanded, waving the gun in front of him. "You . . . walk forward," he said to Ramon. Ramon held his hands up in front of him in surrender and walked forward. "Get on your fucking knees, like the traitor that you are!" Ricky commanded.

"C'mon, Rick. We've been friends for years. Is it really worth all of this?" Ramon pleaded, getting on his knees.

"Friends don't stab friends in the back," Ricky growled, a thick vein bulging from his forehead.

"How did I stab you in the back? Leaving now is what's best," Ramon said.

"Where's the money?" Ricky asked.

"Rick, I don't owe you any money. We split everything down the middle, and you promised to pay Diego," Ramon said, swallowing hard, trying to stay calm.

"Where's the fucking money!" Ricky roared, his voice echoing through the empty warehouse. He placed the gun to Ramon's lips.

"Think about this, Ricky! C'mon, man, Ramon's your friend! You're his kid's godfather!" Bernard pleaded, trying fruitlessly to appeal to Ricky's conscience.

"Shut the fuck up!" Ricky screamed. They were no friends of his. Ricky saw them as a means to a way. His hatred for any other culture other than his own was embedded into him, and it was not going away. "Where's the money?" Ricky asked Ramon again.

"You're going to have to kill me before I tell you," Ramon said, not taking Ricky seriously.

Ricky was sweating and his pupils were dilated. His adrenaline was pumping and he couldn't think. "Did you just say you would turn all of us in?" Ricky asked, blinking rapidly.

"What?" Ramon asked.

"Did you hear that, Baker and Lewis? Aponte has threatened to turn us in!" Ricky announced, sounding deranged. They all looked on confused. Suddenly Ricky rushed forward, stuck the gun to Ramon's lips and fired. *"Bang!"* Ramon's brains burst out of the back of his skull and his body dropped to the floor like a sack of potatoes.

"Oh my God! You killed him!" Lewis yelled, covering his ears with both his hands. Bernard dropped to his knees.

"Now, no one is getting out. We are all in this until I say so. Now, help me find that seven-million-dollars," Ricky said calmly. He was heartless.

Moving like a zombie, Lewis walked over to Ramon's body. He bent down, dug into Ramon's pocket and took out his wallet and keys. Ramon had instructed him to do that if anything had ever happened to him in the field.

Deidre banged her fists on the steering wheel of the car. Tears were running down her face like a faucet on full blast. She couldn't believe what she was hearing. She reached under her thigh and grabbed her weapon. She drew it and placed it at Bernard's temple. "I don't believe you!" she sobbed.

"I'm not afraid to die. I am telling you the truth. Go ahead and kill me," Bernard replied.

"Why?" Deidre cried. Everything Ricky had done for her was a lie.

"I'm sorry!" Bernard cried. He'd finally purged himself.

"So, what does all of this have to do with me?" Deidre asked, sniffling back snot.

"Senator Reeves was a part of the original deal. Diego Esperanza funded his campaign, made sure he got the Senate seat, and in exchange, Reeves was supposed to keep the National Drug Control policy from being passed. Reeves reneged on the deal, under pressure. Ricky decided to take revenge, and used Amber Reeves as an example. The case was a set up from day one. I'm so sorry," Bernard apologized.

Deidre lowered her gun from Bernard's head. She was speechless. All this time she was sleeping with Ricky, he was the enemy. "The fucking criminals are more loyal than the feds!" she screamed.

"I know," Bernard said, hanging his head in shame.

"What about the F.A.B.?" Deidre asked.

"They were just pawns. Ferguson was a part of this, and they had it planned to blow your cover so that the F.A.B. would kill you. They never fixed the tag or set up your identity. They sent gunmen in so that you would blow your own cover, but none of it worked," Bernard said, sorrow dancing in his eyes.

"Did Ricky kill Amber Reeves?" Deidre asked.

"No . . . I did. She bled to death," Bernard confessed in an almost inaudible whisper. In one motion, he took his trembling hand out of his pocket, and before Deidre could react, he placed his gun to his temple and squeezed the trigger. *"Boom!"*

"Aggghhhhhh!" Deidre screamed. Blood leaked from a perfect hole in the side of Bernard's head. It also ran out of his nose and eye sockets. "Oh God!" Deidre yelled, as she snatched Bernard's car keys from his lifeless hand and fought with her car door to get out. "Oh shit!" she cursed, running back to the car.

She reached onto the driver's side floor, with the smell of fresh blood making her want to vomit. She hit the trunk release and popped the trunk, and retrieved the Louis Vuitton duffel bag and her sliver briefcase. Still trembling, she ran towards Bernard's car. Fumbling with the keys and quaking all over, she jumped into the car and reversed out of the dark area back onto the highway. This time she kept heading south.

*   *   *

Sandra Reeves had watched the number of FBI agents that were in her home dwindle each day. She supposed that this was a sign of how much hope they had left to find Amber alive. After the fingers were confirmed, things changed. It seemed the urgency to find Amber had waned. "Richard," Sandra turned in the bed towards her husband. There were things she needed to tell him. She wanted to tell him the truth once and for all about how she felt. He didn't answer. "Richard, I want to talk to you," she shook his shoulder. His back was to her as he lay on his side. Still no response. Sandra moved closer to him and leaned over his shoulder, her weight causing his body to slump all the way over. "Richard? Richard?" she shook him with urgency. He never slept this hard. Sandra's throat became dry as she continued calling her husband's name. After the tenth try at rousing him, she looked around frantically and noticed the pill bottle on the floor next to the bed. "Ri-char-d!" she screamed, knowing that her husband would never answer her again.

VOLUME 20:
THE BITCH'S END

Chastity glanced down at the newspaper on her bed, shrugging her shoulders. She'd just read the newspaper articles about Officer Duke and Tori, and she was unfazed. "One hundred," she mumbled as she continued counting the last of the money she had stashed. Reaching into her Hermes bag, she picked up the two airline confirmations and looked at the clock. R.J. was supposed to be meeting her at five o'clock sharp, and she knew he was never late.

"Sorry, Loca, I couldn't bring you along. Sorry that you're gonna get blamed for the murder too. You were right, there is no such thing as death before dishonor, and no honor amongst thieves," Chastity said under her breath as she bound each stack of money with rubber bands.

Leticia had no idea Chastity was leaving, nor did she know that Chastity had tipped the police off about Tori's murder. While Leticia sobbed uncontrollably over Tori's death, Chastity took the murder weapon from Deidre and slipped it right beside the body. Chastity felt that she had made too much money off of Deidre to blame her. She planned on doing more business with her. The only difference was that Chastity would be in a different country, and she would be making one hundred percent of the profit with Leticia and Tori gone.

Chastity walked over to her floor-length mirror and looked at herself. *Beautiful as usual*, she thought. Straightening the jacket of her cream colored Tahari blazer and sliding her feet into a pair of camel colored Jimmy Choo pumps, she completed her look. She was ready to go. Chastity took pride in her appearance no matter where she was going. She shook her head from left to right, allowing her hair to dance around her head. Satisfied, she picked up her cell phone and called R.J. "Hey, big bro, I'm ready."

"Give me a few . . . I'm tying up a few loose ends," R.J. replied.

"Hurry up. Our plane leaves at seven, and we have to be at the airport two hours earlier for international flights."

"I know. I'll be there soon," R.J. confirmed.

"A'ight. Hey, before you hang up, have you spoken to DeeDee?"

"Nah. I think she went back to D.C."

"Call her. Maybe she wants to go with us," Chastity offered. She really liked Deidre, even more than her own girls.

"I will. I'll be there soon. Love you, baby sis!" R.J. said, and with that, he was gone.

"Where you wanna go eat at?" Leticia asked the raven-haired hottie she had on her arm as they left Leticia's front door. Leticia had been secluded in her apartment, keeping a low profile since Tori's death.

"Anywhere you wanna go, *mami*," the girl answered, stopping to let Leticia lock the door. Just as the girl stepped down the first step on the stoop she heard, "Freeze! Don't fucking move!"

Leticia turned swiftly, only to notice six black Chevy Impalas filled with FBI agents in raid jackets, with guns drawn and pointed at her.

"Leticia Ruiz, you are under arrest! Walk down the stairs slowly with your hands up!" Ferguson announced through the bullhorn. The FBI had gotten to Leticia before the NYPD.

"What the fuck did I do?" Leticia screamed. Her lady friend ran away.

"Put your hands up now!" Ferguson commanded. A small crowd had begun to gather.

Leticia started walking down the stairs. "Fuck the police! I didn't do shit! You got the wrong bitch!" she yelled, and in one motion, she reached into her front waistband and drew out two guns. Lately she never left home without them.

"Gun!" Ferguson yelled, ducking behind one of the cars for cover.

"Fuck the police!" Leticia screamed, extending both of her arms and firing both weapons. She had promised herself that before she went back to prison, she would go out with guns blazing.

"Boom! Boom! Boom! Boom!" Shot after shot rang out. Every FBI agent on the scene emptied at least one magazine into Leticia's body. The first several shots hit her in the chest, sending her flying back into the steps, but she kept shooting. Her body jerked fiercely as more and more shots burned through her skin. Leticia's eyes popped open and blood spilled from her mouth, yet her hands kept firing. Finally, one shot hit her between the eyes, and all motion stopped. Her head banged into the steps and both of her arms dropped. The weapons slid to the ground, as did her limp, dead body.

When the smoke cleared, Ferguson walked over to Leticia's body and looked down into her beautiful green eyes, which were wide open. "A fucking waste!" Ferguson commented. "Get crime scene down here!" she yelled to the other agents. *One down, two more to go*, she thought to herself.

"What's the first thing you wanna see when we get to Mexico?" Chastity asked her brother.

"Maybe the Mayan temples," R.J. answered, looking over at his baby sister. He navigated his BMW X-5 down the Belt Parkway towards the John F. Kennedy Airport.

"You think we'll ever be able to return to Brooklyn?" Chastity asked.

"Not with all this money we owe our connect, and all the shit that's happened," R.J. replied regretfully.

"You just gonna leave DeeDee behind?" she asked.

"Nobody is more important to me than you, baby sis," he replied.

Chastity fell silent and looked out of the window. With each passing exit, she felt worse. She loved New York, she loved Brooklyn, and most of all, she loved the power she had gained and all the money she made. Chastity would miss everything. She wondered what Leticia was doing right now. She wondered if the NYPD had gone and arrested Leticia for Tori's murder, and she wondered if Leticia would ever forgive her for betraying her. Chastity thought about the promise they all had made to each other . . .

"Look at all this money!" Tori said, excitedly.

"Word up! This is more than we ever made boosting," Leticia commented.

"Don't get all crazy. Lay low with this shit for a while. We don't want people to notice us just yet," Chastity instructed as she counted out ten-thousand-dollars for each of them. The money was the result of their first turnover. It was the first time any of them had that much money in their hands, and it felt good.

"Yo, Chazz, you are a mastermind. We are on our way," Leticia said.

"M-o-n-e-y, M-o-n-e-y, M-o-n-e-y!" Tori sang out as she flipped through her bills.

"Everybody got an even split," Chastity lied. She had already set aside an extra five-thousand for herself. She reasoned that it was her hard work that had made them the money; therefore, she was entitled to a larger cut.

"Yo, cash rules everything around me!" Leticia sang, chuckling.

"What you buying first?" Tori asked Leticia.

"A bitch!" Leticia quipped. They started laughing.

"I'm getting my baby back. I'ma buy me a lawyer better than Johnny Cochran," Tori said.

"Ladies, calm down! Ya'll acting like ya'll never had shit before. This is nothing compared to what we will make. I just want one thing," Chastity said.

"What?" Leticia and Tori said in unison.

"Let's promise that money will never come between us. Promise we will always put each other before money," Chastity said.

"We promise!" the other girls said as they all came together for a hug.

"We're here," R.J. announced, breaking Chastity out of her thoughts. She looked up at the terminal sign and wiped a tear from the corner of her eye.

"Get out here. I'm going to park the car," R.J. instructed. Chastity complied, hopping out. R.J. opened the back and set their bags on the sidewalk. Chastity waved for an airport porter to come get their things, and headed into the airport. R.J. looked through his rear view mirror at his sister and stepped on the gas.

Chastity walked up to the American Airlines line and made her way around the dividers. She had three people ahead of her. Looking around she noticed three men in black suits walking in her direction. She didn't think anything of it and kept moving forward on the line.

"Next!" the lady at the ticket counter yelled.

Chastity walked up to the counter and handed the lady her airline ticket confirmation.

The lady looked at the name and looked up at Chastity. "ID, please," the lady said.

Chastity handed the lady her driver's license.

"One moment, please," the lady said, walking to the other end of the counter. She picked up the telephone, looked at Chastity again, and lowered her head.

What the fuck is the problem? Chastity asked herself, tapping her foot nervously. Someone tapped her on her shoulder, Chastity whirled around on her heels.

"Ms. Smith, you need to come with us," a man said, grabbing her arm.

"Who the fuck are you?" Chastity asked, trying to pull her arm away.

"I am an agent with the Federal Bureau of Investigation. You are under arrest," he announced, maintaining a firm grasp on her.

"Get the fuck off of me!" Chastity snapped as the other two men surrounded her. She was escorted out of the airport into a waiting black Impala. "Where is my brother?" she asked, looking around for R.J.

"You tell me," the man replied.

R.J. never came back.

Chastity was handcuffed and placed into the back of the car. "What am I under arrest for? Ya'll don't have shit on me! I wanna see my lawyer!" she growled.

"Ms. Smith, do you recognize this person?" he asked, handing Chastity a picture of Deidre.

"Nope!" Chastity answered. She wasn't snitching on her friend DeeDee.

"Oh, I think you do. You see, Ms. Smith, this is what she really looks like," he said, handing Chastity Deidre's FBI identification photo.

Chastity's mouth fell open in shock.

"Ms. Smith, your friend DeeDee Barnes is really Special Agent Deidre Aponte," the agent said, rubbing salt in Chastity's wounds.

"Bitch!" Chastity screamed, banging her head into the car window.

"Don't be angry, Ms. Smith. Agent Aponte will be happy to see you when she testifies against you," he bluffed. They still hadn't located Deidre.

"You ain't got shit on me!" Chastity screamed, rocking back and forth angrily.

"Oh, we have plenty. You'll never see the light of day again," the agent said maliciously.

R.J. picked up his cell phone and dialed Deidre's number.

Deidre looked at her phone, and although her brain told her not to answer it, her heart told her to pick it up. *Maybe he is the one person I can trust*, she thought to herself. Besides, Bernard said that the F.A.B. was just a pawn. Maybe R.J. was too, she reasoned.

"Hey," Deidre said, her voice raspy from screaming.

"We were meant to be. How could you leave me?" R.J. said deceitfully.

"I'm sorry. I just had to get my head together," Deidre apologized.

"Where are you?" R.J. asked.

Deidre was torn. She wanted to tell R.J. everything, but she didn't. "I can't tell you that. When I get settled, I'll call you back," she said, closing her eyes regretfully.

"C'mon, baby, I need to see you. I need you. A lot of shit has happened," R.J. pleaded.

"I'll call you," Deidre said, disconnecting the line before she got herself in trouble. She tossed her undercover cell phone out of the window on the side of the highway.

R.J. dialed another number. "I just called her. Did you get the GPS trace?" he asked.

"Yeah, she's heading down 95 towards Maryland," he answered.

VOLUME 21:
THE ANSWERS

Deidre pulled up in front of her family's two-story log cabin style cottage in Deep Creek Lake, Maryland. Her eyes burned and her back ached, she was exhausted from driving all night, not to mention all of the information she had received had her nerves on edge. She felt all alone.

Exiting the car, she grabbed her bag and her silver briefcase. She stepped up on the wooden porch, reached into the large white sandstone flowerpot and retrieved the house key. Once inside, she flopped down on the old fashioned plaid sofa and busted out crying. Just being in the cottage reminded Deidre of her father, and knowing that she was right all these years about his death made her angry.

Her private cell phone began ringing, it was her mother. "Hello," Deidre answered.

"Where are you?" her mother asked, concern stringing her words together tensely.

"I can't tell you, but when I get a chance, I will explain everything to you," Deidre said.

"Tell me where you are?" Cassandra demanded as Ricky stood right next to her.

"Mom, I gotta go," Deidre said. She sensed that something was wrong. Cassandra didn't speak that way unless she was drunk, and Deidre could tell that her mother wasn't drinking.

Deidre walked around and made herself comfortable. She locked up all of the doors, and shut all of the window shutters. Walking up the stairs, she stopped and looked at a photograph of her father in his younger days. Her heart almost stopped. She was staring into the face of R.J. "I need to get him out of my head. Shit, I'm starting to think I see him everywhere," she mumbled out loud, continuing up the stairs.

She walked passed the bedroom she used to stay in as a child, stopped and peeked in. Everything was the same. Her ballerina slippers still hung from the wooden mirror. There were still posters and buttons of Michael Jackson everywhere. Deidre was his biggest fan when she was younger. More importantly, the trunk her father had given her was still at the foot of the bed. "My treasure trunk!" Deidre said, smiling. Walking over to it, she rubbed the wooden trunk, running her fingers over the gold lock and accents. She noticed that there was a small lock on the trunk. "Hey, where'd this come from?" she said to herself, flipping up the lock to look at the keyhole. "Daddy?" Deidre whispered, fumbling with her briefcase to get her father's key. She took the key out and rushed to see if it fit the lock. It fit! Deidre pulled the lock off of the trunk and flipped the top open. There was a black wool blanket lying inside. She reached in and pulled the blanket up and her mouth dropped open when she looked inside. The trunk was filled with money. "Oh my God!" she shrieked, her heart racing.

She began taking the stacks of cash out of the trunk so she could count them. When she got to the last stack, she noticed something else in the bottom. There was a letter from her father. Deidre was too angry to read it. She crumpled it up and threw it across the room. "Fucking dirty liar!"

she screamed, clutching her chest. The pain was unbearable. Everything Bernard had told her was true.

Deidre continued to pull things out of the trunk. There were several pictures. The first one was of Deidre at five, when she lost her first tooth. Then there was Ramon and Cassandra's wedding pictures, and pictures of Deidre as a baby.

Deidre kept digging until she came upon a picture of a strange woman. She read the back. It said "Donna". Deidre didn't recognize the beautiful woman at first. Then she pulled out more pictures, and there were several pictures of two children, a boy and a girl. Deidre read the back of one, and it said "Junior and baby girl". She stared at the pictures. She immediately recognized the boy and the girl. It was R.J. and Chastity. "Ramon, Junior!" Deidre said in a low whisper as the answers all came together.

She immediately felt sick. "No!" she screamed, putting her hands up against her ears, rocking back and forth. She had slept with her own brother. "Daddy! You bastard!" Deidre screamed, pulling her hair roughly. Her heart was broken, but now everything made sense. All of the fighting and crying she heard as a child was because her father was living a double life and her mother found out about it. Deidre had the answers to all of her questions.

"Ricky knew all along. That's why he put me under with the F.A.B. He wanted me to find out before he killed me. This must be the money he has been looking for. That's why he never let me out of his sights. He knew my father would leave the money for me," Deidre whispered to herself. She walked across the room and retrieved the crumpled letter and unfolded it:

Dear Cassy,
    If you are reading this, that means I'm dead or in prison. I never meant to hurt you or Deidre. You both are all I ever

*wanted. Take this money and move away. There is enough
money here for you to live for the rest of your life. I only
wanted the best for my family.*

*I know that you found out about Donna and my other
kids. She will not be a problem; I left money for her as well.
I want Deidre to get to know R.J. and Chastity. It's not
their fault that I lived my life like this.*

*You are the only woman I've ever loved. Please take care
of yourself and stay beautiful. Tell the love of my life I said
Recuerda*, que tu eres mi muchacha favorita!

Love Always,
Ramon

"Liar!" Deidre yelled, tearing the letter into tiny pieces.
Flopping down on her knees, she sobbed and sobbed. She
was physically and mentally exhausted, and all she wanted
to do was take a shower, take a sleeping pill and get some
rest. She felt safe at the cottage, but she knew she would
soon have to leave for good.

VOLUME 22:
THE ULTIMATE BETRAYAL

Chastity waited on the other end of the phone for the operator to put the collect call through. She resembled a sick cancer patient. It appeared as if she'd lost about thirty pounds, her skin looked ashen, and her hair was pulled back in a sloppy ponytail held together with cheap gel and a rubber band, not her usual beautifully coifed locks. Fear danced in her once beautiful chestnut brown eyes. She was so nervous that her legs shook visibly. Chastity hadn't heard from her brother in the weeks since she'd gotten arrested. The phone rang three times and she was elated when she heard R.J. pick up the phone.

"Collect call from a Chastity at a correctional facility. Will you accept the charges?" the operator asked.

"No!" R.J. replied, disconnecting the line.

Chastity couldn't believe her ears.

"Ma'am, the charges were not accepted," the operator relayed.

"I fucking heard it!" Chastity screamed, squeezing the receiver until her hand hurt. She slammed the payphone down and turned around to her reality—the gray steel walls of prison that was now her permanent home.

R.J. stuffed another stack of cash into the money counter. He was high from the smell of wealth. He was finally in his rightful position as boss.

"Is this the last one?" the clerk at the post office asked.

"Yes," Deidre replied.

"That'll be eighty six dollars," the clerk informed.

Deidre paid the fee to ship all of the boxes.

"Let me confirm the person who is going to receive these. Is it . . . Cassandra Aponte?" the clerk asked.

"That's correct," Deidre answered, looking around nervously. The clerk looked at her strangely as she processed her requests. Deidre looked like a paranoid nut the way she watched her surroundings.

It had been a month, and the weather had changed dramatically. It seemed like the fall flew by and winter was back again. Deidre had cut off all communications with everyone—even her mother. She'd chopped off all of her beautiful hair and dyed it red. She'd also made plans to leave the country. She had enough money to start over somewhere else; she was just waiting for the media buzz about her being missing to die down.

According to the news reports, Deidre was being blamed for Bernard's death, because he was found in her car. She was also being blamed for Tori's murder, because they found a partial print on the murder weapon, and the crime scene investigators sent it in to the FBI, who matched it to Deidre. There was no place for her to go, so she decided to wait it out a little longer.

She remembered that Ricky had never gotten a chance to come to her parents' cottage; therefore, she was confident that he didn't know where it was located. She also figured that it was that same reason her father had hidden the money there.

Every time Deidre thought about R.J., she became sick to her stomach. But when she thought about Ricky and Ferguson, she became infuriated.

Deidre drove the raggedy green pickup she'd purchased, down the winding dirt road towards the cottage. Pulling up in front, she unloaded the groceries she'd purchased. As she walked in and out of the cottage, she never noticed them watching her.

Once inside, she lit the old fashioned black kerosene stove and placed the cast iron kettle on top to boil water. "That's set. Now let me go change out of these country ass clothes," she said out loud to herself. She'd been dressing in overalls and other very rural style clothing, to fit in around town.

She undressed quickly, and rushed back downstairs to the whistling kettle, and hastily grabbed the handle. "Ahh!" She winced from the heat, dropping the kettle back onto the stove.

Suddenly, she heard a noise. Startled, she rushed to the kitchen pantry for her gun. She crept over to the kitchen window, pulled the curtain slightly and peeked out. She didn't see anything. "Must've been a deer," she mumbled. Breathing a sigh of relief, she placed her gun back in the pantry and settled in for a quiet evening.

After she prepared her coffee, she sat down in the living room to watch television for a while. Deidre hadn't watched television in the weeks she was there. She'd spent all of her time preparing the volumes of her journal, which she'd just mailed off to her mother. She wanted Cassandra to know everything, just in case she wasn't able to tell her herself.

"Huhhh!" Deidre let out a relaxing sigh as she flipped the channels. Something immediately caught her attention:

*"In breaking news today, federal investigators report
that after a one year undercover sting operation dubbed
'Operation Candy Shop', a multi-million dollar designer
drug ring has been brought down. The ring, reportedly run
by three of the most dangerous women operating between
New York City, Newark, Baltimore and Mexico, were
responsible for the illegal sale and circulation of prescription
drugs like Oxycontin, Percoset, and Vicodin. The trio of
woman were also reportedly running a large-scale
methamphetamine distribution conglomerate. In recent
years these drugs have become just as popular and profitable
as traditional street drugs such as heroin and crack-
cocaine."*

*"According to the investigators, the drug ring was
brought down by a joint effort between local police, the FBI,
DEA, and ICE agents. The FBI credits the director of the
Washington field office for the success of the operation.
Investigators would not elaborate on the specific roles the
women played or their expected dates in court."*

*"We will continue to follow this story as it unfolds. For
channel 9 news, I'm Chynna Brown. Back to you in the
studio, Ed."*

Deidre stared at the television screen, anger welling up
inside of her like hot lava in a volcano. Nothing shocked her
anymore, but her heart raced as she listened to the reporter's words. She stood on wobbly legs and the large vein
in her neck pulsed fiercely against her skin. Months of lies,
deceit and frustration sent a rush of heat through her
bloodstream.

"Argggggghhh!" she screamed, sending the coffee mug
filled with her favorite hazelnut-flavored coffee sailing into
the screen. "Fucking liars! Fucking bastards!" she screamed.
The thought of how her life had ended up sent hot tears
streaming down her high cheekbones.

Deidre ignored the sparks flying and the damage she had inflicted on the television. Her mind racing, she ran up the creaking wooden stairs to the second floor of the cottage she had been staying at for the last three days. Reaching the top landing of the staircase, she bolted into the master bedroom. Panting for breath, she began frantically stuffing rubber banded stacks of money into a large Louis Vuitton duffel bag.

She looked down at the expensive brown and beige bag, and she felt her heart sink. The bag had been a gift from Chastity and the girls. A long row of Gucci, Manolo Blahnik and Jimmy Choo shoes peeked out from under the bed. Platinum and diamond jewelry sparkled from the dresser top. All had been gifts—tokens of appreciation for a job well done. Deidre couldn't help but think about the good times she'd had with the crew. All of the shopping trips, parties, vacations, and just the girl talk in general. Deidre felt sick thinking about how everything had played out. She thought about how perfectly she had fit in with the F.A.B.

Being the product of a mixed relationship—a half African-American and Irish mother, and a half African-American and Dominican father, Deidre never seemed to fit in with any one group growing up.

For the African-American girls, she was too light and too cute because her hair was wavy and long. They hated her and let her know it every day.

For the white Irish girls, just knowing she was part Black meant automatic exclusion. Besides, she wasn't loose and nasty enough to hang with them. They'd all started giving blowjobs at thirteen.

For the Dominicans, well, they couldn't really talk because she looked more Hispanic than most of them, but she didn't speak Spanish well enough to fit in.

Exasperated, Deidre flopped down on the bed, snapping out of the past. *Where the hell am I going? What the hell am I? Whose side am I on?* Confusion over her duplicitous loyalties mounted, and suddenly a sharp pain invaded her abdomen and she felt nauseous. Hand over mouth, Deidre ran toward the bathroom, but didn't make it in time. Warm vomit spewed between her fingers and ran down her forearms. Her nerve endings stood on end as she hunched over the old-fashioned porcelain sink and let the contents of her stomach empty into the basin. *I have to pull myself together and get out of here*, Deidre told herself, turning on the faucet to wet her face.

As she finished washing her face and cleaning up her mess, she heard several loud knocks on the cedar wood cottage door. The sound jolted her. Eyes wide, she listened intently.

"*Bang! Bang!*" Then a pause, and another "*Bang!*" The knocks were an all too familiar sound. They all had been trained to knock that way as a code for backup. They were conducting a raid like she was a common criminal.

"Shit!" she whispered, her survival skills catching her around the throat. "How did they find me?" Deidre muttered, her heart racing painfully against her sternum. She'd been taught to get out of situations like this. Looking up at the bathroom window, she contemplated climbing out, but her expertise told her that they probably had snipers surrounding the building. Deidre was now the enemy. The sounds grew louder and closer. "Fuck!" she exclaimed through clenched teeth. Her hands shook uncontrollably. Deidre knew that the information she held would surely cost her her life. *It's all over now*, she thought to herself. *There was no where to go*. However, Deidre didn't plan on going out without a fight.

She inched slowly over toward the bathroom door and locked it. She remembered that she kept her spare weapon hidden inside the Kotex box under the bathroom sink. She reached for the handles of the cabinet under the sink. Before she could retrieve the .357 Sig Sauer, her favorite gun, she heard footsteps and familiar voices thundering up the stairs toward her location. Instinctively, she got low to the ground, just as she had been trained to do, seeking cover as bullets whistled above her head and lodged themselves into the wood panels of the bathroom walls. She balled up into a turtle position, using her back as her shell. Glass rained down on her body, littering her hair, and shattering on her arched back. It was time to give up. If she didn't surrender, the undercover recovery team would surely kill her. In the eyes of the same people she worked for, she was just like the criminals they'd hunted together. What set her apart was that she held too many secrets to live.

Deidre stood up and raised her hands above her head as the door splintered open. "Aponte, it's over. You need to come with us!" Ricky voice yelled over the chaos.

Deidre looked into the eyes of the man to whom she had once professed her love. Just then she caught a glimpse of R.J. behind him. *They were working together this entire time!* The thoughts raced through her mind. "R.J.?" she whispered, staring into her brother's eyes. She knew the jig was up, but still far from over. She tried to think quickly, but the next few seconds seemed to move in *Matrix*-like slow motion for her.

Ricky, her boss and former lover, moved aside to let her see R.J. before he killed her. He wanted her to know she'd been set up. Ricky, dressed in all black stood before her like the Grim Reaper. "Stay back! Stay back! The suspect is armed!" he yelled to the other rogue agents behind him, never once taking his eyes off of Deidre. He wouldn't allow any of the backup anywhere near his location, and Deidre knew just why that was.

"Ricky, don't do it!!" she screamed, throwing her hands up in defense.

"I'm not going to do it," Ricky said, looking over at R.J. who aimed his gun at the center of Deidre's chest.

"Ricky, I'm an agent just like you!" Deidre screamed.

"Drop your weapon!" Ricky yelled deceitfully, drowning out her feeble attempts to elicit help from the other agents on the scene.

Deidra had no idea that all of the agents were a part of the plot on her life. She was unarmed; she never had the chance to retrieve her gun from her hiding place. Immediately, she knew what he had in store for her. She squeezed her eyes together, causing the tears that had built up to leak from the corners.

Suddenly, *"Boom! Boom! Boom!"* R.J.'s gun sounded, hitting the intended target. The bullets burned through Deidre's skin.

"R.J. you're my brother . . ." she gasped as she stumbled backwards from the powerful shots, hitting her head on the edge of the old fashioned lion claw bathtub her mother and father had bathed her in as a child. Her body convulsed as blood spilled from her mouth and ran down her face onto the cold floor. *"Thump . . . Thump . . . Thump . . . Th . . ."* Deidre could both feel and hear her heart beating its last beats. Slowly, the sound began to fade, and the pressure in her chest began to ease. Deidre gurgled for air, as her life began to flash before her eyes.

Ricky walked over to Deidre and stood over her. Looking into her dilated pupils, he smirked. "A traitor, just like your father," he said.

"What is she talking about, I'm her brother?" R.J. asked, confused.

"You are her brother. Ramon, Junior. Your father was a piece of shit that had two families. I made him leave New York and leave your family behind. When I killed him, he begged like a bitch for his life, just like your mother did when I fucked her and then hung her like the spick bitch she was," Ricky said calmly, blowing a ring of cigar smoke in R.J.'s face.

"You motherfucker!" R.J. screamed, rushing towards Ricky.

"Bang! Bang! Bang!" Three shots rang out, and R.J.'s body lurched forward, dropping to the floor.

"Good shot!" Ricky complimented.

"Thanks," Ferguson accepted.

"We did it," Ricky said smiling, as Ferguson led him to the trunk full of money.

"Yep. Now, what are we going to do about all these bodies?" she asked.

"Don't ever doubt me. I'm the greatest," Ricky said, smirking. He ordered the other agents on his dirty team to take all of the money out of the cottage. They made the scene look like a murder-suicide, and they left. As far as Ricky was concerned, he'd gotten away with murder, over and over again.

VOLUME 23:
THE FUNERAL

"*Knock! Knock!*" Pause. "*Knock!*"

Cassandra groggily looked over at the alarm clock sitting on her nightstand. The large red digital numbers read 5:00 a.m. She had been startled out of her sleep by the knocks on the door.

"*Knock! Knock!*" Pause. "*Knock!*" There they were again.

"Deidre?" she mumbled softly as she fumbled with her comforter, trying to rush out of bed. "This girl and her FBI knock. She is a trip. Must've forgotten her keys again. It's pretty early for a visit," Cassandra said aloud as she tied the sash on her red and gold silk kimono. She was excited to see her daughter, who she hadn't seen in weeks. "I'm coming . . . your Mama's coming!" Cassandra yelled in response to the knocking again. She scooted toward the sounds with a large smile on her face. Cassandra wanted to make things right between herself and Deidre after their last meeting.

She reached the last step, and peering through the small triangle panes of glass on her custom-made door, she could see clearly that it was not her baby girl, Deidre on the other side. Instead, she saw two men, one white and one black, both wearing black suits. Cassandra became weak in the knees. Suddenly, the trip to the door seemed like it was taking hours, and the door seemed to move further and further away. This scene was all too familiar for her. A feeling of dread washed over her, and the hairs on the back of her neck stood up. Barely able to twist the doorknob, she pulled back the door.

"Good morning, Mrs. Aponte. I'm Special Agent Harp, and this is Special Agent Rollens. May we come in and speak with you?" the white guy said.

Cassandra could not find the words to answer him. She stepped aside allowing them to enter.

"Mrs. Aponte, I'm afraid we have bad news," Agent Harp continued, not wanting to waste time.

Cassandra felt her legs about to give out and her heart raced wildly. The agent's mouth seemed to be moving in slow motion as he uttered the words, "Your daughter has been killed." He spoke softly.

Cassandra put her hands over her mouth as the words slowly rolled off of the agent's tongue. Moving her head from left to right, she still could not speak. Shock was choking her and had her at a lost for words. All she could think of was her baby girl. She pictured Deidre's beautiful face, and she could even smell the scent of Ralph, Deidre's favorite perfume.

Then, reality began to quickly set in on her. "No! No! Not my baby! Not my Deidre! She was all I had left! *No!*" She screamed, bending over and clutching her chest in great agony.

"Ma'am, please sit down," Agent Rollens said.

It was too late. Cassandra had fainted.

Cassandra sat on the side of her bed, with a pounding headache. She had not gotten any sleep or eaten a solid meal since she received the news. She looked over at her black dress draped across her vanity seat, and became sick to her stomach. Reaching for the bottle of sedatives on her nightstand, she noticed the light on her answering machine flashing. She had been ignoring all callers. She grabbed the bottle and threw three pills down her throat, chasing them down with her "Easy Jesus". The pills alone wouldn't put her to sleep. She had built up a tolerance to them, but they would dull the pain that permeated her heart.

Cassandra pulled it together and slid into her dress. Placing a pair of dark black shades over her swollen and red-rimmed eyes, she stumbled down the stairs and out of the house.

"Good morning, Mrs. Aponte," said the agent standing in front of the black Lincoln Town Car. The Bureau had been very attentive. They had made all of Deidre's funeral arrangements, and they also had someone outside of the Aponte home twenty-four hours a day.

"Good morning," Cassandra mumbled as she climbed into the car. Hands shaking, she lit a cigarette, put it to her chapped red lips and inhaled. She'd begun smoking again, after quitting over ten years ago. She stared blankly out of the window as the driver put the car in drive and pulled out of the driveway. Visions of Deidre as a baby danced in Cassandra's mind, and her tears flowed freely.

"We're here, Mrs. Aponte," the driver announced, snapping Cassandra out of her trance.

Opening her eyes, she never uttered a word as she slid across the cold leather seats, and prepared to exit the car. She bit into the side of her cheek when she noticed Ricky Blum standing in front of a huddle of microphones with, black, green, and orange foam covers displaying each television station's logo. He was giving a statement to the throngs of hungry news reporters that had invaded Deidre's funeral service.

Cassandra definitely wanted to talk to Ricky. She knew this was not the time, but she'd gone over the questions in her mind a million times. She wanted to know what *really* happened to her daughter, and one way or another, she was going to find out. She refused to let the media coverage about the circumstances surrounding Deidre's death sway her belief. She would never be convinced that her daughter had traded her dignity to become a notorious drug dealer and murderer.

As soon as Cassandra stepped foot on the pavement, the reporters turned from Ricky and surged toward her. She lowered her head, and with the help of the agents assigned to her, she forced her way through the crowd, ignoring questions such as:

"Mrs. Aponte, is it true your daughter turned her back on the Bureau and became a loyal member of the notorious F.A.B. crew?"

"Did your daughter ever contact you while she was undercover?"

And, "Did your daughter fire at her colleagues in an attempt to get away with a million dollars in drug money?"

Tears streamed freely down Cassandra's face. Just thinking about how the media was portraying her little girl was heart wrenching. "Don't worry, baby girl! I'm gonna set the record straight, even if it's the last thing I ever do!" Cassandra whispered, lifting her head up and looking at her daughter's casket as she entered the Christ Fellowship Baptist Church.

The day after the funeral, Cassandra sat at her kitchen table, barely able to drink a cup of tea. She hadn't eaten or left the house since she'd found out about her Deidre's death, except to attend the service. Cassandra prepared the tea to prime her stomach for the high dose of sedatives and

E&J she was about to consume. She eased her chapped lips onto the rim of her tea cup and sipped slowly.

Suddenly, the doorbell interrupted her self-pity party. She looked up, deciding that she wouldn't answer it. It's probably somebody concerned about me, she reasoned. Besides, her house was a mess; dirty dishes spilled out of the sink; the garbage was piled high, not to mention she hadn't bathed herself.

"*Bing-bong!*" The bell sounded again. "Go away!" Cassandra grumbled refusing to move. The bell rang again with more urgency. "*Bing-bong! Bing-bong!*" "Go away!" Cassandra yelled again, louder this time.

"I have a package for a Mrs. Cassandra Aponte!" the postal delivery guy yelled through the door. Cassandra ignored him. "This is the third delivery attempt, and there is no return address," he yelled.

"Leave it at the door!" Cassandra replied.

"Ma'am, this is a 'sign only' delivery," the guy yelled back, growing frustrated.

Cassandra finally stood up, her head pounding as she padded over to the door. Cracking it slightly she stuck her hand out for the electronic signature board. She scribbled her name, and pushed it back towards the guy.

"Here you go, ma'am," he said, hoisting a large box and shoving it in her direction.

Feeling weak, Cassandra grabbed a total of three boxes, but could barely hold on to them. She let them drop at her feet. "What the hell is all this?" she grumbled, finally looking down at the package slips. She immediately recognized her daughter's handwriting. Her heart began racing and tears immediately welled up in her eyes. "Deidre?" she whispered as she tore at the tape on one of the boxes. She was too weak to make a difference, so she rushed into the kitchen for a knife. Cutting at the tape, the box immediately flapped open. Inside, the first thing Cassandra noticed was a letter:

Dear Mom,

I know you must be wondering what this is all about, and I'm sorry if you haven't heard from me. I'm not sure if I'll be able to tell you the story, so I've sent you my journals. Start with Volume 1, and read all the way to the end for all of the "answers".

I love you, and I know now that me and Daddy never meant to hurt you.

Love Always,
Your baby girl, Deidre

Cassandra clutched at her chest, her heart was braking all over again. She could feel it stinging inside of her chest, and the pain went all the way down to her stomach. The pounding in her head was superseded by the pain she felt. The tears flowed freely as she opened up the first book, "Volume 1: The Call". She read aloud as her tears smudged the first word on the page.

THE LAST VOLUME: NOTHING TO LIVE FOR

Cassandra sat across from Chastity, separated by the thick unbreakable glass. Chastity looked through the glass at the strange woman, and picked up the telephone receiver. Cassandra did the same. "Hello Chastity," Cassandra spoke first.

"Who the fuck is you?" Chastity growled. When she heard she had a visitor, she was secretly hoping it would be her brother.

"You don't know me, but I know lots about you," Cassandra continued, unfazed by Chastity's rude comment.

"Well, you better say something and quick," Chastity remarked, acting as if she had somewhere else to be. She still couldn't shake her bossy attitude.

"I knew your mother and your father, and you knew my daughter," Cassandra said.

Chastity raised her eyebrows at Cassandra's words. "Knew my mother and father?" she asked quietly.

"Yes. Chastity, you see, my husband, Ramon, was your father," Cassandra started.

Chastity jumped right in. "Look. Who the fuck are you,

lady!" she whispered harshly, gritting her teeth. She was getting pissed.

"This is my daughter, and she is your sister," Cassandra got straight to the point, placing a photograph of Deidre up to the glass.

Chastity pursed her lips, and her eyes hooded over at the sight of Deidre's face. She had trusted Deidre and let her into her life, only to be betrayed. "Your daughter was a fucking fed, and a lying bitch! I have nothing else to say to you!" she said, raising her voice and starting to stand up, which garnered stern looks from the CO standing guard.

"Look, I know you may be upset, but my daughter was doing her job. *All* of you were set up. I have proof, but I need your help. That is why I am here," Cassandra continued.

"Tell me what the fuck you know!" Chastity barked, sitting back down. Their time was running out.

"Do you recognize him?" Cassandra asked, furtively showing Chastity a picture of Ricky.

Chastity's squinted her eyes and bit her bottom lip. She was staring into the face of one of her drug connects. "What is going on?" she whispered. Shit was getting stranger by the minute.

Cassandra had to speak fast. She filled Chastity in on how Ricky had set them all up. Cassandra confessed that she had forced Ramon to leave Donna, R.J. and Chastity behind, and that she knew about them all along. When Chastity found out that Deidre was her sister, she lowered her head to hide the tears that streamed down her face. Not only had her brother betrayed her, so had her sister.

As Cassandra spoke, Chastity was immediately taken back to the last day she saw her father . . .

"Junior!" Ramon called out.

R.J. came running towards the front of their apartment

with his pesky little sister right on his heals. "Yeah, Dad?" R.J. huffed, bouncing his basketball.

"I'm about to go on assignment," Ramon lied, bending down to meet his children at eye level. Donna stood up against the door with her arms folded, trying to hide her tears.

"Awwww, I thought you said you was gonna be here for my game!" R.J. whined.

"Yeah, Daddy. I thought you said next time you go we could go too," Chastity followed up.

"Listen. I'll be back. I have to take care of you all. Junior, you will be the man of the house until I come back. You take care of your mother and sister. Beautiful, Daddy will be back soon. Remember, you are my favorite girl," Ramon said, speaking to his children in his native tongue. He leaned in and kissed both of his children on the forehead.

R.J. and Chastity looked at their father sadly. They'd never gotten used to him coming and going.

"Oh. I almost forgot. Son, take this. Wear it all the time. You are a man now. My father gave it to me, and I'm giving it to you," Ramon said, handing a silver chain link bracelet to R.J.

R.J. grabbed the shiny piece of jewelry and looked at it closely. "But its too big!" he complained.

"You will grow into it," Ramon said, rubbing his son's head. "Okay, I gotta go," he lamented, fighting back tears. He stood up and turned towards Donna. "I love you, and I'll be back as soon as I can," he said, grabbing her and kissing her wet face. Using the back of his hand to wipe tears from her cheek, Ramon moved his face close to hers and kissed her deeply.

Donna returned the passionate gesture as she felt her heart breaking. She always hated when her husband got called to military assignments. Her fear was that he wouldn't return. "Call me as soon as you get there, and write every week," she instructed.

"Here, this is for you and the kids. Use it wisely," Ramon said, handing Donna a black bag.

She slowly unzipped the bag half way and peeked inside. Crinkling her eyebrows, she looked up at her husband, confused. "Where did . . ." she started.

Ramon put her pointer finger over her lips and cut her off mid-sentence. "Just keep it and use it," he instructed. She quickly re-zipped the bag and held it tightly.

R.J. and Chastity grabbed onto their father as he headed out the door. "Remember what I said. I love you all," Ramon said with finality. And with that, he was gone.

"Visit is up, Smith!" the CO yelled, breaking Chastity's train of thought.

"So, we agree to work together on this?" Cassandra asked Chastity.

"Yeah, I'll do it," Chastity said. Although she was angry, revenge seemed like the only thing that would make her feel better.

After Cassandra received the package Deidre sent her, she sprang into action. The thought of the Bureau killing her daughter as they had killed her husband was sobering. Cassandra put down her "Easy Jesus" and set out to finally do something for her daughter.

Ricky had used Deidre's so called murder to get promoted to Deputy Director at the Bureau. And just like Ricky, he took it one step further and made a bid for the Senate. But Cassandra had other plans for Ricky. The day of reckoning had finally arrived.

Cassandra contemplated stopping at the liquor store for some of her "Easy Jesus", because her nerves were on edge.

But she thought about the task at hand, and decided against it.

Arriving at the site for the speech sent chills down Cassandra's spine. The camera flashbulbs snapped ten at a time as Ricky flashed his bright white smile and waved at the throngs of news reporters posted up in front of the speaking podium. Flanked by his wife, Lorna and two beautiful daughters, Ricky stepped up to the microphone. The crowd cheered loudly, showing their support.

"My fellow constituents, I am here to tell you that I will not tolerate crime, drugs, or corruption!" Ricky said into the microphones.

The crowd cheered again. Red, white and blue signs reading "Blum for Senator" were hoisted in the air.

Ricky looked around at all of the banners and buttons with his likeness posted on them, and felt a great sense of satisfaction. He was the town hero. In the public's opinion, Ricky had single-handedly captured or murdered the most notorious female drug dealers, the F.A.B., solved the murder of Amber Reeves, and revealed a crooked agent, Deidre Aponte. All he had to do now was sit back and wait to win the Senate seat so he could finally seal the deal with Esperanza.

Cassandra stood at the back of the crowd as Ricky delivered a captivating speech and the hairs on her skin stood erect. Taking a deep breath, she needed to calm herself down. Walking slowly, she inched her way towards the front of the crowd. She carried a sign in front of her face, trying not to be noticed. "Excuse me! Sorry, excuse me!" she said, as she bumped and pushed her way forward.

Once she made it to the third row, she peered over the rim of her dark sunglasses at the sound guy. The man looked back at her and nodded his head. He had nothing to lose. The money Cassandra had paid him was more than he would make in two years of pushing those sound buttons.

"I want to tell you that I will make sure that something is done about the drugs that plague our . . ." Ricky began.

Suddenly, his voice faded out, and all people could see were his lips moving. The sound in his microphones had been deadened. Hushed murmurs echoed through the crowd, as everyone looked around to see what had happened. The next thing everyone heard were strange voices booming out of the speakers:

". . . *Aponte, I've known you since you were a little girl. I just want you to know that I would've never done anything to hurt you. I respected your father a lot," Bernard began.*

"*What are you talking about, Bernard?" Deidre asked seriously.*

"*Your father, Ricky, Lewis and I were into some things you wouldn't understand. We got in over our heads, and money started coming in all directions. Ricky slowly started taking over things . . ." Bernard began, but Deidre cut him off.*

"*Wait, are you trying to tell me my father was a dirty agent?" Deidre asked.*

"*I know you may not believe it, but we were all a part of it. Aponte, the money came so easily," Bernard replied regretfully.*

"*No. No. I don't believe you," Deidre said.*

"*We got in over our heads, and everybody started pocketing money on the side. It was supposed to be one time, but Ricky kept going further and further. Ramon, Lewis, and myself wanted out, but Ricky wouldn't hear of it. So, your father and Lewis decided to take matters into their own hands, and that is when things got ugly," Bernard stated.*

"*Are you saying Ricky murdered my father?" Deidre asked.*

"*Yes," Bernard answered.*

"*I don't believe you!" she sobbed. "Why?" Deidre cried.*

"*I'm sorry!" Bernard cried.*

"*So, what does all of this have to do with me?" Deidre asked.*

"*Senator Reeves was a part of the original deal. Diego Esper-*

*anza funded his campaign, made sure he got the Senate seat, and
in exchange, Reeves was supposed to keep the National Drug
Control policy from being passed. Reeves reneged on the deal,
under pressure. Ricky decided to take revenge, and used Amber
Reeves as an example. The case was a setup from day one. I'm so
sorry!" Bernard apologized.*

*"The fucking criminals are more loyal than the feds!" Deidre
screamed.*

"I know," Bernard said.

"What about the F.A.B.?" Deidre asked.

*"They were just pawns. Ferguson was a part of this, and she
and Ricky had it planned to blow your cover so that the F.A.B.
would kill you. They never fixed the tag or set up your identity.
They sent gunmen in so that you would blow your own cover, but
none of it worked," Bernard said.*

"Did Ricky kill Amber Reeves?" Deidre asked.

"No . . . I did. She bled to death," Bernard confessed . . .

The crowd was pin drop quiet. Ricky was screaming for
the sound staff to turn off the recording, but no one moved.
He turned a dark shade of red as FBI agents and uniformed
SWAT team officers converged on the podium with guns
drawn. "Police! Don't move!" they screamed.

Ricky's mouth hung open in shock. There was nowhere
for him to run.

Ferguson eased out of her chair, hung her head, and at-
tempted to dip into the crowd. She walked headfirst into a
plain-clothes police officer.

"Ma'am, you need to come with me! You are under arrest
for the murder of Amber Reeves!" the officer boomed.

Ferguson's shoulder's slumped down and she surrendered.

The courtroom was packed. Throngs of reporters lined
up at the back and around the side walls.

Cassandra sat in the first row of hard benches, behind the

prosecutor's table, and Chastity sat right next to her. Sweat drenched Chastity's entire body, and she shook her legs in and out, back and forth as the court officer made his slow amble to the front of the courtroom. Cassandra reached over and grabbed Chastity's hand in support.

"Please rise! The Honorable Judge Melinda Black presiding!" the court officer said perfunctorily.

As the judge took her seat, she seated the crowd. "Order! Let's come to order and begin," she said, banging her gavel twice. A sickening hush came over the room.

Chastity glanced over at Ricky standing shackled behind the defense table. Her heart immediately began pounding as he glared in Chastity's direction. She avoided eye contact, and hung her head. Suddenly, the boom of the prosecutor's voice startled her.

"The prosecution calls State's witness, Chastity Smith to the stand!" the short, balding middle aged prosecutor called out.

As she stood up to walk to the stand, she could feel eyes burning holes in her back. The courtroom was pin drop silent.

"Please raise your right hand," the court officer requested.

Chastity complied, raising her hand. She was sworn in, and as she took her seat, her eyes locked with Cassandra's. Chastity knew what she had to do. Being a snitch under any circumstances wasn't in her nature, and she felt like throwing up right there in front of all of those people. Instead, she was able to swallow the lump that burned her throat, and remember how Cassandra had kept her promise to help her.

Chastity quickly turned her eyes away from Cassandra and decided to find something else to focus on throughout her testimony. Looking at the front row behind the prosecutor's stand, she focused on the face of a three-year-old girl. It was Akayla. This little girl would give her the strength to do what she knew was right. Chastity thought that maybe God would forgive her for what she'd done to Tori and Leticia.

"Ms. Smith," the prosecutor began.

"Yes . . . ahem! Yes?" Chastity replied in a raspy voice, trying her best to get rid of the ball of fear stuck in her neck.

"Please tell us how you know the defendant," he continued.

"I bought drugs from him—he was my connect, as we say in the street," Chastity mumbled. Out of the corner of her eye, she could see Ricky leaning in to his attorney. She moved uneasily in the burgundy leather swivel chair at the left of the judge.

"Please tell the court where you met the defendant," prosecutor said.

"I got introduced to him through Amber Reeves," Chastity said in a low, barely audible voice.

"I'm sorry . . . Did you say 'Amber Reeves', as in Senator Daniel Reeves' daughter?" the prosecutor asked for clarity.

"Yes. She also sold drugs for him," Chastity said in rapid succession, letting the uneasy words roll off her tongue.

"Ohhh's" resonated through the crowd.

"Can you please tell us who the F.A.B. crew was, Ms. Smith," the prosecutor said.

"Yes . . . Yes I can," she replied.

"Please begin," he said flatly, taking his seat back behind the prosecution table.

Chastity looked over at Ricky before she spoke. Ricky shot her evil looks; if looks could kill, she would have been six feet under. Averting her sight from him, she then looked at Cassandra, and filled in the missing pieces to the story.

Ricky's trial went on for six weeks, and throughout the entire court proceedings, Cassandra remained sober. She hadn't indulged in the "Easy Jesus" since the trial had begun. She wanted to be sharp and astute when she avenged her husband and daughter's deaths.

Lorna Blum sat on her living room sofa in a daze, watching the breaking news. Her eyes swollen from crying and lack of sleep, she took a long drag of her cigarette as she awaited news of her husband's fate. She hadn't been to court for the last four weeks of the trial. She couldn't stand to hear how her husband had slept with so many woman, murdered so many people, and sold drugs. Staring at the screen, she watched as the creamy-skinned African-American reporter began speaking:

> *"After twelve hours of deliberations the jury in the murder, conspiracy and racketeering trial of former FBI Special Agent in Charge, Ricky Blum has returned a verdict. The twelve-person jury, made of up four African-American women and eight white men, returned a unanimous guilty verdict on all counts just after ten a.m. this morning. Ricky Blum is slated to be moved from the courthouse shortly. As you can see behind me, a crowd has formed outside of the courthouse. We will continue live coverage . . ."*

Lorna stared at the gun on her coffee table. It sat atop the asset forfeiture papers she'd been served with just the day before. She and her children would ultimately be left with nothing. The government had orders to seize her home, cars, clothes, jewelry, artwork and anything else of value. She was penniless. Lorna picked up the gun and slid it into her black leather Chloe purse. Inhaling, she rose from the sofa and left her front door. "He left me nothing to live for!" she screamed as she headed towards the garage.

* * *

Cassandra and Chastity sat together in Cassandra's family room, camped out in front of the television set. They'd been watching the news telecast since the verdict, and now they waited to see Ricky being hauled off to jail.

"How are you feeling?" Chastity asked, rubbing Cassandra's arm.

"I'm okay. How about you?" Cassandra replied softly.

"I'm okay too. Before you came into my life, I was lost. After my brother betrayed me, I felt like I had nothing to live for. But thanks to you getting me the immunity offer, I can start a new life," Chastity said gratefully.

"You also gave me a reason to live. You're a part of Ramon no matter what, so therefore I can accept you. We will keep each other strong," Cassandra said with tears welling up in her eyes. For the first time, she had truly forgiven her husband, which made life easier. She no longer had a reason to drown her pain with alcohol.

"Look, they are bringing him out!" Chastity screamed, pointing to the television. They'd been waiting for hours to see Ricky handcuffed like a common criminal. Cassandra shifted her attention to the screen and turned up the volume:

"*. . . As you can see here a large crowd has gathered to see Ricky Blum off to jail. His lawyer is scheduled to make a statement shortly,*" the reporter said, pointing to the courthouse steps.

"Look at that dirty bastard! To think I had him in my home, around my family!" Cassandra screamed, banging her fists on the arm of the sofa.

"There he is!" Chastity said, moving to the edge of her seat. They both watched as the detectives, uniformed police and several layers of people escorted Ricky down the courthouse steps towards the waiting Department of Corrections of van.

"Back up! Back up!" one of the detectives screamed, extending his arms to move the crowd back. Ricky held his head down, hiding from the cameras.

"Ricky! Ricky! It's me!" Lorna screamed out, struggling through the crowd.

Ricky lifted his head before he stepped into the van. He hadn't seen his wife in weeks. "Wait! That's my wife!" he called out.

Lorna rushed forward, and the detectives hesitated letting her get close. As soon as she got near Ricky, she raised her hands in front of her. "I thought you loved me! You left me nothing to live for!" she screamed, firing the gun griped tightly in her hands. *"Bang! Bang! Bang!* The shots cleared the crowd.

"Gun! Gun!" the transporting officers screamed as they drew their weapons and unloaded on Lorna.

The media cameras captured the entire scene. When the smoke cleared, Lorna and Ricky both lay dead, and two officers wounded.

"Oh my God! Did you see that?" Chastity yelled to Cassandra. They watched most of the melee on television, but weren't able to see Ricky go down. The cameras all went black.

"I think someone shot Ricky!" Chastity screamed excitedly.

"I know she did. I went to visit her last night, and we talked about it. I helped her get that gun," Cassandra said calmly. She was elated inside. Justice for her daughter and husband had been served.

REST IN PEACE:
RAMON APONTE
DEIDRE APONTE

Cassandra and Chastity both stooped over the gravesite and placed their flowers as a show of respect. Cassandra sobbed and Chastity comforted her. "They're in a better place," Chastity consoled. She thought about her mother, Leticia, and even R.J. and Tori—all casualties of war.

"Yes. I know. I'm just glad that they both got to tell their stories from the grave," Cassandra replied.

"Well, they say that everybody has a story to tell. The dead speak volumes, while we, the living just learn page by page," Chastity said as they held onto each other and headed out of the cemetery. They had a trip to take, and a few more graves to visit.